The Legacy of Lucy Harte

Emma Heatherington

A division of HarperCollins*Publishers*
www.harpercollins.co.uk

Harper*Impulse* an imprint of
HarperCollins*Publishers*
1 London Bridge Street
London SE1 9GF

www.harpercollins.co.uk

A Paperback Original 2017

First published in Great Britain in ebook format by Harper*Impulse* 2017

Copyright © Emma Heatherington 2017

Emma Heatherington asserts the moral right to
be identified as the author of this work

A catalogue record for this book
is available from the British Library

ISBN: 9780008194864

Find out more about HarperCollins and the environment at
www.harpercollins.co.uk/green

Emma Heatherington

Emma Heatherington is from Donaghmore, Co Tyrone where she lives with her children - Jordyn, Jade, Dualta, Adam and baby Sonny James. She has penned more than thirty short films, plays and musicals as well as seven novels for Poolbeg Press, two of which were written under the pseudonym Emma Louise Jordan.

Her latest signing with Harper Impulse (HarperCollins) saw the re-release of *Crazy For You* in 2013 and three new releases lined up in the near future.

Emma loves spending time with her partner (the talented artist and singer/songwriter Jim McKee), all things Nashville, romantic comedy movies, singalong nights with friends and family, red wine, musical theatre, new pyjamas, fresh clean bedclothes, long bubble baths and cosy nights in by the fire.

Find Emma on Twitter @emmalou13 or on Facebook at emmaheatheringtonwriter.

For Ciaran and Ashley
#donatelife

Prologue

I thought I saw you once on a train to Dublin.

You were about six years old. You were slurping on an ice-cream, your face covered in chocolate sprinkles and you were laughing so hard at the little boy beside you that I thought you were going to choke.

I thought I saw you a few years later, but this time you were a curly-haired toddler in a park throwing a high-pitched tantrum when you couldn't reach the swing. A handsome man scooped you up in big strong arms and took you to a pram, where you kicked and screamed, your little arms stretched out, your hands opening and closing and reaching back towards the play area.

I thought I saw you as a lanky teenager one sunny afternoon when I was in London as you shopped for clothes with your mother, arguing with her over a pair of ripped jeans versus a pretty floral dress.

I think I see you all the time, even though I have no idea what you look like, who you are or what your story might have been.

You are inside me. You are part of me. You are within my every move.

I feel like I know you, Lucy Harte, I really do.

But you will never, ever know me.

Chapter 1

Monday 10th April

I am dying.

I am drowning, or else I am having a heart attack, but either way, whatever it is, I can't breathe and I'm definitely dying this time. How ironic it would be for me to die today, of all days...

Oh God, please help me.

I sit up on my brand-new bed and automatically fall back again, my squinted eyes unable to open just yet and my shaking body needing much more time to recuperate from my latest 'party for one'.

This is no ordinary hangover. Hell, no. My head is like a bowling ball, I can't open my dried-out mouth, the phone is ringing off the hook and I wish whoever it is would just stop already because I don't want to talk to anyone.

Not Flo, not my parents, not my boss and definitely not my excuse for a husband.

I really can't listen to lectures or 'I told you so', not today, not today of all days, please no. Plus... I can't remember where

3

I was or what I did last night and I'm afraid. I am so afraid that if I answer the phone I will hear what I did last night and I can't face up to that truth ever.

Did I do something wrong? Did I leave my apartment? I can't remember!

No, no I didn't. I definitely didn't. Not this time.

With relief I get glimpses of flashbacks of turning off the TV, stumbling into bed in my pyjamas (always a good sign when you wake up wearing pyjamas), so I can't have done that much damage, can I?

Unless I was texting everyone about how miserable I am or sharing my suffering on Facebook. Please no! Or even worse, I could have been texting *him*.

Ah Jesus! Oh why do I do the things I do? It wasn't me, it was the wine. Oh, for God's sake Maggie *get it together!*

But I can't get it together and the phone won't stop ringing! Why can't they leave me alone? I don't want to talk to anyone and I just can't bring myself to look at it to see who has woken me from my deep, drowning, drunken sleep so I shove the phone from its usual perch on the bedside locker and feel instant relief when it hits the bedroom floor in silence and falls into three pieces – the front, the back and then the battery.

There now. All is quiet at last.

But the constant pounding of my head from dehydration, and the voices of my nearest and dearest echoing, remind me of how, no matter how quiet it is here, I am so not at peace at all these days.

'Are you sure you're okay, Maggie? We're really worried you

aren't able to cope with this stress.' (My mother/father – delete as appropriate.)

'Why don't you come and stay with me for a while? I have a spare room?' (My best friend, Flo.)

'Are you on some sort of death wish or what? Get a grip, Maggie!' (My ever-sympathetic brother, John Joe.)

'What? Ah Maggie! Why do you need to work from home again?' (My boss/colleagues.)

'You are going to have to move on, Mags! Get over it! Get over me and you!' (My husband, I mean, ex-husband, Jeff.)

'You really need to stop drinking so much. It's not helping' (All of the above.)

I really should stop drinking. I really should stop avoiding them all.

I really should just answer the phone and face up to their concerns, or at least reassure them that, yes, I am certainly having a shit time coping with this whole marriage break-up thing and, yes, I know my job is suffering and, yes, I need to pull myself together and get back on track, but I'm not just ready to. Not just yet.

Ah, sweet Jesus, not the landline now too! Whoever it is they are pretty bloody persistent!

'Stop! STOP!' I shout into the emptiness of my new apartment.

Its IKEA shininess and anonymity makes me want to smash it up and crawl out of my skin or at least under the covers, where I don't have to be constantly reminded that this is where I live now and it doesn't feel like home. I don't feel like me.

I don't know who the hell I am any more.

I am alone, '*separated*', desperate and miserable in a hazy, drunken limbo between marriage and dreaded divorce and I have no idea of who I am or what I'm supposed to be doing.

'Please stop calling me! Please *stop!*' I sob into the spongy new pillow that smells like lavender – a tip from my mother to help me sleep, but the scent of it makes me want to retch.

'It's much better than wine, love,' were her words, but what would she know? She's been teetotal all her life.

The phone continues to ring, piercing my fragile brain and I picture the caller, determined to 'do the right thing by poor Maggie' and check in on me at every bloody turnaround.

Have they no stupid lives of their own? Do I constantly barrage them with phone calls and concern every time they screw up? No I don't.

But then they don't really screw up, do they?

And then I realise it's Monday. Ah, Jesus. It's Monday.

I have no idea what time it is or if I am meant to be in work right now. Normally, on waking up like this, I would already be in the shower in a blind fit of panic and praying for time to stand still so that I could get to my latest appointment or show my face in the office and convince everyone that I am fine but today... today is different.

I don't care if I am late because there is somewhere else I need to be and, at the risk of losing my job, which is no doubt already written on the cards, the place I have to go is much more important. I hate my job. I hate everything right now, but most of all I hate Jeff and his new 'girlfriend' and how he has made me into this shell of nothingness, desperate and empty and drunk and sad.

I sit up on my bed again and focus.

The phone has stopped ringing. There is a God.

I open my eyes slowly and steady myself and consider what to wear, but I don't really care about that either.

It's time for me to go. It's time for me to talk to Lucy Harte.

It's weird thanking someone from the depths of your soul when you can't see them, have never met them, when they can't hear you and when they have no clue who you are.

It's a bit like talking to God, I suppose. It takes faith and belief, so here I am an hour after my latest meltdown of loneliness, in a church, lighting candles, saying prayers and thanking Lucy Harte for my life – and she can't hear a word I am saying.

I hope she is here somewhere, floating invisibly like a little angel with a smile on her face and taking in my every word, glad to have given me part of the life she left behind.

I like talking to Lucy, even if it's via my mind and not aloud and even if it is only once a year when I get the chance to really dig deep and have a good old chin wag. I think about her every single day, but it's always on this date that I feel her closest.

I talk to her like an old friend. Well, she *is* an old friend if you consider that our one-way conversations have been going on for exactly seventeen years today. Not many friendships last that long, especially when, like ours, they are totally one-sided.

Even my marriage didn't last that long – seventeen *months*

and ten days, to be precise, but then again, that was pretty one-sided too.

I wanted to be married to him. He didn't want to be married to me. Pretty simple, when you think of it that way...

'Elizabeth Taylor was married eight times and had seven different husbands,' my father reminded me when I told him that Jeff was leaving. *'And you're even more beautiful than Elizabeth Taylor, I've always said it, so I wouldn't worry too much about Jeff bloody Pillock.'*

Yes, Pillock. Thank God I didn't take his name.

He's ever so slightly biased, my dad, but then again, I am his only daughter. He has to say nice things like that. It's kind of his job.

My mother's reaction, on the other hand, was a bit more traditional.

'But he can't just leave you!'

'He can, and he did,' I told her.

'But not so soon!' she said, bewildered, as we both sobbed uncontrollably for days over endless cups of tea in her kitchen, then damning Jeff to a life of misery without me and insisting that karma would one day come to bite his sorry ass. *'Marriage is so throwaway these days. And all that money on the hotel and fancy dresses all down the drain. Disgraceful. Promises and dreams down the feckin' drain.'*

She is right, of course. All those big promises and dreams just thrown away before the real hurdles of life had even set in. And, as for the money... I shudder to think what our wedding cost. It was wonderful, but hardly worth it for seventeen months and ten days...

The Legacy of Lucy Harte

It's cold in the church and I hug my jacket around my waist. There are a handful of others in here, older people mainly, whose whispers sound like they are whistling as they chant with rosary beads clasped tight around their wrinkly hands.

I close my eyes and focus on Lucy again. Today is our special day. Today is the day she gave me life, a life so precious that I am reminded whenever I feel her heart beating in my chest. This heartache I am experiencing right now, as painful as it may be, reminds me of the gift of life her family gave me when they gave me her heart seventeen years ago.

I want to thank Lucy for everything I can remember in this thirty-minute window I have allowed for this encounter. It's important for me to thank her on this day, at this time every year. It's the nearest I get to gratitude, I suppose, and it keeps me sane and positive.

I try to focus on the good times from the past twelve months since we last 'spoke' and I can't help but smile at the irony. The good times are hard to come up with, believe me –but with some reflection they begin to roll off my tongue, silently, of course. I'm sure the little old ladies and gentlemen who sit around me with their eyes shut don't want to hear my life story and I find strange comfort in my thoughts over their repetitive whispery chants of the rosary.

I thank Lucy for my promotion in January, which was mega and which means I have actually got spending money at the end of each month and savings. Actual *savings*. My father always told me that money burned a whole in my pocket – I would either spend it straight away or give it away by buying random presents for everyone and anyone I could, but now that I am totally all on my own in the big bad world I'm starting to put some away for a rainy day and it's starting to look good.

I give thanks for my apartment. I'm getting used to living on my own again *(I am so not, but I keep telling myself that and one day it will be true)* and it even has a garden. Well, it has a window box and a small, decked balcony with potted plants, but it's enough of a garden for me, for now. I can barely look after myself these days, never mind tend to a real garden with weeds and growing grass and other living things that need attention.

Then I get to the really good bits, where I tell her of all the crappy parts of the past year and how they have turned my once pretty-damn-fine life on its head.

I tell her of the night I embarrassed myself in front of my now ex-husband's family by singing Britney Spears 'Hit Me Baby One More Time' along with a full-on dance routine wearing his dad's tie with my skirt hitched up after five-too-many glasses of Prosecco. I don't even like Prosecco. Hell, I don't even know if I like Britney Spears that much, if I'm honest, so God knows where the idea to imitate her came from.

I have a feeling that night was the beginning of the end for Jeff and I. Maybe that's when it all started to go wrong? Who knows? I've kind of blamed everything I can at this stage and still can't get my head around it. But, for now, let's blame Britney and Prosecco...

I tell her about the last few months I spent with Jeff as his wife, which was mainly made up of a) me checking his phone and b) me finding what I didn't want to see, and I pray to Lucy to help me find acceptance that he is now with her, the one he left me for only ten weeks ago. Her name is Saffron, she is an air stewardess who speaks with a lisp and they met on Facebook. Lovely.

That's as much as I know so far, despite my full-time mission to suss her out through social-network stalking but her bloody pages are all private and the most I can see is that she seems to really like cats. This makes me happy. Jeff is allergic to cats – they bring him out in hives and welts. *Delighted.*

'She must have done something wrong,' I overheard my mum say to my dad a while ago when she thought I couldn't hear her. *'A man doesn't leave his wife for no reason. There must have been something.'*

Once again my father's logic put a different spin on things as I listened from the kitchen.

'I never really liked him anyway,' he told her from behind his newspaper. *'He dyes his hair that colour, you know. Weird blacky brown. I could never trust a man who dyes his hair, especially the colour of cow dung. And he wears heels on his shoes.'*

My dad is so on the ball. Jeff does dye his hair and he has a 'special' cobbler who he visits every time he gets new shoes...

'Jeff? Heels? Are you sure, Robert? I never noticed that.'

'Yes, heels,' my dad said. *'Put it like this, a man who needs inches there probably needs them in other places too. Nah. I never liked him. Let him get on with it. Our Maggie's way out of his league.'*

I haven't told my parents about Saffron, the stewardess, and I probably never will. That would totally put my mother over the edge and we can't have that. She may wonder if any of this was my fault, but she is old-school and sweet and innocent to the ways of the modern world and she would never get how Jeff was able to fall in love with someone he met just once in a sweaty gym and then wooed through private messaging on Facebook, while I was still admiring our wedding photos and choosing names for our future family.

Instead of telling my parents the real reason behind my big fat failure of a marriage, I spill my heart out to a dead fourteen-year-old just as I tell her my secrets every year on the same date and same time of the morning, when the rest of the world is doing school runs or in rush-hour traffic heading to work or having coffee in front of early-morning television.

I tell all of this to Lucy Harte, a fourteen-year-old girl who I never met but who gave me a second chance at life, even though she has no idea that I even exist. I pray for her family, whoever they are, and I thank them from the bottom of my borrowed heart for the day they said yes to organ donation.

Then I bless myself quickly and aim to get out of the church before someone mistakes me for a real Christian and I leave Lucy to do whatever it is dead fourteen-year-olds do up in heaven, while I go back to my new life of singlehood, meals for one and real estate, which is highly pressurised, fast-moving and a far cry from the soft Irish countryside where I was brought up.

I am being brave.

I am being brave but I am not brave.

I am not brave at all. In fact I am bloody scared stiff.

Fuck you, Jeff.

I want to scream and shout and kick and cry so loudly but I am in a church so I can't and it's so damn frustrating.

Fuck you for leaving me and fuck her for taking you away. Why? What the hell did I do that was so bad?

I think I am going to cry and I so don't want to cry in public.

I close my eyes, breathe in and out, in and out, in and out and focus on Lucy Harte. I am not here to think about Jeff. I am here to say thank you to Lucy.

It's been a long time, Lucy Harte. Seventeen years is a long, long time for you to beat inside of me. Why do I have the feeling that we haven't very long left?

I really should get to work.

Chapter 2

'Are you *sure* you are okay? You don't *sound* okay? I've been calling you all weekend, Maggie!'

And don't I know it...! My mother's voice is always high-pitched, but today it is more frantic than ever.

'I'm fine, Mum. I'm driving,' I tell her. I shouldn't have answered. My head...

I'm not really driving but it's the only thing that might get her off the line. My mother would talk the hind leg off a donkey but she sees right through the whole *'I'm sorry, you're breaking up'* or *'I'm in a bad area'* or *'I have an important call coming through'* excuses I usually make when I can't be bothered with conversation.

'You're not fine. I know you're not fine. Robert, she says she's driving and she's fine.'

'Lies!' my father shouts back. 'She's not fine. Maggie, you cannot do *stress*! You need to rest. No stress!'

'You should have taken the day off and done something nice, Maggie. Even your father says so. You can't afford this stress.'

'Yes, she should have taken the day off and done something

14

nice,' I hear him echo in the background. I can just picture him, standing in his green wellies and baggy old-man trousers with his braces over his checked shirt, hovering by the ancient navy-blue landline phone that is attached to our kitchen wall back home in the big farmhouse I grew up in. He will be chewing on something, the end of his pipe, probably, and he will have a pen behind his ear (chewed also), just like I always do when I am doing something I enjoy and he will smell already of manure and sawdust.

'I'm going out for dinner with Flo after work and she is meeting me outside the office at six, so it's best I'm there,' I lie. 'I'm really looking forward to it.'

'Oh, that's nice. Where are you going for dinner? Robert, she is going for dinner. With Flo.'

'We're going to... um, we're going to that new place,' I waffle. 'You know, my favourite. On George Street.' More lies. 'You see, I'm keeping busy, Mum. Busy, busy, busy.'

'Well, I suppose that's better than having too much time to think. Did you go to the church?'

'Yes.'

'Robert, she went to the church.'

Oh, Christ.

I hear a rustle as my dad takes the phone.

'I hope you weren't making an eejit out of yourself in front of those people,' he says in a fluster.

By 'those people', he means 'a man of the cloth'. By 'eejit' he means going to what Catholics call 'Confession'. There is no one my dad hates more in this world than the Clergy.

'I wasn't.'

'You could say your piece in your own apartment and it would do the same good than telling 'them' boyos your problems. None of their bloody business. Nosey –'

'I didn't even see a priest, Dad. I just said what I wanted to say to Lucy, lit a few candles and left. I'm about to walk into the office now, so I'd better go.'

That bit wasn't a lie. I was standing outside our office block and Davey, the porter, was winking at me as he did every morning and checking out my boobs, legs, bum and everything in between. Davey loved a good old perv.

'You're a good girl, Maggie O'Hara,' says my dad and I can hear his voice shake. 'A really good girl and you deserve the best and you deserve to be here. God bless wee Lucy Harte, but you deserve to have a life too and a great one at that. Now, push those guilty feelings to the side and have a good day, do you hear me? And look at Princess Diana. Charles didn't want her but it didn't stop her finding a man again, did it?'

'No, it didn't, but then she died,' I remind him.

'Well you're not going to die, are you? You're even nicer than Princess Diana. You're even nicer than Princess Diana *and* Elizabeth Taylor. You're nicer than the whole bloody lot of them rolled into one and don't you ever forget it!'

I turn my back on Davey. I feel his eyes burning on my backside.

'I hear you, Dad,' I say and feel tears sting my eyes. 'I am absolutely fine and as much as I wish I looked like Lady Di or Liz Taylor or the whole bloody lot of them, believe me when I say that finding a man is the least of my worries. Now, stop worrying! I am thirty-three years old. I can cope with being dumped and having my heart broken. I've coped with a lot worse...'

I know that he is pointing his finger through the air in front of him as he speaks. I can just see him.

'Well, I'm just saying that when the time comes to find love again, you'll have no bother,' he tells me, 'so don't be worrying that you are going to be on your own because you won't be on your own for long. You've been through enough in your life and if I was talking to the man upstairs if there even is such a thing as the man upstairs I would be telling him that enough is enough and it's about time he left you alone! Enough is enough!'

And at that I burst out crying.

'Yes and *that* is well enough, Robert!' my mother shouts in the background. 'Enjoy dinner with Flo and send our love to her, Maggie. Is she crying?'

'I'm not crying,' I say, wiping black blobs of mascara onto the back of my hand. 'I love you both, okay? See you soon. I will come visit really soon.'

'Do. Yes, see you soon, love,' says my dad and I can tell that he is crying too.

This makes me feel even worse because every time my second-hand heart breaks, I think my parents feel my pain even more than I do.

'Morning, Maggie,' chirps Bridget, our long-serving receptionist who caters for the six businesses who share our building, diverting calls and taking appointments and basically minding other people's business. 'My God, what happened? You look a mess. And you're very late!'

Bridget is salt of the earth, but she couldn't tell a white lie to save her own life. I know I look like shit. I don't need her to remind me. I also know I'm late too! I fucking hate this place right now.

I stop in my tracks. I am not just late for work. I am late for a really, really important meeting. Oh shit!

'Can you tell the guys I will be up in two? And give my apologies, please, of course. I've had a rough morning.'

Bridget looks back at me somewhat reluctantly.

'A speedy two-minute fix-up in the bathroom isn't going to make much difference, is it?' I say.

She shrugs and lifts her phone while I quickly nip into the bathroom and see her honesty staring right back at me. I have a face that would scare babies, all blurred mascara, and I am as white as a ghost. Ah well, nothing that a hairbrush and some good old war paint won't fix. Thank heavens for make-up. I need to compose myself and then forget what day it is.

Lucy Harte, just for now, I will have to try and let your sweet memory go.

A few minutes later I am in the elevator. My eyes are only slightly puffy but I've made a good job of looking as normal as I possibly can under the circumstances.

I'm half an hour late for a meeting with Will Powers Jr. I should be terrified. I urge the elevator to speed up. My heart begins to race. See, it works. It may be broken but it works and I am reminded of its presence every day as it breaks into tinier pieces over Jeff and that cat-loving smurf he is living with...

But anyhow...Will Powers... the boss's son... the smooth-talking, suit-wearing, stereotypical rich kid who was born with a silver spoon in his mouth and was blessed with brooding good looks to boot is waiting for me and he is probably foaming at the mouth in temper.

Will lives in Spain most of the year but comes back and forth to deal with mainly human resources matters and is always tanned and tries his best to be nice but would stab you in the back if you didn't watch yourself. You could say he has it all really... until he opens his mouth and talks the biggest load of shite you ever did hear in a fake American accent. He has it all, apart from a heart, that is. He could be doing with a transplant too, I often think. Swap his swinging brick for something that actually shows some compassion now and again.

'Sorry I'm late,' I say, trying to sound convincing but I'm not really sure that I'm sorry. I can't feel sorry for anyone, only myself, these days.

Will looks at his watch, then, like a Mexican wave at a football match, the rest do too. Copy-cats. Five faces stare back at me and I feel my face flush.

They are waiting on my excuse. Their silence tells me so.

'I... I was...'

'Sit down, Maggie,' says Will.

I wasn't expecting such a gathering and I have no idea what this meeting is even about. I was probably informed in advance, but, surprise, surprise, I can't remember.

The company directors, all of them, are here in one room. I bet I have big red blotches all over my chest, which always bloody happens when I'm under pressure, but, more importantly, what on earth is going on?

Will pulls out a seat and I do as I am told. I sit. He smells of posh cologne and flashes an uber-white smile. 'I know this is a difficult day for you.'

'Sorry?'

'Just try and relax, Maggie. Thirty minutes late is not going to change the world. Have a seat and chill.'

Chill? Who does he think he is, Jay-Z? Who even says 'chill' these days?

Why is everyone staring? And what on earth does he know about my difficult day and its relevance to my life? I hadn't told anyone that it's my heart anniversary and I keep my private life very much private. No one even knows I broke up with Jeff. Well, apart from Bridget downstairs whose brother knows Jeff's family and, yes, I told Diane who sits opposite me and... okay, so I may have told a few people. Maybe they all know more than I thought they do about me. But what the hell is going on?

'I'm sure you have been wondering what this meeting is all about, Maggie,' said Will. 'I hope I haven't been causing you sleepless nights.'

Sleepless nights? I haven't had a full night's sleep since Jeff dumped me. It's not easy to sleep and stalk mutual friends on Facebook for clues on his whereabouts at the same time.

'I haven't been sleeping well lately but...'

The five faces are staring at me.

Will looks up at me from beneath dark knitted eyebrows that I notice are the exact same as his father's. No, Will Sr's are even thicker. But greyer. Why am I even thinking about eyebrows?

'Maggie?'

'I'm fine. Just the odd sleepless night, but yes. I'm... I'm fine,' I say, screwing up my forehead. I think I have overused that word for one day but it's all I can think of. I reach out my hands in front and clasp them together. I wish I had papers to shuffle, or a diary to check or something to do with my hands.

'You don't have to pretend you are fine,' says Sylvia Madden, one of the CEOs, from across the table. 'You have been through quite a lot personally lately and no one expects you to be fine.'

They are all staring at me. I need to get out of here. I don't want to be here any more. I feel the room closing in.

'I can't do this any more,' I say, but I barely recognise my own voice. I stand up. 'I need to go... I need to quit. I can't do it. Sorry.'

I am going to cry. Will shakes his head. He is smiling. Why is he smiling?

'I understand why you would feel like giving it all up, quitting,' he says. 'But you're not a quitter, Maggie.'

Now, I really *am* crying. Big sobs just like I was earlier when I was on the phone to my dad. I sit down again.

'I have to... I just need some time to get through this.'

I manage to blurt out the words semi-coherently as Sylvia hands me a tissue across the table.

'Yes, I can see that,' says Will. 'Your work has slipped since the promotion and having done some homework, we think you need a break, but only for a while, for health reasons.'

'Slipped?' I splutter. 'I suppose that's one way of putting it. I feel like a failure. I should probably go.'

I try to recall how my work has 'slipped' and I cringe at the realisation. Sure, I'd taken some days out after the break-up with Jeff and before that, when things weren't going well with us, I'd had to leave early a few times and then there was the day when I broke down in the coffee room, but that was it really. Oh, apart from the day when I was showing a client around a property and I cried because he reminded me of Jeff and I might have flirted with him a bit more than was professionally advisable... crap. And that day last week when a potential buyer from America had to wait while I got sick in the bathroom of a boutique hotel I was showing him round after drowning the poor man in the stink of vodka from the night before. Oh shit.

'Yes, it has been poor lately and not like the vibrant go-getter we know, Maggie,' says Will, but he is still smiling. He is not mad. 'Days off, working 'from home', late arrivals, missed appointments... but your health comes first and foremost and you are too big an asset to our team to take any chances on. You seem very stressed and upset so I'd like to offer you some time out, with a payment plan, of course, to get yourself together and when you feel like coming back, the door is always open.'

Stressed? Well, of course I am stressed. My husband left me for a younger model and seventeen years ago today I lay on an operating table and I've outlived any expectancy the doctors could have given me, and believe me, the reminder every year of another year of survival is a big burden and a huge heap of gratitude to carry around.

But time out... a payment plan? I think I am going to choke and the walls are moving towards me again. Why are they offering me this lifeline? I don't deserve this.

'Can I get you some water?' asks Sylvia. I wish they would stop staring and smiling. Why do they have to be so nice? It's making me worse.

I look up to see Will Powers Sr enter the room, apologising too for being late. Sweet Jesus, this really is serious. *Very* serious. To have both 'Wills' in the same room always indicates a crisis. In fact, it is a sight that's enough to put the fear of God into any working member of staff.

Sylvia gives me the glass of water and I sink it in one. I didn't realise I was so thirsty.

Will Sr pulls a chair out right beside me and clasps my cold, sweaty hand tight. I always admired him so much and he knows it and he has nurtured me through my whole time at the company, giving me opportunity after opportunity. I feel like I have let him down.

'Maggie, we don't want to lose you,' he says gently, reminding me of my father. They are about the same age, but their lives are worlds apart. My dad drives a tractor while Will Powers Sr drives a Jaguar. My dad holidays in a caravan in Donegal while Mr Powers takes his wife on Caribbean cruises. Yet there is something about him that reminds me of old Robert back on the farm with his cows and sheep and love of a good old fry-up on the weekends and his current obsession with celebrity divorce.

'I'm sorry, Mr Powers. I'm sorry if I've disappointed you in any way. I know I have missed quite a few days and my work probably has um, *slipped*, but I can assure you that I will make it up to you. To all of you.'

Here I am, almost thirty-four years old, in my fancy suit and expensive shoes, at almost the peak of my career and I feel like a schoolgirl who hasn't done her homework or who has been caught cheating in an exam.

'You have let no one down,' says Mr Powers. The others move their heads like nodding dogs. 'And don't be panicking and thinking we have called a crisis meeting which is all about you. We have a few major projects to discuss today, which is why we are all here together, but it is because you are so special to us that we wanted to show you our full support in helping you get through whatever it is you need to get through.'

I think of other incidents; the car accident I almost had when I arrived at work a little tipsy from the night before... the days I had turned up so hung over I could hardly string a sentence together... there were many little things I had chosen to ignore and now they had all come to the forefront, like an abominable snowball rolling down a hill towards me. The day I sent an email to a wrong client and put 'x' like a kiss at the end of it, again due to a boozy lunch, and the time I called another a wrong name throughout an entire meeting because my head was too fuzzy and full of anger with Jeff to have done any preparation.

And they are giving me a lifeline. Instead of telling me to clear my desk and never come back, they are giving me a chance to put my life back together. Wow.

'We were thinking of six to eight weeks, initially,' says young Will Powers from the head of the table. 'If this isn't long enough, just let us know. We all need time out, Maggie. Hell, I know I do from time to time. I don't want to see any of our staff burn out, least of all someone as valuable to the team as you are.'

My God, the Man of Steel does have a heart after all and a pretty big one at that.

'I... I don't know what to say.'

'Do you agree it might help?' asks Sylvia who sits opposite me. I always thought she was a bit of a self-absorbed snob and now I swear I can see her eyes fill with tears in empathy.

'Yes,' I mumble back to her and nod, wiping my nose. 'Yes, I do. I didn't think that things were so bad, but now that I'm here... well, yes, I do think it will help.'

'That's good,' says Will Sr. 'I want to see you get back in the hot seat here at Powers Enterprises as quickly as possible and if there is anything else we can do to help, just give me a call.'

I look at the business card he presses into my hand and flip it over to find his personal number written in his own handwriting. I am overwhelmed with a flurry of emotions, like a slow-motion movie is unfolding as I watch on in disbelief.

'Thank you, Mr Powers,' I whisper, still staring at the card. 'Thank you. All of you.'

He walks me to the door but instead of stopping there, Will Powers Sr walks me through the open-plan office, past my colleagues, who don't even lift their heads (no one ever does when he is around) and down into the foyer. Thankfully Bridget isn't at the front desk. We walk outside and the rain has stopped and Davey the porter must be on a cigarette break, so I have a clear path to the car, but Mr Powers stops just before we reach it.

'Sometimes, Maggie, life moves too fast and we can't keep up no matter how hard we try. Before you know it, you're facing retirement and kicking yourself, wondering how on earth you've missed out on the simple things in life. Take some time and *breathe*. Do at least one nice thing every day, something for yourself. Build yourself back up again and then I want you right back here where you belong. Do you hear?'

I nod back at him and smile. Carlsberg don't do bosses...

'You're a very special and very kind man, Mr Powers,' I tell him. 'I will never forget you for this. Thank you.'

'I'll see you back here really soon,' he tells me and for a second, I think he is going to give me a fatherly hug, but he stops and pats me on the shoulder and then walks off towards the tower block where I have spent most of my life for the past five years.

I sit in the car for a few moments and breathe right to the pit of my stomach, trying to digest what has just happened on today of all days. I feel a weight lifting off my shoulders, a pressure gone already and I take my time before I drive off and don't stop until I reach the off license.

I need a drink.

Chapter 3

It's almost ten at night and I am watching my wedding DVD all on my own and I keep rewinding it to the part where Jeff reads out the poem he wrote especially for me and there's a big close-up on me and my eyes are stinging red from crying at his overwhelming love.

Now they are stinging red from overwhelming love for Sauvignon Blanc. Isn't it amazing what a difference a year or two makes?

'You lift me up when I'm feeling down. You light up my world when you smile. You are my one and only, the one I love and the one who I want to grow old with.'

Vomit...

I can see that it's straight from Google, or else a Ronan Keating song, now that I have snapped out of my starry-eyed romantic honeymoon phase. I am now in a 'bitch of darkness phase' after my afternoon of sleeping and drinking and sleeping and drinking and ignoring more phone calls. (It's Flo this time. She will be grand, as they say here in Ireland. *Grand.*)

I switch off the DVD, put on some eighties' classics and sway to the beat of Rick Astley, then look out the window

27

onto the city below me and I raise my glass to my freedom and my future. I have got to be positive. I am merry and positive and I am on a 'career break' – that's what they call it these days. I have it all at my feet and the world awaits, starting with this city I call home.

Plus it's still my heart anniversary, isn't it? On this day, seventeen years ago I was at death's door and then a miraculous gift of life from a little girl in Scotland and her totally amazing family gave me the chance to grow into adulthood. So what if I don't have a husband any more. So what if I almost lost my job by acting the eejit lately. I still have life! I don't know how much longer I have it, but for now I do and it's for living!

'I still have life!' I shout out through my open window and a couple below me shout back at me to fuck off. I smile at them and wave. I am drunk again. And I am loving it! I love everything right now!

Mostly, I love Belfast. I love the buzz, the people-watching, the culture, the accents, the shopping, the night-life and the sense of community that still exists, even though it's very much a big city to a country girl like me with its universities, cosmopolitan quarters and bloody dark history.

I think of all the men I have loved and lost since I moved here in my university days and I start to laugh and laugh and laugh at the memories.

There was Bob, the engineering graduate (or Bob the Builder, as we all called him), who moved to Australia when I was in the thick of my studies and who never returned. There was Martin, an accountant from Dublin, who said he loved me but that with my temporary tattoos and purple hair at the time, he could never see me being the 'wife' type; there was Andrew who worked in sales but who turned out to have a criminal record the length of my said long legs and more, and then there was Jeff, the teacher who, as already mentioned, left me for Saffron the Stewardess quicker than the shine wore off his wedding ring.

My love life has been, let's just say, colourfully complicated.

'I love being colourfully complicated!' I shout out loud and continue dancing with myself.

'Fuck off', shouts Mr Smart Ass from below again. This time I give him the fingers, then laugh my way to the sofa, totally absorbed in Wham!, who are now playing on the music channel. This is fun. No work tomorrow, a white-wine buzz and Wham! What more would a girl want? Who needs a husband and a job anyway? I'm drunk and I'm on top of the world! I've got this! I've finally got this!

I see my mail on the coffee table. How exciting! I've got mail! Real snail mail. I lift it up and try to sort it while still dancing, but my vision is blurred and I have to set down my wine glass to focus.

A letter from my mobile-phone company, a credit-card bill... I fling them on the floor.

A list of offers from the local supermarket? A voucher with a pound-off washing powder. How exciting?! And it's on the floor it goes too!

But then a handwritten letter catches my eye and it stops me in my tracks.

I study it, knowing almost immediately that this is of some

sort of huge importance but the words are moving, dancing before my eyes. I squint to focus. No good. I close one eye. The writing is neat, all in capital letters and in blue biro. It reminds me of the letters I used to get from a pen pal I once had who lived in Brighton and who drew lines on her envelopes with a pencil and ruler and then rubbed them out when she had written the address in perfect symmetry. Weirdo.

I try to read the postmark on the letter and eventually it comes clear. It says the letter was posted in town of Tain, near Inverness in Scotland.

Scotland, right? *Tain?* Oh holy shit!

My heart stops. Quite ironic, really, but it literally skips a beat and when I find my breath again I reach for my wine and take a long gulp, draining the glass.

There is only one person I know from Tain. One person I know, but who I never have met and never will.

That person is Lucy Harte.

And Lucy Harte is dead.

Chapter 4

I wake up in daylight with the letter in my hand, still unopened. I must have collapsed into a drunken coma – again – or else from the shock of what could lie inside this envelope.

'Just open it, Maggie,' Flo tells me when I call her. She doesn't even get mad that it's just gone seven in the morning, but then again, her son has probably been awake for at least an hour so it's like the middle of the day to her. 'There's no point staring at it and wondering. Are you sure you don't want me to come over?'

I am still holding the letter and I try to sip the last glass of wine from last night which tastes like vinegar and makes me gag. I am not yet totally sober. But unfortunately Flo can't just 'come over' – as much as I'd want her to. As a single parent, she can't exactly up sticks and leave with a two-year-old on her hip at this time of the morning. He goes to school. No, he is only two so he doesn't go to school. He goes to day care. I am such a crap friend.

'Don't be silly,' I tell her, even though I would give my right arm for her to be sitting here with me now. 'You have Billie to get sorted. Do you really think it's from them?'

I can hear Flo inhale deeply and finally she replies.

'Well, unless it's some sick joke, yes I do think it's from 'them'. I mean, Tain is hardly the centre of the universe and from your description of the envelope, it's not a bill or one of those random marketing leaflets or charity letters. It has to be them.'

'Them' are the Harte family. Lucy Harte's family. I don't know how many of 'them' they are or if they are men, women or children; her grandparents, her mother or her father and despite my efforts in my early twenties to find 'them' to thank 'them' by going through the official route via hospitals and social systems, this is the first correspondence I have ever had and certainly not the way I expected to hear from them.

But why would they be writing to me? Why now? And why not when I wanted them to in years gone by?

'They aren't supposed to get in touch with me directly, Flo,' I say, looking around the kitchen now and searching in every corner for a cigarette. I don't smoke and never have done, but I need something to ease my nerves and Jeff used to have the odd smoke when he felt anxious, so maybe it would work for me. 'It's a delicate process. It's supposed to go through the hospitals if there is to be any correspondence.'

'That doesn't say they won't find you if they want to,' said Flo. 'The world is tiny, Maggie. You know Lucy's name, so I'm sure they could have found out yours if they wanted to. A quick Google search or a nosey on Facebook and *voilà*. It's not rocket science.'

'I suppose,' I mumble. 'But what would they want from me?'

'Well, what have you always wanted from them?' asks Flo.

'Closure, maybe? A chance to say thank you for my shitty life.'

'You don't have a shitty life,' Flo assures me. 'It's just temporarily shit.'

I light up a cigarette I found in a box in a drawer. I knew there had to be one from the house-warming/birthday party I had. The morning after left all sorts of evidence of a heavy night.

'Are you smoking?' asks Flo.

'Are you psychic?' I retort. My God, she doesn't miss a beat.

'I sometimes think I am a bit. Do you think I am?'

'No. Yes, I am smoking and I'd take stronger stuff if I could get my hands on it, believe me,' I say, which is so not true as I am petrified of anything stronger than a menthol cigarette, in reality, and Flo knows it.

'Anyhow, are you going to open the letter, or are you not?' she asks. 'No matter if this is the official way of doing things or not, you are going to have to open it before you send yourself crazy and me with it.'

'Okay, okay, I'm on it.'

I stare at the handwriting again and put the cigarette on an ashtray, then exhale smoke from my lungs, polluting my beautiful kitchen. I start to cough. Guilt and an urge to vomit make me put the cigarette out after one puff. Disgusting.

'I thought this was what you always wanted, Maggie?'

'It is what I've always wanted,' I whisper and, as if on autopilot, my fingers start to pull the envelope apart as I nestle my phone under my ear. 'But I'm absolutely petrified, Flo. I think I'm in shock.'

'Okay, pause a second. Wait!' says Flo. I am totally convinced she can see me. The woman should have been a detective. She can read me like a book.

'What? I'm in the middle of opening it, for crying out loud!'

'I just want you to think of what it is you would like this letter to say. What is it you had ever hoped to gain from meeting with, or talking to, the Harte family? You say closure. Is there anything else?'

'I suppose... I suppose I just want to let her go,' I say and I close my eyes as my own made-up images of Lucy flash through my mind. 'I want to be able to close the door on Lucy Harte and get on with my own life. And I guess the only way I've ever felt that would be possible was if I got a chance to say thank you to whoever it was who decided to offer up her organs to someone like me when they had just suffered the ultimate tragedy of losing their own child.'

'Well, that's certainly it in a nutshell,' says Flo and, before I know it, I have the letter unfolded and the words blur before me. The writing inside, like on the envelope, is handwritten in neat black ink. I am impressed.

'Oh God, Flo.'

'Oh God Flo what? *What?*'

'It *is* them. It really is them! Will I read it out?'

'Well, I can't see it from here, can I?! Yes! Read it out.' She stops for a second. 'Only if you want to, of course... I can hang up and hear from you later if you want to do this your-self?'

There is no way I want to do this myself, which is why I

called Flo in the first place. I have read the first line twice but still haven't digested a word.

'Okay, here goes,' I say, clearing my throat, as if I am in front of a huge audience. 'Dear Maggie...'

Dear Maggie,

I hope I haven't shocked you too much by contacting you directly and to your home address but I have work connections in Belfast and, with a bit of poking around, I found you at last. We have a mutual friend, believe it or not, and he was able to give me your address. At least, I hope it's you and not some other random lady called Maggie O'Hara, who will have no clue what I am talking about.

My name is Simon Harte and I am the older brother of Lucy, who died on 10th April 1999 and who was your organ donor. I still remember that day and those before it like I do yesterday, but I won't burden you with the details of how she died as it's not essentially why I am getting in touch.

I know you tried to contact us a few years back and I'm sorry that we only got so far and the process stopped, but my father, well he wasn't capable of it, Maggie. He wasn't capable of a lot since our family was torn apart that day. He was a broken man from that day on – a broken man who never was fixed.

He thought donating organs was the right thing to do at the time, but he cursed himself for years afterwards, having nightmares about his decision. I hope you understand that meeting you would have not given him any comfort. In fact, it might have tipped him over the edge.

However, the decision to reply to you is no longer in his hands. Sadly my dad, after years of suffering, passed away last month and now it's just me left… just me, my memories of my family and an Irish girl who holds the heart of my dead sister. There are others, I suppose, who are out there, but you are the only one to ever look us up.

This week marked Lucy's anniversary and the first one I had to face up to on my own. And now I am writing to you…

I don't want to freak you out, Maggie. I ask nothing from you and if you don't reply I will try and forget that you exist and do my best to move on with my life.

But you contacted us first and now that the next step of the process is in my hands and mine only, I want to let you know that I'm up for a chat if you think it would help you move on or close a chapter that I can imagine has been haunting you for years, as it has done me. I would love to see how my sister's legacy has lived on.

My contact details are on the page enclosed. We could chat on the phone or even email if you prefer? Don't worry – I won't land at your door! And you can take my offer or leave it.

I hope you take it.
With very best wishes,
Simon D. Harte

I put the letter onto the table and slowly let go of it, but my eyes are superglued to his signature. Simon D. Harte. Lucy Harte's brother. And a mutual friend? Who could that be?

'Christ almighty,' says Flo. 'What do you think of that, Maggie? Are you alright there?'

I'm not sure if I'm alright. I'm not sure if I am even still breathing. I need to read it again and again. It is both heart-breaking and breath-taking and so different to how I imagined this moment would happen. I never really believed the day would come when I would hear from the Harte family and now it has and it's even more overwhelming than I expected it to be.

'Are you going to get in touch? I'd be itching to if I were you. But have a think about it first. He seems nice. But then I thought Damian was nice and he fled before Billie was out of nappies. I hope he is nice,' says Flo. She is rambling. Flo always rambles when she is nervous.

'Yes, I am going to contact him,' I say, and of that I am sure. 'In fact, I am not going to waste another second. I am going to contact him now.'

I stand up and the room starts to spin, so I sit back down again and try and regain some focus. Am I crazy? Am I even ready for this? It's something I have always dreamed of happening, but I've just taken time off work to get myself together and I'm not sure if this is the way to do so. Or maybe it is. Maybe this is what's meant to be...

'Now? Are you going to contact him now?' says Flo. 'Maybe you should wait... you know, sleep on it.'

'Sleep on it?' I ask her. 'Sleep on it? I can't sleep on it!'

'Okay, okay. What are you going to say to him, then?' asks Flo.

I stand up again, this time more slowly, and lean against

the worktop for support. What am I going to say? What *am* I going to say? I have absolutely no idea...

'I'll tell you when I do. Thanks Flo.'

'Keep it simple, Maggie. Polite and simple.'

She says goodbye and hangs up and I am left in my kitchen with an empty glass of last night's wine, a smoky room and a mind full of whirlwind thoughts. I have so much to say, but where on earth do I start? I have absolutely no idea.

At 8am I am in bed and on my third draft of what I'd decided, on Flo's advice, was meant to be a very polite and simple reply – in which I would thank Simon Harte for getting in touch, hope he was well, give sympathy to him on the death of his father and take it from there. As in, wait for a reply and see how it goes. Simple.

But it wasn't simple at all. I have so many questions I want to ask him and they just won't stop gushing out. What was Lucy like? What happened to her? Did she die suddenly? Did she suffer? Does he resent me like his father did? Are there other people walking around with Lucy's organs inside them? What about her poor mother? Where is she now? Is she still around? Did knowing about me make him feel like Lucy wasn't really dead? Has he tried to contact me before or even thought about going behind his father's back to do so? How long did it take to find me? Who told him my name? Who the hell is our mutual friend? Was he doing this through grief or was it something he had thought about properly? Had he sought professional help before even considering such a decision?

I write and delete and write and delete and my eyes are starting to drop again but I won't give in to sleep until I press send. Eventually I settle for this...

Dear Simon,
First of all, I am so sorry to hear of your loss. I cannot put into words how thrilled I am to hear from you.

Thrilled. No, I'm not thrilled. That sounds desperate. I start again.

Dear Simon,
Thank you so much for getting in touch. How brave of you to send your letter. You have indeed found the right Maggie O'Hara and I am delighted to hear from you after a long time searching and wondering.
I am so very sorry to hear of the loss of your father.
I have so much I want to ask and say and I've written this email over and over again to avoid waffling and now here I am doing exactly that... waffling.
Anyhow, yes, it's me.
I too have listed my contacts below, should you want to chat further.
God bless you,
Maggie

I press send. *God bless you?* What? I must be turning holy. My stomach is in my mouth as I close the laptop and curl up under my duvet in a mixture of delirium and exhaustion.

I re-read the email. Shit, but it is awful. It's bitty, it's nervy, it's rushed. Shit. But it's done.

I need to sleep.

Simon D. Harte. I wonder what the D stands for. Derek? David? Daniel? Yes, I bet it is Daniel. Why am I even wondering that? What difference does that make?

I wonder lots of things. I wonder where he is right now. Well, he is in Tain, I suppose. But where exactly?

Is he a sad and lonely man who is clinging on to a last-chance family connection and is going to want to meet me like I'm long-lost family? Is he lying right now in bed with his arms around an oblivious woman who has no idea of his pursuing me and will go nuts when she finds out in case it takes him away from her? Maybe it's been a lengthy obsession with him to find the people who carry parts of his dead sister around?

My mind continues to race furiously.

Maybe Lucy Harte was murdered or killed in a freak accident and he is out for revenge and will now track me down in a fit of rage and jealousy that I am alive and she isn't! Oh, good Lord!

Maybe he is outside my door now and has been following my every move in some stalker-type way and is going to break in and kidnap me and hold me to ransom!

Or my parents! What if he has tracked them down too and wants to blackmail them in some sick kind of way and threatens to kill them all!

Maybe I am the one going nuts!

Maybe Flo was right and I should have slept on it.

I lie and stare at the ceiling. It's going to be a long, long day.

I wake up later that morning with a crick in my neck and a thumping headache and check my phone with the same dread that comes with every hangover.

I turn to say good morning to Jeff but he isn't there, of course.

It's just me and the plush, unslept-on new pillow beside me and this strange room that I am so trying to get used to with its new pale grey-and-white gingham bedcovers and matching curtains and clean white walls that I am trying my best to suit the new me.

I scroll through Facebook, but it only serves to annoy me as I read of people I hardly know and their pretend-perfect lives, then turn to Twitter for a snapshot of random thoughts from more people I don't know. And then I check my emails and a rush of excitement fills my veins when I remember the early-morning message I sent to Simon D. Harte.

I have two messages in my inbox, so I'm guessing that the emails, or at least one of them, are from Simon.

But they are not. One is from a finance company offering loans at a ridiculously high interest rate and another is offering me Viagra for a discount price of $5. I'm gutted. Why hasn't he replied?

Probably because he hasn't read it yet and is at work or doing whatever people do in the north of Scotland like eating a late breakfast or an early lunch or reading the paper or on a train to a meeting somewhere?

Yes. Probably.

I sneak another look at Facebook, despite how much it aggrieves me these days. Jeff and I have lots of mutual online friends and I know I run the risk of his photo popping up on my newsfeed is a huge probability and I will sink into further self-pity when it happens. Especially if it is one with 'herself' in it. I wonder, do they take selfies and post them like we used to? I wonder, does he take her picture at every turn like he used to do with me?

And then my phone pings and I open my Inbox, wide-eyed and hoping.

This time it isn't junk mail. It is him.

It's Simon D. Harte. Oh, good God above.

I bless myself and press open, then I bless myself again. I will be joining the golden oldies in the church soon and saying the rosary in whispers if I keep up this rate of acknowledging God, but somehow it feels like the right thing to do.

Dear Maggie,

I take a very deep breath.

I don't know when the last time was that I cried.

I don't even think I cried at the funeral way back then but, to be honest, that's all a blur. I was only seventeen and I think I stayed in shock for at least a year after that. What I am trying to say is that I am really not a man who cries easily, or even when pushed, and believe me I have been pushed to the limits many times. My wife is having our first baby and is very emotional, so I need to let her do most of the crying these days!

I cried, however, when I read your email. I have never been so relieved about anything in my whole life as I am now that I have heard back from you and that you are not mad or telling me to butt out of your life or reporting me to the medical authorities for contacting you directly.

I too am trying not to waffle but there is so much to ask you, so much to say. Do you feel the same?? Please be honest. I can't emphasise this enough – I don't expect anything from you. You don't have to reply again if you don't want to. I'm just so happy to hear from you and to know that you are well. You are well, aren't you? I really hope you are.

Now I am so waffling.

I will go and wish you a great day.

Best wishes and most of all, thank you for getting in touch.

Thank you

Simon

No 'D' this time. Just Simon. Just plain informal chatty 'Simon'.

I read it all over again. And then again. And then again.

He seems pretty normal, right? Not too serial killer-ish, so I think I'm pretty safe for now. He has a wife. They are having a baby. I picture him, sitting at a breakfast table, or maybe on a train. He is somewhere out there, pressing send and waiting in the same anticipation as I have been on a response. Even in my dreams I was waiting on a response. What does he look like? What did Lucy look like? My mind is racing. I have so many questions! Where do I start? I haven't even got out of bed and there is so much I need to say and do!

I start typing back immediately.

Dear Simon…

So lovely to hear from you again. If you want to talk, any time, please feel free. My number is on my signature at the bottom of my email, so do give me a buzz anytime.

We all need to talk. I know I really do right now.

Chat soon,

Maggie

And then I send. And I wait.

Chapter 5

M y mother calls me later that afternoon when I am toying between a bunch of lilies or a bunch of tulips in Tesco.

'And I just told her that when it comes to John Joe, he will do what he wants when he wants and no one, not even her, will stop him,' she says.

'Told who?'

'Vivienne!'

I am still none the wiser. 'Who?'

'*Vivienne*! John Joe's girlfriend!'

I have no idea why my mother thinks the domesticities of my older brother and his latest squeeze hold any interest for me, but I try and keep up with her.

'Right, okay,' I mumble, checking the price tags on the flowers to help me decide. Tulips it is.

'I mean, even your father says that John Joe is his own worst enemy when it comes to relationships. He can't handle sharing his space. He can't handle sharing a bag of bloody chips, never mind anything that might dare last longer! So I thought I did right by setting the poor girl straight. What do you think? Did I say too much?'

'What?'

'Did I say too much? I mean, it's not as if I have even met her, but she called me for advice and I could barely make out her accent. I think she is French. I always try to give good impartial advice, even to the lovers of my own two children, no matter what their nationality.'

I put the tulips back and pick up the lilies. I should probably get a basket. I fancy a browse around the clothes section for Billie.

'You did the right thing, Mum,' I reassure her, even though I have barely listened to a word she was saying. 'Is this the girl who had his name tattooed on her chest?'

'Lord no,' she says. 'She was last year's model. This is the girl that his friend Clive, the country singer, introduced him to. You see, our John Joe was working on Clive's ranch shoeing horses near Nashville for a few weeks and he met her. Poor girl. She is in for an almighty fall.'

'Oh men! They are all filthy rotten lying fucking bastards,' I say a little too loud and a passing stranger gives me a dirty look.

'Exactly!' says my mum. 'I couldn't have put it better myself. And speaking of men. . . any word from –'

'No, Mum, no word from Jeff,' I reply quickly. 'I don't want to... oh no!'

I trail off. I freeze. Ah Jesus. Ah Jesus no.

'Maggie?' my mother calls. 'Maggie, are you there?'

Please no. Don't do this to me. Not now. No.

My skin goes cold. I didn't think that could actually physically happen but every part of me tingles with angst from my very toes to my fingertips. Fizzy, prickly, pins and needles of anxiety.

'I have to go, Mum. I've just spotted... someone I used to know. I'll call you back.'

I stand there, bunch of lilies in one hand and my phone in the other, in the kids' clothes section of my local Tesco watching, as if in slow motion, as Jeff, my 'husband' and his fancy woman walk obliviously towards me, laughing and looking into each other's eyes as she pushes a trolley full of fucking groceries.

I think I am going to actually vomit as an invisible wrench clasps my whole insides. Oh God!

She leans on the trolley and he stands behind her, playfully putting his hands on her waist as she walks along, scanning the aisles with a love-struck smile on her face.

He used to do that to me.

'Are you okay, love?' asks a little old lady. 'You look like you've seen a ghost.'

Jeff sees me.

Our eyes lock and he raises his hand, a desperate look of guilt replacing the smug look of love from seconds before. I can't move. I don't want to look but like one does at a car crash I can't help but stare and stare and then she follows his eye line and looks towards me and her face sours and she looks panicked up at him and I just want to go home. Now.

'Have some lilies,' I tell the old lady, handing her the flowers. 'You're right. I have seen a ghost. I have to get out of here.'

I make it to the car before I burst into tears and huge unapologetic cries of despair empty out from my lungs.

I hit the steering wheel.

'Bastard! Seventeen fucking months! What does she have that I don't have? What?'

I turn the ignition. I am in no fit state to drive. I want to go to Loch Tara, far away, and lock myself in my room and hide under my duvet and hug my mum and dad and just crawl out of my own skin.

I want to punch him. I want to punch her.

I have no energy to punch anyone.

A message comes through on my phone but I don't dare look at it yet. If it is Jeff... if he has the audacity to apologise in a text message, I don't know what I will do. I don't want to hear from him. I want to hear from him, but I don't want to. I don't know what I want.

I look at the phone. It's not a text, but an email and it's from Simon Harte.

'Can I call you?' is all it says.

I put the car into reverse and speed out of the car park.

I need a fucking glass of wine.

I dash into my apartment block to avoid the late-afternoon April shower, kicking myself for being so upset at seeing Jeff and that giraffe-like bitch who he was all over like a rash.

I am bigger and better than that, I say, as I climb the stairs to my front door, stomping up each step with vengefulness. How dare he? How dare he?

I fling off my coat and throw my bag on the floor, then bend down to get my phone and contemplate messaging

Simon back. I don't know if I have the energy for Simon and Lucy Harte.

I will shower, get freshened up and then I will reply to him. Maybe.

I am towel-drying my hair when the phone rings and I look at it in disbelief. It's him. It's his number, glaring at me, urging me to pick up and actually... well, talk, I suppose. Actually speak instead of typing bravado questions and messages. *Talk.*

I quickly tie my hair back.

'Hello?'

'Maggie!' says a very rich, more mature and confident voice than I had expected. But then he breaks slightly. 'My God, Maggie.'

I don't speak. I can't speak. I sit down on the bed.

'Are you okay?' he asks, but I don't know what the answer to that question is. Am I okay? Probably not. Is it anything to do with him? Probably not.

Or maybe it is. I don't know anything any more.

'I'm looking at flights to Belfast,' he says eventually. 'Are you free this weekend for a coffee? I need to see you, Maggie. In person.'

I stand up again. Then I sit again. A coffee? With him? Here? In Belfast? What the actual fuck? Already? What?

'*Flights?*'

'Yes,' he laughs. 'You know those things that take you from one country to another in an aeroplane. Flights. At least that's what we call them in Scotland.'

This has floored me. We only found each other yesterday

and now he wants to fly here and get together over a coffee? His accent is delicious. He sounds like Gerard Butler. He is not Gerard Butler, I remind myself.

'Are you sure you want to meet me? Isn't this all a bit –?'

'Soon?' he asks.

'Yes, soon.'

'Maggie, I have waited for years to find you,' he says. One minute his voice is an emotional quiver and then it extends into an almost overactive excitement. 'There is a football game this weekend I need to cover in Belfast – well, that's not exactly true. I don't need to cover it but I could if I wanted, so I figured I can mix business with, well, with finally getting to meet you. Only if you want to, of course. If you decide after this that you don't want to hear from me again, that's fine. It just feels amazing to have been able to chat to you.'

I seriously do not know what to say. I can't really argue with what he has said. Why wouldn't we meet up for a coffee? It's what I have always wanted. Closure. A chance to say thank you to someone related to the mysterious Lucy Harte.

But the weekend... that *is* soon. I need to prepare myself. I need to prepare the apartment. Will he want to come here at any time? I look around my bedroom. It's an absolute tip. The spare room is a mess. The living room is a mess and the kitchen resembles a bombsite. Is he expecting to stay here? I did tell him about my apartment and that I had a spare room. I feel a bit claustrophobic with it all.

'I can book in somewhere nearby,' he says, as if he read my mind.

Oh, thank God.

'Oh-okay,' I say with relief. 'Well, then, yes. Why not? Let's meet for a coffee. I know a great B&B on the Lisburn Road. It's lovely and it has real chandeliers and a library. Yes, okay. No harm in that at all.'

Real chandeliers and a library? What the hell am I on about?

'Perfect,' he says. 'You had me at chandeliers. Send me the name and I will book in. I'll check out more flight options and text you when I get into Belfast on Friday afternoon. I can't wait to meet you in person and I can't wait to tell you all about Lucy.'

I relax again. Simon is cool. Any pressure I felt for that moment has passed.

'I can't wait to hear about her too,' I tell him and I really do mean it.

I am in Flo's kitchen, freshly applied *au natural* look make-up on my face and rollers in my hair. Yes, rollers. Not the little-old-lady type but the big giant ones that promise volume and lift to my long hair, which is in need of some TLC. Flo is tweaking and checking the rollers as Billie vies for my attention, wriggling like a worm to get up on my knee and then immediately wanting to get back down again. He then ditches me for *Peppa Pig*.

Story of my life, being ditched for a pig – so no surprise there...

'So let's go over this all again,' says Flo. She is beginning to sound like my mother.

'Honestly, Flo, there really is no need. It's not like this is some dodgy online date, you know,' I retort. 'You are being over-protective.'

'I am not being over-protective. I am being sensible and wise,' she says, undoing one of the rollers and then putting it back in its place. 'Now, the signal is, you tweak your right earring if you need help and I will call your phone.'

'Who said I was going to wear earrings?'

'You always wear earrings. That way, you can make an excuse and go outside to take the call if you think he is a nutcase and I will follow you out and make up an escape plan.'

She is beginning to sound ridiculous.

'Flo! Simon is not a nutcase! He is the same as me in this whole situation,' I explain, picking a sticky stray Cheerio courtesy of Billie from the edge of my jeans. 'He just wants some closure and, on top of it all, he seems really nice, so there is no need for you to come along and sit at another table in the bar like some undercover detective. And besides, what will you do with Billie? There is no way he will sit for any length of time in a public place and he will probably make it clear that he knows me.'

Billie gives me a knowing look. He goes bananas when he hears my voice on the phone and is always hyper at first sight. I guess that's something to do with the treats and toys I brought for him, but as his godmother I believe that is my duty.

Flo rolls her eyes. There is no way I am putting her off.

'Billie is going to Ursula's for the afternoon. You know, Jack's mum from the mother-and-toddler group? We take turns when things come up to arrange a quick playdate to allow us both the odd hour off here and there out of daycare hours. I don't know what I would do without her.'

Now it is my turn to roll my eyes. I have heard it all now. A play *date*.

'So you mean, Ursula is going to babysit for a while at her place? Why didn't you just say that? What's with all these fancy 'new-age mummy' terms? What is happening to you?'

Flo laughs. She knows I have a point. It's the type of thing the two of us would have sneered at before Billie came along, only because we were secretly jealous, of course, and would love to be in the whole baby club. Now she is in that club up to her neck, though it's not exactly how she had planned it.

'Oh your day will come, Miss Power Suit,' she tells me. 'I bet you will be making up your own terms for mummy issues when you have a little ankle-biter. Now, let me see you.'

She has unravelled all the rollers and, I have to say, she has done a great job on my hair and my make-up is so subtle and effortless, which is exactly what I wanted for today. For the last ten years of her career, Flo was one of the city's most sought-after top stylists and beauticians, but had to work part time from home when little Billie came along and the aptly named Damien (think The Omen) she made him with did a runner. It's how I met her. She cut my hair for my job interview at Powers and we have been best friends ever since.

'Oh you're a star,' I tell her, loosening the curls with my fingers. My hair is well grown down, which is just how I like it and the curls give it just a little bit of bounce. 'I could never have done that in a million years. Now, do you still think jeans and a nice top? Or should I go summer dress? It's not too bad outside. Or maybe I should glam it up just a wee bit? You know, show an effort?'

Flo is concerned. I know she is. She does this thing with her nose, like a tiny twitch, when she is hesitant or a bit anxious about something. I'm trying to control my nervous excitement but we know each other too well to keep any secrets.

'Remember, Maggie. This is not a date.'

'I know it's not! He has a wife, for goodness sake, and a pregnant one at that. Plus, in case you didn't notice, I am in no fit state to be on a date, but I just want to look nice. You would too!'

'I just want you to be careful,' says Flo, hoisting little Billie on to her hip like it's the most natural thing in the world. I'm constantly amazed at how motherhood totally transforms a woman and I can't help but wish that woman one day soon will be me. Though not like Flo. I want the man too, if you don't mind, but I'm not exactly going in the right direction for that – with a failed marriage behind me.

'It's like this,' I explain, hoping to reassure her. 'Simon is the brother of the little girl who gave me life. I have had so many issues and struggles with trying to close the door on Lucy Harte for seventeen years now. She has haunted me forever and this might be my ticket to let her go.'

I sigh from the tips of my toes and get my coat, ignoring for now the chocolate finger prints that Billie has kindly left on it for me. Just as well this coat wasn't part of my planned outfit for later this afternoon.

'Simon gets into the city at two; we are having some pub

grub and a chat at The John Hewitt after that. It's all very cool and it's all very casual and if you insist on sitting at a table in a corner in case he murders me in a public place, then so be it. I know what I am doing, Flo. Believe me.'

She walks me to the door and I give her a light hug, then kiss Billie very quickly on the cheek. There is no way I am risking kid snot or dribble on my newly applied make-up.

'Say what you want but I will be there just in case,' she says.

'Say what you want but you're just nosey,' I say, walking to my car. 'You're dying to check him out all for yourself.'

She expertly pinches Billie's snot and wipes it on her shirt.

'Believe me, sunshine,' she says in earnest. 'Gawping at a man is the last thing on my mind right now. Go get ready. I'll be the one in the long trench coat. Just call me Jessica Fletcher.'

Chapter 6

I am early. I couldn't settle at home and I've been 'ready' for at least an hour, so I thought the best thing to do was just come here and wait. I do feel like it's an awkward blind date, even though I know it couldn't be anything more different. I chose my outfit carefully, a little too carefully perhaps, but I think I've got just about the right balance. Not too dressy, not too casual. The sun was shining and there was a hint of summer in the air as I drove here, which made my white jeans and pale-blue chiffon blouse feel just perfect for the occasion.

The occasion... what on earth is this occasion anyhow?

I am pondering this to myself when I see Flo come into the bar and she takes a seat and then hides her face behind a menu. I catch her eye and shake my head in laughter. She orders a drink from the waiter and then gives me the thumbs-up. I may have wound her up for doing this but now she is here I actually do feel a bit more settled. I am meeting a total stranger in very emotional circumstances, after all, so it's good to know she has my back, should it, for whatever reason, go horribly wrong.

I get the waiter's attention and ask for a tall gin and tonic.

I need some Dutch courage now – more than I've ever done in my entire life.

Are you there yet? It's a text from Simon.

I'm here, I message back. *I'm early.*

Good, so am I, he replies. The waiter returns and is just placing my drink on the table when I see him.

Jesus.

It really is him. Not Jesus, no, but Simon Harte, Lucy's brother, walking towards me right here, right now. I smile. I breathe. I glance over at Flo who is staring at him like he is the Second Coming.

I wave. He waves back and smiles and runs his hand through his hair, looking as nervous as I feel.

This is so, so surreal. I stand up to greet him. He is tall. Boy, but he is tall. I swallow back a rainbow of emotions and I can't hear anything now. The muffled sounds of cutlery and background music and people chatting fade into the background. Everything sounds and looks like a blur. I can see nothing and I can hear nothing. Nothing. Only him. It's like time has stood still and it is making me very dizzy.

'Maggie,' he says, in his soft Scottish brogue. 'Maggie, Maggie, Maggie.'

His eyes fill with tears and mine do too. He keeps saying my name, whispering it and then he kisses me lightly on the cheek.

'I... I have to say thank you, Simon,' I mumble. 'I just really want to say thank you to you and your family for what you have done for me.'

He stands back, his hands holding my wrists lightly and

his eyes dancing, like this is truly a moment he has been longing for as long as I have. I am afraid that if he lets go of me I might fall. The room is really spinning. I focus on his face. His beautiful, smiley, friendly face.

'You're real,' he says. 'You're Maggie.'

I feel my heart beat. My lonely, borrowed heart. I think of Lucy and I wonder if she is watching. Does she feel what I feel, what he feels – her very own big brother, who she left behind when she was much too young, has found me? A piece of her is inside of me. I feel guilty and grateful all in one big blow of emotion.

'I can't believe you are here,' I manage to whisper.

For some reason it's like my own world finally makes sense, like I make sense now. It is Lucy Harte's brother and his family is the reason I am still alive.

'I can't believe I am here either,' he says and I know he means it. 'I can't believe I am here... with you. This is... this is... pretty amazing.'

I feel so unsteady. If Flo looks at me now she will be calling an ambulance as I'm bound to be a deathly shade of white. He purses his lips and breathes in long and hard, then exhales and smiles and his eyes wrinkle and I can tell he is finding this just as overwhelming as I am.

'Thank you for seeing me,' he says. 'I have wondered about you forever. I think we should sit down. Will we sit down?'

'My heart is racing I'm so totally nervous,' I mutter and when he looks at me I can see the pain etched in his eyes as the reality of my heart, Lucy's heart, racing sinks in for him.

He guides me to my seat and I sit down slowly, then take

a sip of my drink, hoping it will bring me round. We stare at each other again and smile and stare and smile and stare.

'You look different to what I expected,' he says. 'Not in a good way or a bad way, just different. God, I am waffling again.'

'Well, you look... you look more tanned than I expected,' I say with a nervous giggle. 'Have you been on holiday? I feel very pasty and... well, Irish in comparison.'

He takes a seat opposite me, still smiling, still staring.

'Yes, I thought I'd mentioned that,' he says and his eyes wrinkle again.

'No, you didn't,' I reply. I am shaking, but hearing his voice is soothing and I get a real sense of familiarity just being in his company.

I am nervous. I am emotional and I am in awe of this moment. It's like I am meeting a long-lost family member, someone who has been looking for me and I have been looking for them for years and years and we are finally finding each other and it's so darn overwhelming.

I signal the waiter's attention again and Simon orders a beer as he tells me of a week in Greece he spent just after his father's funeral. He went alone, which impresses me greatly.

'Do you travel alone much?' I ask. 'I'm a bit of a chicken when it comes to going places alone. I always drag Jeff, well used to drag Jeff along or my mum and dad or a girlfriend. Some people prefer it. Do you?'

'No, not normally,' he says and his eyes divert from me slightly.

'Did I say something wrong?' I ask. He looks sad now. 'God I'm talking too much. Sorry, I'm just so –'

'No, you're not, you're not at all!' he says, brightening up a bit. 'It was more of a time to grieve than a holiday, that's all, but anyhow...'

He goes quiet and the waiter thankfully breaks the brief silence by serving Simon's beer, a Budweiser, by the bottle, like he asked for it. I stir my gin and tonic and feel butterflies in my tummy. Where on earth do we go from here? Food. Yes, food would the next stage, though I don't know if I can actually stomach food right now.

'You must be starving,' I say, handing him a menu, which I realise I have two of. 'I had a sneaky peek while I was waiting so I kind of know what I want. Though I am so nervous I don't know if I can eat.'

'I'm nervous too but I'm always hungry,' he says. 'My mum used to say...'

He trails off again and I notice him bite his lip.

'Go on...'

'Ah, it doesn't matter,' he says. 'I won't bore you with trips down memory lane just yet. Now, what do you recommend? I'm normally a steak-and-chips kinda guy.'

I glance over at Flo, who seems to have forgotten her detective mission and is wolfing down a humongous burger. Unlike me, she didn't have small talk to go through before placing her order, so is well ahead with her grub. It's just as well I'm not in any despair over here.

I realise that Simon is looking at me, waiting on my answer regarding the food.

'Oh, sorry, do excuse me!' I say. 'I thought I recognised someone there but it's an uncanny lookalike. Yes, recommendations. Well, I'm having salmon. I had steak here before and it was really good, so I'd say go with your usual.'

He flashes a smile at me and closes the menu. We are slowly beginning to relax now. It is a huge relief as my tummy starts to settle and my senses come back to me. I never felt nerves like that in my life, not even when I met Jeff's fancy-pants-rich parents and, believe me, that was nerve-wrecking because they hated me and I knew it and that was way before my Britney Spears impression.

'Steak and chips it is, then,' he says. 'Sorry if I'm staring. You're shaking. Are you really that nervous?'

He keeps looking at me. Yes, staring, but I am doing the same back.

'I'm something but I don't know what it is,' I confess. 'I am nervous, yes, overwhelmed more so, but I am slowly starting to come around now, very slowly. You?'

'Same,' he says and his eyes smile. 'I'm just in awe that this has finally happened. It's like this was always meant to be. I just had to find you...'

He fidgets a bit and then continues.

'Maggie, I hope I haven't frightened you by landing so soon.'

'No... God, no.'

'I'm in deep grief once again in my life,' he explains. 'I am vulnerable at the minute and raw but I just needed to see you. I wanted to see that in some strange way, I still have part of my family alive. Does that make me sound like some freaky weirdo?'

I look at Flo. She is still attacking her burger. If she was Jessica Fletcher she would be sacked by now.

I look back at Simon. I look at the table. I look at my hands. And then I find my voice.

'No, I don't think you are some freaky weirdo,' I tell him softly. 'I have always wanted to meet you, or someone connected to Lucy, so that I could say thank you. I wanted to thank you, thank Lucy, for my life.'

He really looks like he could cry. If I am vulnerable, he is even more.

'My wife thinks this is a bit crazy but I need to do this,' he says. 'I suppose that when my dad died, part of me died too and I just had to find something to hold on to. I'm making this all sound so desperate, but Lucy, well she was special to me and I wanted to see she... well, how she lives on. In you.'

I purse my lips and he puts his hands to his face in sorrow. Oh God, we should have met somewhere more private. This is all too much for a public bar. I don't know what to do. I don't know what to say.

'Are you okay, Simon? Do you want to go somewhere else? We could go to the park? For a walk?'

'No, no, of course not,' he says, taking a deep breath. 'I'm sorry. I kind of knew this would happen but... sorry, it's just a big moment for me, that's all. I'm very raw right now, Maggie.'

Of course he is. It all makes perfect sense. His little sister, to lose her so young must be the worst thing ever and now watching me, living, breathing, drinking, talking, sitting opposite him. This is a big moment for him, for sure. And for me.

'I hope I'm doing a good job with her heart,' I whisper, 'but to be honest, it's been broken quite badly lately and I really need to fix it.'

He looks up at me with tears in his eyes. I shouldn't have said that.

'Let's eat first,' he says as the waiter finally brings our food. 'Look, I am going to make this meeting positive because it *is* positive and there's no point us both sitting here blubbering over our food.'

He attempts a smile.

'It would be a shame to put this to waste,' I say, looking at the delicious steaming dishes that are set before us.

'It surely would. *Bon appetit*, Maggie,' says Simon Harte. 'I won't bombard you with everything too soon, but I have something for you that might, just might, help fix your broken heart. Or at least point you in the right direction.'

Chapter 7

After a fairly quiet but relaxed dinner, we decide to move on to somewhere new and as we walk through the evening sunshine I feel the warm fuzziness of the alcohol kicking in.

Before we left the bar, I gave Flo a discreet 'thumbs-up' when she finally had finished her burger followed by what looked like a chocolate sundae. She paid her bill and when Simon left the table to use the bathroom I sent her a text to tell her that he was very nice and very attached so that she could settle in the knowledge that I wasn't about to jump his bones and then find myself embroiled in yet another messy relationship in which I try to sprint before I can even crawl.

She replied with a lecture on not drinking too much and not to divulge too much information on the first meeting, but I could tell she was much more content about me spending the evening with Simon, as was I. Plus she had just herself indulged in her mighty chocolate sundae so she was, indeed, very happy and content with her full belly, never mind my predicament.

If only Simon Harte knew how much I had allowed my errant husband to tramp all over Lucy's precious heart and leave me in such a mess. If only he knew...

We walk past city hall and I do my best tourist-guide impression, pointing out different streets and hotels and interesting facts about Belfast. I tell Simon about Jeff and Saffron, about my job and how our break-up affected me, despite my denial at the time. I don't mention my growing alcohol problem, of course. He doesn't have to know *everything*.

'Sorry but Jeff sounds like a right plonker,' says Simon as we cross the street and head towards the Europa Hotel. I suggest the Europa because it's less noisy and not as stuffy as any city centre pub and we can have a proper chat in civilised surroundings without a live band or jukebox ringing in our ears. Plus they have a pianist in the lounge which I think will complement the mood nicely.

'That's one word for him. A plonker,' I joke back. 'I can think of a whole range of others. But maybe he is happy now. Maybe I didn't make him as happy as I wanted to. I am trying to believe in fate and that everything happens for a reason. Mind you, at this stage of the game, I have to believe in something.'

We go inside, take a seat in the piano lounge and order our drinks – Simon sticks with his Budweiser and I decide to treat myself to a Cucumber Cooler from the cocktail menu.

The pianist tinkles the ivories in the background at just the right volume and after a brief argument about what he was playing, which Simon wins – it was not a nineteenth-century classic, which I suggested, but a rather toned-down funky version of an Ellie Goulding song – we finally get down to business.

'Do you want to tell your side of the story, or shall I go first?' he asks. 'I'd love to know how a girl in Ireland needed a new heart and I'm sure you want to know what happened on our side of the pond.'

Since mine is much less complicated, I decide to take the reins.

'Well, rather than bore you to tears with my whole life story, which is completely irrelevant anyhow, I will fast-forward to when I was sixteen and where our story begins, when I was apparently a very healthy, normal teenager.'

'You were normal?' he says in mock surprise. So he has a sense of humour...

'Very funny,' I say and have a sip of my delicious cocktail. The mood is slowly loosening up with the help of good old alcohol. 'I do share a birthday with Amy Winehouse. Same year and everything.'

'Cool,' he says. 'That's pretty impressive. Can you sing?'

'In the shower I'm a rock star.'

'Snap,' he says with a smile, and then it's time to tell him my story.

I haven't really spoken to anyone in depth before about how I became the keeper of a borrowed heart – well, it might seem like party piece-style entertainment, but most people shy away from the subject as quickly as their eyes divert from the light scar on my chest – should they spot it – so talking to Simon, who is all ears and who has a genuine interest, is a whole new experience.

'I was quite the athlete back then,' I explain. 'I won most of the prizes on every sports day and the farmhouse was like a shrine to my achievements on the track and field.'

'Really?' he says, seriously surprised. 'I had visions of you as a really sick kid for years, or someone who was born with a heart condition.'

'Not at all,' I explain. 'Had I had any warning signs, what unfolded would have been less of a shock. It all happened very suddenly. Totally out of the blue.'

'Go on.'

'I have one brother, John Joe, who is a bit older than me,' I explain. 'My parents had gone to the market one Saturday and left us both to take care of things on the farm, just as they had been doing for years.'

The piano man is playing an Elton John favourite and in other circumstances I would stop to listen, but I know if I don't keep going I will never finish and I want to hear about Lucy as soon as possible and get my side over and done with.

'John Joe and I, well, we used to be really close before I got sick. Looking back, I think he resented me for not only coming along and ruining his status as an only child, but also for then totally stealing his thunder for taking most of my parents' attention when I almost died,' I explain, realising that I am talking very, very fast. 'I was helping him on the farm and I remember feeling ill, really ill. So, so ill.'

I slow down now and Simon is taking in every word, sipping his beer.

'I went into the house, despite John Joe's insistence on labouring me with more chores,' I tell him. 'He kept telling me I was faking it and being lazy and saying I looked okay and to just get on with it... I suppose he was just teasing me like any brother in charge would, but...'

'Take your time, Maggie,' he says. Everything feels like slow motion. The piano man has gone silent and things are blurry. Simon takes my hand.

'These... these,' I whisper, 'well, they were like really heavy flu symptoms, were becoming more and more severe. I couldn't breathe. I was sweating. I was so, so hot. I felt like I was shutting down inside. Because I was shutting down. My whole body was shutting down.'

I feel my voice break slightly so I decide to keep going and push on through the pain barrier that comes with reflecting on that dark day. If I stop talking now I will never be able to tell this story again.

'I had to lie down, so I went to the house and when it got even worse, I called for my brother, but he didn't come,' I tell him, and I feel all the hurt and resentment for John Joe rush through my veins again. 'He says he didn't hear me but I know he did. He heard me, Simon. He heard me and he didn't come.'

'Oh, Maggie, he couldn't have. He mustn't have heard you.'

My tears flow now and I look around, not wanting to cause a scene in such a warm and social environment. I can hear the piano again. I am going to be okay.

'Everyone says that but I think he did. I don't know. It doesn't matter... well, it does matter...'

God, this is harder than I thought it would be.

'Take a deep breath, Maggie,' says Simon. 'We have all night. Take your time.'

He puts his hand on top of mine again and I want him to hold me so badly. I want to lean in on his manly chest and cry and cry and never stop.

But I can't. So I do what he says. I take a deep breath and continue as best I can.

'They say I passed out and when I woke up, I could literally see that my heart had swollen in my chest,' I explain. 'It looked like it was going to burst. I tried to scream but I couldn't get a breath. And then everything went black again and I woke up in hospital, where I lay attached to a machine for almost two weeks waiting for a transplant – and then a miracle occurred. And that miracle was your sister's gift. To me.'

'Wow...'

'Yip. Wow indeed.'

I stare into my glass. Simon is still holding my hand.

'So, who found you?' he asks. 'Who came to your rescue? Was it John Joe?'

I see protection in Simon's eyes and it makes me want to never let go of him.

'My parents found me,' I tell him. 'When I got to hospital my heart was failing pretty rapidly. Turns out I had a congenital condition that would have killed me had they not came back when they did. I was inches from death and I needed a heart transplant to save me. Basically, I needed someone to die to keep me alive. And that someone was your sister. I'm so sorry.'

We both sit in silence, absorbing the moment. I have a flurry of emotions running through me right down to my toes. Relief, gratitude, love, grief, sorrow... but, most of all, guilt. Why did Lucy have to die and I got to live? Surely that isn't fair?

'And what happened since then? Could it happen to you again? Could Lucy's heart fail?'

It's the question I am asked the most and the one that I can never bear to answer.

'I take immune suppressing drugs every twelve hours and will do so all my life,' I explain to him. 'It's so my body doesn't try to fight the foreign cells, which would send me into rejection, which would be the worst thing ever.'

He knows what I mean. 'So, is there a life expectancy? Sorry, I shouldn't have asked you that.'

'It's okay, Simon,' I tell him. 'I know my special heart won't last forever and that someday I will need a new one to live and I see my consultant often enough to keep an eye on things. If that doesn't come my way, I'm grateful for all I have and all I got to see and do. Me and Lucy, well we just take one day at a time and so far we are doing just fine.'

Simon has gone to the bathroom and I sit there waiting, hoping my side of the story hasn't upset him too much. I feel like I have cheated him, like I have cheated Lucy and all their family. Why should I have survived when she didn't?

When he finally comes back, I see tiny beads of water on his forehead. It's not sweat because he didn't have it before he left. He must have splashed his face with cold water in the bathroom.

'Is this too much?' I ask him.

'No, please, no,' he says with such sincerity. 'It is why I am here. I have wanted to know this for so long. Tell me about your brother. Tell me the rest.'

'I feel so guilty, Simon. I feel so bad that I am here talking to you and Lucy isn't. You must resent me so much.'

'Maggie, Maggie, Maggie,' he says, sounding just like he did when he first came into the bar to meet me a few hours ago. 'Lucy died and that was nothing to do with you. You have given me hope. To find you is like finding a missing jigsaw puzzle piece that I lost all those years ago. She lives on in you and to see you in real life is something I have always dreamed of! Please tell me the rest of your story and then I will tell you mine and I hope that, in some way, all of this can help both of us. Please, go on.'

And so I continue…

'It took a long, long time to get the full story of what happened that day and then more time to forgive my brother,' I tell Simon. 'Years, really. Mum always idolised John Joe and she forgave him slowly once I had the operation and the transplant was a success. For my dad, it took a lot longer, but they managed to work together in some sort of civilised manner and then John Joe moved to America and has been womanising… I mean, working there ever since.'

Simon looks puzzled.

'That was my idea of a joke,' I say with a shrug. 'He seems to go through a *lot* of woman. Anyhow, I've stayed out of his way and he's stayed out of mine. With that unspoken arrangement in place, we all get along fine. At least we had a happy ending, thanks to your family and the brave decision your parents made.'

We sit in silence again for a few moments, both taking in the incident that I have just relived – something that I have avoided talking about for years and yet which kept me awake at night after night.

'I'd love to give you a hug,' says Simon.

'I'd love you to as well,' I say. I need a hug really badly.

I lean into him and he holds me and I close my eyes, my chest moving up and down as I focus on breathing in and out, in and out.

'I can feel your heart beat,' he whispers and I close my eyes and breathe.

Then I excuse myself and it is my turn to go to the bathroom. I need to compose myself before I hear Simon's side of the story. Apart from my grievance with my brother, at least my story *has* a happy ending.

His doesn't.

Chapter 8

'My sister Lucy was wise way beyond her years,' Simon tells me later and I lean on my hands, my eyes dancing in reflection of his happy memories. 'She was so clever, so tuned in and she looked after me and our younger brother, Henry, like we were precious jewels. She really was a special kid. I know I'm biased, but she was.'

He gulps and his mood drops a little.

'Her death, it happened at such a weird time for us,' he explains. 'My sister, our brother, Henry, and I were close, so close and we'd had such a brilliant few days as a family, which unfortunately was pretty rare for us. Mum and Dad were in top gear, you know, really flying after a few tortuous years when they had depended on others to come and pick up the pieces, but at that time... at that time, we were good, you know?'

He rubs his eyes. He is tired and it is getting late and we are both getting a bit tipsy by this stage. I contemplate stopping him, asking him to pause and tell me this when we hadn't consumed alcohol because, to be honest, I am afraid that when I wake up the next morning I will forget what he had said thanks to the amount of gin and the level of emotions that are swilling around in my head.

'My mum was an alcoholic,' he tells me.

Oh God. Ouch.

'... and for most of our childhood it was misery, but on that day, everything seemed, ironically, perfect, like she had finally put us before the bottle. But she hadn't.'

Jesus. I don't know what to say. This is not what I was expecting from this strong, beautiful man who has contacted me out of the blue. I think of my own drinking and the selfish way I have brought misery and worry onto others. I push away my glass. Then I reach for it again and feel the familiar glow the alcohol brings – like an old friend who is really your worst enemy.

'Are you sure you don't want to leave this until tomorrow?' I ask him. 'You look tired. You don't have to tell me this at all if you don't want to.'

'I want to,' he says.

Simon's childhood sounds so painful and worlds away from the idyllic upbringing I had on the farm with my older parents, despite my clashes with my big brother. My life sounded perfect compared to what Simon, Lucy and wee Henry had gone through and I feel like such a spoilt brat for complaining about John Joe.

He pauses for a second.

'I think I need to get this out of my system. It helps talking about it. Do you mind?'

'I don't mind at all,' I reply. 'Tell me anything you want to.'

He smiles. I am so touched by his honesty, about his pain,

about the heartache he has lived through and I totally respect that he has been to hell and back and has taken the time to find me and tell me Lucy's story.

'So Mum was insisting that Lucy had a haircut that day, which in any other family would be no big deal, right?'

'Of course,' I say, remembering in a flashback the time my own mother made me have my hair cut in a 'page-boy' style, which was all the rage. I looked like a cross between Lady Diana's bridal party and a cocker spaniel. I want to tell him that, to try and make him laugh, but now is not the time.

'Lucy had refused for so, so long. She didn't want to have her hair cut but that day she finally gave in. So Mum, Lucy and Henry set off and the mood was good. She seemed happy but we had no idea that she had been sipping away at her vodka all that morning,' he goes on, with deep sorrow in his voice and his eyes drop. 'I have gone over and over that morning since then, analysing her every move. Wondering what would have triggered it. A row with Dad? Or another crazy notion that his eyes were roaming towards any random woman that came his way? But there was nothing. Even Dad said there was nothing. He had gone to his conference that morning in high spirits, confident that when he came home, it would be as it had been for the last few days... I had sneaked my girlfriend around and was too worried about how she might feel if I kissed her for the first time. Just a normal, pretty nice day, but of course it didn't end that way at all.'

The barman signals to us that last orders are being taken and the piano man is packing up his song sheets. The room goes quiet as punters filter out and welcoming low-key house music fills the stillness in the air.

'Would you like another drink?' he asks and I shake my head.

'I think I have had enough.' His mother was an alcoholic. I can't go a day without a drink lately. Like John Joe said, I need to get a grip.

'Two whiskies, then,' he tells the barman.

'Whiskies?' Ah, Jesus.

'I think we might be glad of them. What is it you say in Ireland? One for the road?'

I can't really argue with that, can I?

'Okay, then,' I tell him. 'Let's have one for the road.'

I dread to think how bad his story will end, but no matter how much I anticipate, the real story is a whole lot worse.

'Mum drove into town after a morning's drinking behind our backs,' he tells me. 'We found her stash in the hot press, under the kitchen sink, in her old handbags, everywhere there was evidence that she had been topping up all along. They hit a car in a head-on collision and she was killed instantly. Lucy lived for two days, but her injuries were too much for her to survive.'

'Oh my God!' My hands cover my mouth. 'Not your mother too! No...'

'The other driver escaped almost unmarked, which was lucky for him. He was as devastated as we were.'

'And Henry? Was he okay?'

I am almost afraid to ask.

'Henry is... well, Henry is alive,' says Simon. 'Well, as alive as he can be. He was in a coma for three weeks with a brain injury and he stayed in hospital for two months after the accident. He needed special care after that and has lived with our Aunt Josie in Glasgow ever since. I see him when I can but he remembers very little really. He doesn't speak much. He exists, but he doesn't really live any more. He is twenty-eight years old but has the mind of the little boy he was on that awful day.'

We sit together, numbed at the story that has unfolded and for once in my life I am truly lost for words. Simon seems to be too as we stare at the table, at each other, at the barman who is wiping down empty tables and at the piano, which is now idle and without a tune.

'I think we should go,' he tells me.

'Yes,' I say. 'I think we both need some sleep.'

We have thrashed out enough, more than enough, for one night and our minds and bodies need to rest and digest all that we have told each other, though, to be honest, despite the rush of alcohol that fills my veins, I doubt there will be very much sleep for me tonight.

I say goodbye to Simon Harte and watch him from the back seat of my taxi as he walks towards the Lisburn Road to the B&B with the real chandeliers.

He looks so lost and lonely and his sister's heart aches inside of me with longing to ease his pain. I only hope that meeting me can give him the closure he so desperately needs so that he can look forward to his new life with his wife and their baby.

77

Chapter 9

I count sheep. I count them in English and then in French and then *As Gaelige* and then backwards in each language, but still sleep won't come. I see her every time I close my eyes. I see her freckled nose and her glasses and her long wavy, tatty hair that needed to be cut so badly that day. I hear her voice, or what I think it might sound like, and I feel... well, I feel her heart beat inside me and it makes me very sad.

'God bless you, Lucy,' I say out loud. 'God bless you poor, poor Lucy Harte.'

I think of Henry and his wide-eyed innocence. A little boy at only twelve years old, now orphaned and trapped in a man's body and fully depending on his ageing aunt. I think of Simon, sat that morning with his young girlfriend and worrying about how he might kiss her, when the police arrived at the door. I think of their father, now dead and buried too, and all the pain and regret he must have lived with for so many years. And I think of their desperately addicted mother, who probably thought she was doing the right thing that day by taking her daughter to have her hair cut, topped up in Dutch courage by the dreaded drink.

Life is cruel. Life is crap and cruel and I can't sleep.

I get out of bed and take my insomnia to the living area, where I curl up on the sofa under my throw again and turn on the TV. Shopping channels. Yes, that should do it. I lie there and squint at the screen, the rush of gin pumping through my veins and my head begins to spin. I am going to be sick. No... I am not. Yes I am... no... should I get up? What time is it? I feel dizzy again... I'm so...

The TV has gone onto standby and I wake up to the sound of a car radio booming outside. I lift my head from the sofa. Ouch. Damn you Cucumber Coolers. Then I remember about the whiskey. My mouth is like sandpaper. No bloody wonder. Yuk.

I am raging to be awake as I was having the most glorious dream where Jeff came to my door, totally unannounced, but looking oh-so handsome apart from needing a haircut, and like someone had waved a magic wand, he told me that Saffron didn't even exist and it had all been a big mistake. There was no affair. In fact, there was no one in this entire world called Saffron. No one in the entire universe called Saffron, in fact. *Saffron who?* He kept saying this. *You must have been dreaming, babe! You're my wife and I love you.*

He wanted to take me back to the place we called home, the terraced house we bought in Stranmillis until we decided where to build our dream pad, and the place where we would bring our first baby home to in just a few months' time because I was already pregnant and didn't even know it. It would be a girl, he said, and we would call her Lucy Harte.

Will Powers Sr was with him at the door and he was laughing at the idea of me thinking they had told me to take time out from work. *Don't be so silly, Maggie,* he had said and offered me another pay rise. It was a lovely dream, all in all.

I sit up and rub my face. I lie down again. It's only 6.30am. Thank God I don't have to face the world today. Well, not yet, anyway. Simon and I have planned to meet again for dinner before his night-time flight, but that is ages away. I can sleep again for now. Phew.

The doorbell wakes me what feels like ten minutes later, but when I look at the clock I am shocked to see it is nearly lunchtime. I head to the door, reminding myself of my mother as I mutter to myself as to who it might be at the door like it is one big mystery.

'Just answer it and see and stop wondering,' my dad would always tell her and lo and behold, it always worked. She would open the door and find the very answer to all her questions.

It's too late to be the postman and I haven't ordered anything that would come by special delivery so when I open the door, still tightening my dressing gown and squinting as I attempt to wake up, it is like a blow to the stomach when I see my husband standing there with his hands behind his back and his head lowered, just like in my dream.

'Jeff? What on earth are you doing here?'

Was this my dream coming true? He does look like he needs a haircut...

'Maggie, I had to come and see you,' he says, looking up at me under an overgrown, sticky-up fringe. He speaks so gently. It's just like my dream, but there is no sign of Will Powers Sr and although I know it is Jeff and he sounds like Jeff, something about him looks different. Has he lost weight? No. Actually, he looks a bit fuller around the face, if anything. It's his clothes, I realise. He is dressed like a Spice Boy in his zippy sports top and trendy jeans and Converse trainers. What on earth has Saffron done to my forty-year-old husband? My head is banging as usual and I'm not sure of what is real and what isn't right now.

'You need a haircut,' I tell him sharply, and automatically think of Lucy Harte's poor dead mother, who said the same moments before she died. I hope I don't die soon. I am not ready to die yet. Am I still dreaming? Is he going to try and take me home to Stranmillis? Should I start packing now?

'I know I do,' he says and he flashes me a smile, the one that used to turn me on so much. 'It's been a while since I had a decent cut. Can I come in?'

I want to be mad at him. I should be mad at him, but that stupid dream has confused me. I want him to come in, so badly. I want to fall into his arms and get my old life back and just pick up from where we left off, but I am a mess. My apartment is a mess also.

I glance back over my shoulder and survey days of sheer neglect and, well, doom and gloom, I suppose. Damn you, Jeffrey Pillock. I would have had the place shining clean and myself dolled up to the nines if I had known you were coming!

'I'd love you to come in but it's not really a good time,' I tell him. 'Can you come back later, like in about four hours or so and we can have a good chat then?'

81

'Four hours?' he asks. 'That's a bit of a random time frame.'

Well, it would take me at least four hours to get organised, I figure in my cloudy mind. I am not dressed and the place is like a tip and now that I think about it, I actually don't appreciate him calling like this unannounced, even if it is to try and win me back. He is going to have to at least bring flowers when he returns. None of this empty-handed shit is going to wash with me. I am going to play hard to get for once when it comes to my husband and his attempts at apologies.

'Look, Maggie, I don't think there is such a thing as a good time for what I have to say,' he says emphatically. 'I need to talk to you. Now.'

Oh, so it's like that, then! Oh, he is keen! I fold my arms.

'Talk to me about what?' I ask him. If he thinks I am going to make this easy for him, he can think again. He will have to do more than just turn up like this and say sorry! And he needn't tell me that Saffron doesn't exist because I saw them in Tesco with my own two eyes. He is going to have to beg to get me back!

'It's about... well, it's about how we have both moved on in the past few months,' he says, darting his eyes around anywhere but my face. 'Or, maybe, how you haven't... moved on.'

'*Moved on?*' my voice squeaks. 'Excuse me if it has taken me a little bit of time to get my head around what has just happened. It's not as easy as that, to just 'move on'. We were married, Jeff. You said you loved me with all your heart.'

This is the part when he tells me he doesn't want to move

on... where he says he still does love me with all his heart. I wait. And then he speaks.

'Yes, I understand it must be difficult,' he says, avoiding my eyes. 'Which is why I wanted to speak to you face to face about... about moving on. I wanted to tell you that I want a div... I want a divorce, Maggie. As soon as possible.'

Silence.

I can't speak. I do speak. At least I think I do.

'A what?' I mutter.

'A di... a divorce,' he replies. The bastard can barely say the words.

'A divorce,' I repeat. I feel a blow of reality has punched me and my rose-tinted glasses crash to the floor as I see him for what he really is again. A lying, cheating, good-for- nothing tramp! A divorce? A fucking divorce?

'How fucking dare you?' I say to him, my guts twisting like I might heave at any minute.

'I thought you might say that,' he mumbles. 'Please, just let me in. I wanted to see you in person but you never seem to be here.'

He glances around in frustration as if he doesn't want my neighbours to hear and then he checks his phone like he is on some sort of timer. Like he is in a fucking hurry!

'Hold on a minute,' I say to him, forgetting that I probably look like something from a horror movie as I haven't taken off my make-up from the night before. I don't actually care any more what I look like. 'Is she *with* you?'

My eyes are like saucers and I know I am spitting as I speak but I do not care if I shower him in saliva. I try to remember some anti-panic attack exercises but at this present moment I can barely remember how to breathe.

'She isn't with me, no, but she is waiting in the car.'

'You brought her *with* you! In the car! Here! What are you trying to do to me?' I am shouting now. 'What the hell are you trying to do to me, Jeff?'

I am crying buckets and I want to murder him, right here, right now. Like, really murder him. I don't care if I go to hell for it. He is messing with my head and I can't look at him standing there at my new front door like he has literally poisoned every single step I tried to take to get over him. He has polluted my new home. He has polluted my new life and I hate him for it.

'Maggie. Can you please keep your voice down and let me come in and explain?'

I don't want him to explain. There is no explanation. I know enough. I saw enough in fucking Tesco. In the very store where we met I saw enough and I don't think I can take any more detail of their fine romance.

I don't know what to do. I can't look at him. I think I am going to be sick. So I do what my instincts tell me to. I try and get rid of him. I slam the door in his face.

'Maggie, for goodness sake, will you be an adult about this and let me in?'

He calls in a hurried whisper through the letterbox. Jeff would shit himself if any of my new neighbours heard us arguing, even if he didn't know them from Adam. Where he comes from, no one raises their voice in public and no one ever speaks through a letterbox. This pleases me greatly.

'Fuck off to fuck!' I tell him from my hiding place on the floor on the other side of the door.

'Is this how you want me to tell you what I have come to say?' he asks and I literally dig my heels into the ground and then cover my ears. Childish, I know, but very, very satisfying. 'Through a damn letterbox?'

'I'm not listening,' I sing back to him. 'I am not listening, not even one little bit.'

'Okay then, Maggie, be like that,' he says. 'But don't say I didn't try and do the decent thing. I tried to tell you to your face but you have given me no option.'

'Not listening!' I say again, my eyes now shut tight as I try my best to block him out.

'Saffron is pregnant,' he says through the letterbox.

Now I *am* listening. My hands drop to the floor and I think my whole body has turned to jelly.

'What?' I'm definitely going to vomit.

'You heard me,' he says. 'We are having a baby.'

I slowly stand up and like a boxer who has just been punched in the ring, I stagger and reach for the door handle. I open it slowly and I look at my husband, who less than a year and a half ago told my family and friends in a fancy hotel that he was the keeper of my precious, precious heart and that he would be there for me, his best friend, until death us do part. He said it in a poem he had written himself only days after we met. That's how sure he was. And we all believed him.

And now she is having his baby. *She* is. Not me. Her. The one he hardly even knows. The one who swept in from nowhere and destroyed our future with the flutter of her eyelashes and a quick flick of her hair, like it was just another day and no big deal.

Oh, my God, please help me. I can't see straight. I'm having another weird dream, right? My stomach tightens into a giant ball of sick and the room starts to spin.

She is having his baby. My husband's baby. No, please no! I can't... but... no. No! I had names chosen and had scoured books and websites to find them. I had joined online forums and chatted to other newly-weds who were trying and mums-to-be who had just found out the most magnificent news of a new arrival.

I had pictured myself with a bump and how much I would glow and how he would tell me how beautiful I was even when I was big and bloated and hormonal as hell. I had the nursery colours chosen and I even had scraps of fabric pinned on a cork board in pinks and blues to see how it would all look together. I took tests every month. I prayed it would happen. But it didn't. And now this. Now *this*?

I try to speak. To react. To say something.

'How could you, Jeff?' It comes out in a croak and the tears start to fall and I want him to hug me and tell me he is joking or at least that he doesn't really love her the way he loves me and it's a mistake and he never meant it to happen and he's sorry.

But he doesn't do any of that. He doesn't even speak. So I do, again.

'How could you do this to me?' I mumble. 'That was meant to be what we –'

I don't have time to finish my sentence.

'Don't say '*we*' Maggie,' he says firmly. 'I love Saffron and we are starting a family. There is no '*we*' any more. Move on. Please.'

I inhale deeply. Move on. I exhale slowly.

Then I stare him out and he squints in... is that fear? I nod my head. He knows what he has done. He knows he has just dealt me one deadly, almost fatal, blow with his grand revelation of Saffron and their fucking family!

So I do what any boxer on the edge of defeat would do.

I take a step back, I look at my opponent, I raise my fist and I knock the fucker out.

Then I go to the bathroom and I am very sick indeed.

Chapter 10

'I can't believe I hit him,' I tell Simon later that evening after his football game, which he admits he could barely concentrate on. We have ditched the going-out-for-dinner idea and are having Chinese in my living room. 'I am so ashamed of myself for hitting him. I don't have a violent bone in my body and I obviously don't know my own strength.'

'That's all that farm work standing by you,' says Simon. He looks so relaxed, like he has been here forever.

'Gosh, I actually feel so, so bad.'

'I'm sorry but I can't stop laughing when I imagine you actually knocking him out,' he says, piling rice and curry sauce on top of a prawn cracker. 'What happened after that? Did Saffron come to his rescue?'

I start to snigger now. It is quite funny, when you take the extreme violence out of it.

'I honestly have no idea,' I tell him, covering my mouth, which is half full of noodles. 'I just closed the door and put on Amy Winehouse full blast and tidied up this place so that it is now unrecognisably clean and put all my energy to good use. I assume he wasn't still lying in the corridor when you arrived?'

Simon shakes his head and we swap foil containers. It really is like we are totally co-ordinated, like we are connected, somehow, and it feels surreal but oh-so comfortable.

'There was no sign and no trace of evidence, so your secret is safe with me,' he says. 'Have you heard anything from him since?'

At that I really do start to laugh when I recall the text message I received a few hours later.

'*Seriously, Maggie, you need to sort out your anger management,*' I read aloud from my phone, much to Simon's amusement. '*You could have broken my jaw.*'

Simon is doubled over now, in hysterics laughing, and I fear the remainder of the delicious chow mein he is holding is going to end up on the floor. I take it from him so that I now have two foil containers in my hand.

'Gosh, I needed that laugh,' he says when he finally gets rid of the giggles. 'You have no idea how good it feels to laugh again.

We finish our Chinese and watch the clock, knowing that our time is coming to an end.

'I really better get going, Maggie,' he says. 'God, it's going to be so hard saying goodbye. You're going to be okay, you know that?'

I don't want him to go. I feel safe when he is here and I know that when he leaves I am going to crash and it's not going to be pretty.

'Thanks, Simon,' I tell him. 'I will be fine. Time heals, isn't that what they say?'

He puts on his coat and gets his bag from the hallway. His

taxi will be here in just a few minutes and in a way I wish this moment would just hurry up and pass because it's going to be hard.

'Remember I said I have something for you,' he says. 'Something that might help?'

Did he? There has been so much discussed over the past twenty-four hours that I can hardly remember him saying that.

'I was kind of holding out until the last minute because I didn't want you to open it when I am here,' he tells me.

I pull a face. Uh-oh. Has he bought me a farewell gift? I didn't get him anything! I curse myself for being so disorganised.

'You know, if the wind changes your face will stay like that,' he says as he goes to his overnight bag. I look away and when I look back he is holding what looks like an old biscuit tin.

'I didn't get you anything,' I say, for a moment actually believing that he is giving me... biscuits?

'It's not biscuits,' he explains with a smile. 'It's a biscuit tin with just a few things I want you to have. It belonged to... it belonged to Lucy.'

Oh, Jesus.

'Are you sure...?'

'Please don't say anything,' he interrupts. 'Just take it and have a look and if you don't want to have it you can maybe post it back to me, or give it to me when you come and visit.'

'Come and visit? I would so love to come and visit!'

He smiles.

'You better.'

I take the box.

'My... okay... thank you, but I hope there is nothing of real value in here,' I warn him. 'I'm not very responsible at the minute and would die if I lost anything belonging to you.'

Simon shakes his head.

'I think you should have it. I just thought it might let you get to know her a bit more, hold her closer or maybe even... maybe even let her go, if that's what you feel like you have to do. I have a feeling, though, that it might help you more than you know.'

I stroke the box, feeling tiny dents along the side and along the rim. It is a decadent navy-coloured Cadbury's tin with a Christmas design and it has her name neatly scored into the bottom-right corner. I want to open it now, right now, and get lost in Lucy's child-like innocent world and forget about all my troubles and the mess that seems to follow me these days.

'Are you sure you want me to have this?' I ask him and my voice breaks as I stumble on my reply. He is giving me some very sentimental stuff and I am touched beyond words.

'I'm totally sure,' he tells me and our eyes meet and we both smile and sigh deeply at the same time.

We hear the taxi horn from the street and we both take a deep breath at the same time.

'It's been a rollercoaster but I have loved every minute of it, Maggie O'Hara,' he says. He reaches out his hand and I hold it and then he pulls me in for a hug. 'Come and see us really soon.'

'I will,' I sniffle, trying not to get tears or snot on his nice grey jumper.

I let go and clutch the tin to my chest.

'Look after her for me,' he says, nodding at the box and he takes a few steps back, delaying the inevitable. 'I hope it helps you to get the closure you need and rebuild your life. You deserve the best, Maggie. The very best.'

'You better go,' I tell him. I open the door, wiping my eyes and he walks away. I hate goodbyes. 'Text me lots!'

He makes a hat-tipping gesture and blows me a friendly kiss and we keep waving at each other until he is out of sight and I hear his footsteps on the stairwell that lead outside. I go to the window and watch him get into the taxi, but before he does, he looks up as if he knew I would be watching.

'Goodbye Simon!' I mouth and he blows me a kiss.

I hold the biscuit tin and Lucy's heart aches inside me as I watch her brother go and I try to be positive. I feel so full up and I glow inside when I think of how I now have Simon in my life, but also an emptiness of the life I have to face alone without leaning on him or interfering too much in his world. He isn't mine. He is just connected to me in the most surreal way and it's great for what it is.

It's time for me to get back to my own reality and start picking up the pieces of my broken existence. But first, I have some catching up and letting go to do with a little girl who has made my life, as messy as it might be right now, possible at all.

Chapter 11

I am looking at her for the very first time. I am in my pyjamas on my sofa (with pizza) and I am staring at her face from a newspaper clipping in which she has circled two spelling mistakes in red pen. I like that. I like that a lot.

It is a school photo in which she is proudly holding a shield that says 'Most Improved Player – Girls' Netball' and beside her is a boy whose plaque reads 'Player of the Year – Boys' Football.' According to the date, she is seven years old in the photo and her front teeth are missing and her strawberry-blonde hair is in pigtails. She looks like a little toothless rabbit with her freckles and cheeky grin and I want to shout at her *please don't get into the car when you are fourteen and your mother tells you to get a haircut! Please don't die, Lucy Harte!*

I want to warn her of what is going to happen, but then if it didn't happen, if she didn't die, I wouldn't be here, would I?

This is crazy. It's like looking back in time into a crystal ball. It's like watching a movie that you've seen before and you know the ending but still want it to change until the ending comes and then you know that it was for the best. It was what was meant to be. It is painful, it is strange, but it is healing me in a way that I never thought I would ever experience.

The tin which Simon left with me has enough contents to keep me busy for days and I don't want to rush it. I want to savour every picture, every scribble, every piece of her life and relish in this strange comfort that she brings me.

I check my phone and messages from earlier as I tuck into a steaming-hot slice of pizza heaven. One is from Simon, as I expected, telling me that he has arrived safely and I send a quick reply, but it is the other message that gets my attention. It's from my brother, John Joe.

My mood dips.

'I need to talk to you,' is all it says.

I am not replying. I don't need his negative energy, especially not now when I am clinging to Lucy for distraction on what is going on in my real life.

I have not heard from John Joe since he last told me in a message to stop drinking and get a grip, and I have no head space for his random interest in my life. Not today, anyhow.

It saddens me that I feel this way because as a very young girl, no matter how much he taunted, teased or ignored me, my brother was my knight in shining armour. He was the one I literally looked up to. My big brother. My flesh and blood. My hero.

But he isn't my hero any more.

He is arrogant, he is flighty, he changes his mind as often as he changes his girlfriend and that is a *lot*. He appears on the outside to be overly ambitious, yet he doesn't know what he wants to be when he grows up and he was always jealous of every single thing I do. Everything.

In a sickening and immature way, he never could give me credit and always brought me down as soon as I began to become a person and not just the little girl in the corner who happened to share the same home as he did.

'Why do you hate me so much?' I remember asking him once when I was about nine and his attitude towards me was becoming more and more horrible.

I had just won a prize for show-jumping and he hid the rosette but Dad found it in his room.

He looked at me in a way I will never forget, his black eyes staring from a face I no longer recognised.

'I don't hate you,' he said. 'Grow up, Maggie. You're not the only one in this family.'

Since he moved to the States a long, long time ago, I have to admit that life at Loch Tara has been a whole lot easier – well for me anyhow. No more pretending we got along for Mum and Dad's sake. No more awkward family dinners or Christmases when we would both rather stab each other than share a turkey. No more false 'Happy Birthdays' and exchanging gifts when we would rather exchange punches.

Yes, that bad.

I spilled my guts to a counsellor about our so-called 'relationship' years after my life-saving operation and we worked through all the nooks and crannies of our otherwise idyllic upbringing.

I wanted for nothing throughout my childhood, nothing

that is, aside from a brother who loved me back and who wanted me instead of always seeing me as a threat, or worse – not seeing me at all.

John Joe never messages me. Never ever. The only reason I have his number is because Mum insisted I put it in my phone in case something ever happened to her or Dad – and I assume she has done the same with him.

I just wish I didn't miss him so much.

I have a hot shower and I use all my favourite toiletries so that I smell delicious in a bid to erase my old childhood memories and get back into Lucy's world. I have lit candles in my bedroom and I have some soft music playing. I feel quite relaxed. I am being kind to me and it feels good.

I open the box again and lift out a bundle of notes and letters and photographs for me to look through and get to know better the little girl who saved my life. They are held together with an elastic band and I take it off, feeling a rush of warmth run through me when I see her face, her gorgeous face, staring back at me.

'Hello, Lucy Harte,' I whisper, running my fingers across her beautiful smiling face.

She looks like a Lucy, that's for sure, if you know what I mean. She is petite and friendly and smiley and I know from her astute record-keeping that she was a very clever little girl. There is a photo-booth strip of her with a friend and they pull faces and laugh and pose as everyone does when they pull that little curtain across. Amy and Lucy, it reads on the back of the strip and a date that is faded, but I think it says 1997.

There is a picture of her in her school uniform, looking very proper. Another of her with her two brothers and I smile when I see Simon in his youth and little Henry. How my heart breaks for Henry – more than them all.

Another picture of the whole family this time and another lady whose name is Marilyn, according to Lucy's very neat handwriting on the back of the photo. Their father was a handsome man and he looks proud with his arm around his wife but she looks desperately distracted, like a woman with a lot on her mind. I wonder, if she was around now would she have had more help to deal with her addiction and any other mental illnesses that she appeared to have battled with.

There are drawings in the box too and I giggle at Lucy's interpretation of Van Gogh's sunflowers and her caption, which indicates that, as creative as she was, visual art wasn't her strongest subject.

Her humour is definitely her strongest point and her ramblings on paper make me laugh out loud. It is like reading your favourite book and not wanting it to end and I devour every aspect of Lucy, getting to know all the things she loved and loathed and the boys she fancied and those she would rather 'stick pins in her eyes than kiss'.

She had lists of favourite foods, lists of favourite songs, lists of favourite movies, even a list of favourite teachers. Apparently Miss Davison, the pretty PE teacher needed to sort out her crush on Mr Thompson and just get a room together! I wonder if they ever did.

I text Simon.

Your little sister was a real hoot! Wise beyond her years, just like you said! Thank you for sharing this with me. It is helping a lot!

He texts back immediately.

I thought it would! Lovely to hear from you. I hope you are well. Thinking of you lots.

Hours pass and I am totally enveloped in everything I am finding. She certainly liked to record her feelings and what an amazing writer she would have made one day. I am almost at the bottom of the bundle when I come across a separate notebook and I lift it with the same anticipation as I did every other item she had stored in this box.

It is red in colour and it is neatly titled in Lucy's distinctive handwriting, but this one is different from the others. This is not a memory book or scrap book from her past. This one stops me in my tracks because it is about her planned future.

This one is entitled '*Things I Want to Do When I Grow Up*' by Lucy Harte. It is a diary of entries but she has summarised her thoughts with a list on the inside cover, each item written at different times with different pens but each referring to the diary that waits for me to read it.

I stop. I wasn't expecting to get a glimpse into her non-existent future and my mood drops to the floor. All the warmth and excitement drains from my body at the thought of her wanting to do so much and planning it but never having the chance.

I read the list, slowly anticipating the sorrow and pain that I am set to experience by reading a little girl's hopes and dreams that never were to come true.

I text Simon again, needing to communicate with someone who will understand my sadness.

Life is cruel. I just read Lucy's list.

He texts back within a few minutes.

Would you do it, Maggie?

Do it? Do what?

Do the things that Lucy planned to do?

A cold shiver runs through me and Lucy's smiling face stares up at me from a photo by my side. There is a cheeky look in her eye, one of strength and sheer will and determination.

Do it! I hear her whisper. *Do it for me! Do it for you! Go on, Maggie. Do it!*

I read again through the list of things to do and I feel a new energy run through my veins at the prospect of it all.

Find the world's tallest bridge… learn to play guitar… spread your wings and travel far…

And so it went on…

Could I? Should I? It could be a challenging, crazy distrac-

99

tion to see it through. I certainly have the time. I have the money. It would give me something to do and take my mind from what has happened between Jeff and I, never mind his impending fatherhood with Saffron. Plus it would allow me to give something back to Lucy. It would let me do the things she never got to do and enjoy them and show my gratitude to her for giving me a second chance in life.

Is this what Simon had planned all along? It could help us all, really, couldn't it? It all makes sense. I am excited. I can feel her with me, cheering me on, telling me to do it and have fun and do all the things that she never got to do.

Yes, I'll do it! I am going to do it! I'm nervous, I'm scared stiff, but I won't allow that to take over.

'Let's do this, Lucy Harte!'

I read the first thing on her list again, then I close the book, kiss its cover and I pick up my phone and text Simon.

Where is the tallest bridge in the world?

Tarn Valley, South of France, he messages back in the blink of an eye. *I already checked that one out for you. Good luck, Maggie! Who knows where it will take you? Don't be afraid to travel alone. I'm so proud of you x*

I feel a new energy, new blood pumping through me as my whole insides take on a new lease of life. This is not just any old list of dreams and ambitions. It's a story as well and it brings me right into the heart of the little girl who saved my life once.

Maybe she is going to do it again.

Lucy Harte, age 10½

~ April 1995 ~

I *have a secret that no one knows.*

Well, no one but Henry, but he won't tell because if he does, I can tell that he ate some of his Easter egg the other day and then covered it up in the red foil and put it back in the box so that Mum wouldn't notice.

Or I could tell that he says bad words when he thinks no one is listening. I saw him just this morning standing in front of the mirror in just his underpants and saying the 'eff' word like ten times as he wiggled his bum and made silly faces.

Or, last of all, I could tell that he picks his nose and eats it and Mum would go totally chicken-oriental mental if she thought he did that. It would, as Simon says, 'gross her out.'

Anyhow, my secret is this (please don't tell anyone or I'm dead meat)… my secret is that when I am sad, like when Mum and Dad are arguing and even when Simon turns the telly up and we can still hear it, and even when Marilyn says they are only playing but we can still hear it – well, my secret is that I go outside and away, way down the lane and across two fields where I sit on the edge of the stone bridge and I dangle my legs and I look at my reflection in the water for ages and ages and no one even notices that I am gone.

It's a secret because I am not allowed on the stone bridge. No one I know is allowed on the stone bridge. Not even Simon is allowed and he is thirteen and a half.

This may sound weird but I love bridges. If I am ever caught, if Mum finds out, then I would be grounded again and there is nothing I hate more than being grounded and stuck in my bedroom all day. Except frilly dresses. I hate frilly dresses.

Here are four reasons why I love bridges:

1) *They are high up and you can see for miles, like you are on top of the world*
2) *They bring you to the other side of somewhere you don't want to be*
3) *They can be a little bit dangerous, which is bad but cool*
4) *I just love them*

If you are reading this (I am talking to you, Simon and Henry Harte) please do not tell because Mum says my grounding is becoming 'a bit of a habit' and she will either ground me again or else kill me.

I'd rather be killed than grounded sometimes.

The last time, which was only four days ago, was for bringing a mouse into the utility room. It's not like I was going to keep it for a pet or anything. I just wanted to see how it liked sleeping in the warm laundry basket and it wasn't my fault that Marilyn almost had a heart attack when she lifted it out thinking it was one of Dad's socks.

I had to stay in my room and read books that I had read a hundred times before and it was a sunny day and Simon and Henry went swimming with Dad but I wasn't allowed to (harsh!).

The grounding before that was on Sunday and it was just because I tore my horrible pink frilly new dress that Aunt Josie had bought me for my birthday. I hate that pink dress as much as I hate Aunt Josie. And that is a lot (another secret, so don't tell. Aunt Josie thinks she is my favourite but she so is not).

The only tricky part about going to the stone bridge is trying to figure out when it is safe to go back home.

Too soon and they would still be fighting; too late and I would be noticed missing and that would be big trouble.

Sometimes Henry comes with me to the stone bridge but he is only eight and he really annoys me the way he hums and sings when he sits on the edge and then he gets scared and wants to go home. He doesn't have any sense of adventure. I think I get that from my dad. Henry is like Mum. He likes sticking to the rules. I like breaking them.

When I am older, I am going to find the highest bridge in the world and I am going to sit right at its edge so that I can see for miles and miles of water below and no one is going to stop me. Not Dad, not Simon and definitely not Mum.

Today is another one of 'those days' when Mum is having a lie-down and Marilyn is having a sleepover. This is not good news because when Marilyn stays over to make sure Mum is okay, it means that Dad won't come home for a few days. I know this because Mum was meant to make us chicken drumsticks but now Marilyn is making them downstairs and it's past six and Marilyn is meant to go home at five.

I have a tummy ache. I better go and eat my dinner.

*Note to Lucy Harte: Find the tallest bridge in the world. (Bring Henry... maybe.)

Chapter 12

I am sitting on my bed munching toast and reading Lucy's diary as the rain pelts down outside and for the first time in a long time I feel warm, cosy and... safe. Yes, I feel safe here in this little apartment I never thought could feel like home.

I hear the hum of traffic from outside but I can honestly swear that the real world and what is going on out there is of no interest to me at this time. I am engrossed. I am right back there with Lucy on that bridge and I can feel her breathe in and out and lap up the peace and quiet that she got when she went to her little runaway place.

I can feel the knots in her stomach as she worried so much about her mother's drinking that she had to hide away and wait for it to subside, only to go home to find her mum hiding in bed, her father gone and this Marilyn lady filling in the gaps of her parenting.

I've never thought of bridges as a thing of passion but I love how she saw them in the most simplistic way – a thing that gets you to the other side of somewhere. A place to sit on top of the world. A place to escape from all your troubles.

I open up my laptop and Google the Tarn Valley region of

France and for the first time I see the huge viaduct that stretches across the river. At 343 metres high, it is known to sometimes sit in the clouds, which is bound to feel like the top of the world, for sure! My eyes widen at the prospect of actually going there, just like Lucy had hoped to one day.

My phone rings and instead of avoiding it like I normally do, I smile when I see that Flo is calling me for an update. For once, I am ready to talk about something positive instead of dwelling on all the usual shit that has masked the real me for too long.

'I am so bloody insanely jealous, is it wrong for me to say that?' she asks. 'I just think this could be the best thing that has ever happened to you. It's so exciting and my life is so boring, but you deserve this, Maggie! You so deserve it!'

I hear Billie in the background making his usual random aeroplane noises and I can just picture Flo trying to hear me over his drone, blocking one ear with her finger and concentrating.

'Don't be jealous, not yet anyhow,' I reply to her. 'I haven't done anything with it yet. Oh, Flo, she was such a little sweetheart and so endearing and so, well, she was real, you know? This is making her real to me.'

I can hear Flo gulp on the other end of the phone.

'Did you just gulp?'

'I did just gulp. Oh, I am thrilled for you, Mags,' she whispers. 'Billie will you be quiet!'

She doesn't whisper the second part of her sentence. She screams it so loudly I have to pull away my phone from my ear.

'So, now you've perforated my eardrum –'

'Sorry!'

'It's okay, I have another one. Anyhow, I've been looking up the tallest bridge in the world so that I can go and visit it for Lucy and it looks like a really beautiful place in France. I'm going to go there soon and – is Billie okay?'

There are weird sounds coming down the phone now and I'm not sure if Flo is still listening to me.

'Yes, yes,' she says. 'He's just pretending to be a walrus. It's his latest phase. All good. Anyhow, back to you and Lucy. So, France, Maggie? Wow-wee! When are you going?'

I flick through Lucy's little notebook as I speak to my best friend.

'I'm not sure. I don't know where to start with all this, to be honest,' I tell her. 'There are about ten things in this book that I want to get through but the tallest bridge is just the one she started with. It's a lot to take in. I swear, I can't believe Simon left this all with me.'

'He sounds like a really sweet guy,' says Flo. 'And, believe me, there are few of those around, from what I can see.'

A sweet guy, unlike Jeff…

I allow Jeff, for just a fleeting second, to enter my mind and then I shut him out again and turn my attention back to Lucy and my conversation with Flo. I haven't told anyone apart from Simon about Jeff's baby news and I am not up to telling it just yet.

'You're sounding more like the old Maggie already,' she says. 'And you're not even drunk.'

I could take that the wrong way, but she is right. I am not even drunk. I have not had a drink since Simon left. And, best of all, I hadn't even noticed until she pointed it out just now.

'Ah, Flo, I'm still a bloody wreck, but I'll get there,' I whisper down the phone to my best buddy.

I look across at Lucy's notebook. Just the sight of it gives me great comfort and, strangely, it's like companionship, like I am not alone.

I hear Flo gulp again, which means she is worried again. I wish I didn't make the people who love me worry so much.

'You get back to your list and all of your amazing, exciting planning. Go back to Lucy Harte and let her innocence and ambitions mend your soul. You deserve it, pal.'

We say our goodbyes and I put the phone down and lie back on my pillow. Flo is right. This is a new beginning for me and something I would never have imagined in my whole life. Lucy Harte and her little diary are presenting me with a glorious opportunity to make things better. Her red notebook lies beside me on my pillow and I open it again and read her tender handwriting, which almost speaks to me, begging me to hurry up and start where she left off.

Lucy

~ July 1995 ~

We are in Donegal in Ireland, where it is raining and raining and raining, but who cares about rain anyway. We are staying in a little cottage on top of a cliff and across the beach *there are rows and rows of caravans and nothing really else but it doesn't matter because I have two new secrets…*

My first secret is this…

I, Lucy Harte, am In. Love. Yes, L.O.V.E!!

Secret number two is who I am in love with (Simon or Henry if you are reading this, stop right now!)

Well, his name is Tiernan Quinn, he is from a place called Galway in Ireland and I am writing this from my little bedroom, where I can see him play football with my brother outside in the pouring rain. Tiernan and his family are staying in the cottage next door and my mum and his mum have conversations in the porch that go something like this:

'Isn't the weather just so awful?' (My mum.)

'Yes, isn't it just so shite!' (His mum.)

I like his mum.

So as I write this, Tiernan is playing football wearing a black biker jacket and ripped jeans. He looks like a rock star even in the rain. Oh, and he sounds like a rock star too because he actually plays guitar. Swear to God, he actually does!

Here are the reasons I love Tiernan Quinn:

1) *He has dark spikey hair and I like dark spikey hair*
2) *He plays guitar*
3) *He says bad words*
4) *He has a (fake) tattoo – more on that later*

Simon brought him in here yesterday and I nearly peed my pants because he said 'shite' in front of my mum and she was horrified. She says his family would need to wash out their mouths because they swear a lot. My mum thinks people who swear a lot are crude and ignorant, but I think it's a bit funny.

Henry was being a right pain when Tiernan was here and he kept asking me to play cards with him, which made me look like a big baby when all I really wanted was to talk to Tiernan, but then when Tiernan asked my name I realised my voice wouldn't even work and Henry had to answer for me. Henry said I was ten but I am not ten, I am ten and a half! In fact, I will be eleven in November!

That was last night and I haven't stopped watching him since I got up this morning. It is now tea time, so that's a pretty long time to be watching him play football in the rain but there isn't a lot to do here so I'm not missing much.

Dad is taking ages to get chips in the village and Henry thinks he must have gone to Chip Land or somewhere, but there is no such place as Chip Land. I know exactly why he is taking so long. Anything for some peace from Mum, who is... anyhow back to Tiernan and how I fell in love with him...

His hair was wet from the rain when he came in here last night and Mum said he would catch his death of cold.

She nearly passed out when he replied.

'Will I shite!'

She gave him one of Simon's Oasis t-shirts and he went to the bathroom and got changed and he smiled at me when I said Oasis are cool. He actually smiled. At me! He has a tattoo of a cross drawn on his arm, but it's not really a real tattoo because it's only drawn in black marker, but of course Mum thought it was real and said later that maybe Tiernan was a bad influence. She has no clue.

I think we are going home tomorrow and Mum says she will never spend a summer in Ireland again because it is 'shite' – only joking, she didn't say that, but that's kind of what she meant, so like most lovers, Tiernan and I will probably never meet again.

I hope I don't go home with a broken heart.

*Note to Lucy Harte: Find Tiernan Quinn and kiss him. Proper Kissing!

** Note to Lucy Harte: Learn to play my favourite song on guitar

I am going to make a start on her list... so I choose the easiest place to start, which, in this case, is to find the mysterious Tiernan Quinn.

I lift my phone and click on to Facebook and search for his name. Of course, just as I'd imagined, there are quite a few people with that name and more than one who claims Galway as his home place.

I do the maths to realise he isn't a teenage boy any more so that rules a couple of young lads out straight away and I eliminate a few from my investigation. I feel like an armchair detective and it is fun.

I click onto the first one who may match who I am looking for. This Tiernan looks like he is in his early thirties and is from Galway, or at least lives there now, and is in a relationship... with a man. Still. Could be him. I make a note of him and go onto the next one, who is living in Dublin and looks like he plays in a band. His profile picture is of a guitar, so I add him as a maybe. The third and last one who fits the age bracket is an ex-pat in San Francisco and is married with twin girls. Again, it could be him. I don't think my budget stretches to San Francisco, so I'm kind of hoping the man I am looking for is one of the other two, but, hey, if it is, I can always send him a message and tell him he is cool, which is all Lucy really ever wanted to do.

How's it all going, Mags?

A message from Simon.

Well, I suppose I have made a start, I tell him. *I'm stalking someone called Tiernan Quinn on Facebook. Lucy planned to check him out. Any clues?*

I really want more toast, so I walk to the kitchen as I wait for his reply. I am just popping the bread into the toaster when his message comes through.

Ah yes, he replies. *He was my holiday buddy in Donegal many moons ago. Ha, I knew she had a crush on him and Mum hated him. Cool lad. Played guitar. Look him up, for sure.*

I think it could be the Dublin guy...

I need my laptop to get a proper trawl on his page and see if I can pluck up the courage to message him. But what the hell am I meant to say?

What will I say to him? I ask Simon

Simon replies straight away.

Decide that when you see him.

See him?

Well, yes. Go see him. Facebook messages are a cop-out. Go.

The toast pops and makes me jump. I butter it and a smile creeps over my face. I have loads of old friends in Dublin, so a night or two down there might be good. I'm not going to go knocking on doors looking for some random stranger who Lucy probably met for less than five minutes, but maybe Simon is just trying to give me a nudge to take some new directions in life and have some fun.

I get my laptop and sit at the kitchen table looking at Tiernan Quinn's page. His page and photos are private, so I can't tell what he looks like and I'd have to add him as a friend if I wanted to know more, however there is a link to a band page called 'The Madd Mollies', so I take a snoop on that page to see what I can find.

They obviously need a new publicist, I think to myself as I scroll down their postings, which are way out of date. There are no great photos to speak of, either, just graphics and quotes and a list of upcoming gigs. Well, at least that's something. I could be barking up the wrong tree, but it's not like I have got anything to lose, is it?

Ooh, at last I have an opening... they are playing in Temple Bar in Dublin tomorrow night. I feel a rush of excitement as I contemplate just jumping on a train and going there for the craic of it all. I could stay with my cousin Roisin. She is always asking me to come visit, so why not now? It's less than a three-hour train ride or I could take the car.

I message her to suggest a last-minute visit. I know it is short notice, but who knows? If you don't ask and all that...

While I wait I move on to my next challenge, which is to find this big tall bridge somewhere in the south of France. I've never travelled alone before, apart from on business, and I have butterflies at the very thought of even getting on a plane and wandering around a country where I can't speak the language. It would be strange to go and not really know what I'm going to do when I get there, but hey, I'm up for anything that keeps my mind occupied and my adrenalin pumping.

Just then Roisin messages me with a very enthusiastic reply.

You beauty! She writes. *I will meet you off the train. I'm a jobbing actor with no current job, remember, and it's dole day tomorrow so I have funds for fun! Call me!*

So I call her...

'Cousin! My God, I am so excited you are coming to the Fair City! What's the story?'

Roisin, may I add, was born and bred in Belfast but has adapted a Dublin twang as well as their slang after only a year of being there. She is about five-foot nothing, has the maddest throaty voice and short red hair and has done every job under the sun, from waitressing to dog grooming to pub singing, to fund her ambition to be a regular theatre actor. She has lived in London, Glasgow, Edinburgh during the Fringe every year, New York for a short while and is now in Dublin following a stint in a one-act play at the Gate Theatre, where she played a prostitute who fell in love with her client. According to social networking updates, it was her best role to date, but I'm nearly sure she said the same about the last one, and the one before that.

'I'm going through a bit of a shit time at the minute, as you've probably heard,' I explain. 'And I just fancy a change of scenery for a night or two. Do you mind?'

'Do I mind? Do I *mind*? Maggie O'Hara, you're like my favourite cousin ever and I know you are having a shit time, so don't even bother explaining! Just get here and we can have a good old catch-up and a good old piss-up, if that's what you feel like. Give me a rough time and I'll be right there at Connolly Station to meet you. And you can stay as long as you like. It's not the Ritz where I live, but it is cosy.'

I log onto the train timetable online and give her a few options. There are a few trains to choose from early morning till late afternoon and though I may have become used to lie- ins lately, it won't hurt me to get up a bit early for a change, so I go for one that will get me in for lunchtime.

'Meet me at 1.15 – is that okay?'

'Perfect. That's just perfect and we'll have great craic. It's been way too long.'

I say my goodbyes on the phone to Roisin and log off my laptop. My head is spinning with all this spontaneity – I used to be so much more 'fly by the seat of my pants' type when I was at university, but the past few years with my job and life with Jeff has been, dare I say, a bit rigid and routine. Work, sleep, work, sleep, work, sleep and visiting relatives or shop-ping at the weekend was as good as it got, but I liked it at the time. Now, all of this last-minute decision to get up and go with no one to answer to and no one to even tell, even if it's just to Dublin, on a wild-goose chase to find a man I am not even sure is the right one, is just a little alien to me, but I am adamant to go with it and see what it brings.

Lucy Harte, my darling girl, I hope you are guiding me in the right direction.

Chapter 13

I have always loved travelling by train. Maybe it's the lack of responsibility, maybe it's the people-watching opportunities or maybe it's the sheer sense of freedom it gives me since it reminds me of day trips and holidays or going to big national football games and concerts in Dublin.

The railway network in Ireland isn't very extensive outside of the main city routes so perhaps I love it because it's a bit of a novelty for a country girl like me.

On the train! See you soon! I text Roisin and I get a flutter of excitement.

Hurry, can't wait! She messages back and I glow inside.

I have a novel and headphones packed in my overnight bag to keep me company, but I'm almost too nervous to concentrate on anything else right now. So when I find a seat with a table attached, I take out Lucy's red notebook, but instead of reading her little snippets and thoughts and dreams, I just stare at the front cover and then close my eyes and breathe to feel her near me.

I already feel like my life is changing, just by getting on

this train, just by getting away from that apartment and from Belfast, even if it's just for a day or two.

I take out a pen and notebook of my own. I need to connect with Lucy right now. I need to explain my mission.

Dear Lucy

I pause and look around me, wondering at first what it is I want to say, but then the words flow out and I begin to write...

I hope you are with me now. I like to think you are from time to time...

I'm on a train to Dublin from Belfast, in case you haven't caught up with me yet, but I do hope you come along for the ride.

You see, I'm on this crazy mission to find the lad you met on holiday so many years ago – Tiernan Quinn, the guitar-player who was your very first crush. It was kind of Simon's idea that I go through with your 'to-do' list, so I hope you don't mind but I'm in this really weird place in my life right now and he thinks, and I agree, that it might help me re-focus my whole direction and also do something in your honour.

It's a bit way out, I know.

Chances are, had you lived on and not had that tragic accident, that your words in this book would have been something you barely ever looked at as an adult. You may even have forgotten that you wrote them. You would, no doubt, have forgotten all about this Tiernan guy, but for some reason I am going to try and do a few of the things you said you would like to do in my bid to move on with my own life and also in a bid to set you free.

I've been holding on to your memory for so long now, and although I will never forget you, I guess I need to find what it is I really want in life and go get it, rather than always feeling this sense of being half alive, of always owing my life to you.

I hope you understand and maybe, in this way, you can help me.

It wasn't very hard to track down all the Tiernan Quinns from Galway and, with some online searching, it's leading me to Dublin, so here I am on a train, cross country on this magnificent wild-goose chase and it's already so liberating and fun.

And I think I may have found him. The power of social media, eh? It's quite surreal to think you didn't get to experience any of that and how we can peer into the lives of strangers, find out where they are and what they are up to, what they look like and what they work as and they don't even know it. I bet you would have loved it.

If and when I manage to see him (he is playing a gig tonight in a city bar) I will be subtle, of course, and try and say hello to him, just for you. If you thought he was hot back then, then I'm pretty sure he is still hot now.

I'm sorry but I won't be able to kiss him even if he is still hot, but I hope you understand that. I say that for my own reasons as well as the fact that he is more than likely in some sort of relationship, or even married, and also the biggest reason of all is that he would really think I am some sort of lunatic if I even suggested it. So the kissing is out, but a hello is definitely in!

No matter if I find him or not, I'd like to thank you for taking me on this little journey to spend time with my cousin, Roisin, who no doubt will look after me like she always does and distract me a bit, which is just what I need right now.

A lot has happened over the past two weeks and I think I'm in shock. I probably am losing the plot doing this, but hey ho. Nothing to lose and all that...

Please stay with me, Lucy. Stay with me just a little while longer. I'm thinking of you every step of the way.

Your friend,

Maggie

I put down the pen, tear out and fold the piece of paper then tuck it into the back of Lucy's red notebook and lean back to relax, lap up and enjoy the beautiful Irish scenery on my way to the big smoke.

Lucy

~ Autumn 1998 ~

*T*oday, *I am having a party. There is no one at the party, only me and it's in my bedroom, but I have spent the evening* *dancing around my room and playing my music loudly and I don't care that Simon is mad and that I am embarrassing him in front of his stupid friends. I am also playing my new favourite song, 'Songbird' by Eva Cassidy, on repeat, which is annoying him so badly.*

Simon has called me three names so far since I came home from school:

5) *Loser*
6) *Double loser*
7) *Freak*

He called me a freak because I have decided to become a vegetarian and he thinks it's the funniest thing he has ever heard in his entire life just because when Dad was getting pizza I asked for pepperoni, but I just made a mistake.

I meant pineapple.

Pineapple and pepperoni do actually sound alike and it's very easy to get mixed up in your words when you have two brothers who act like they are going to die of starvation if you don't hurry up and decide what toppings you want.

I am fed up with everyone in this house. Mum is back in her room and all she ever does is be very quiet or else she cries, Marilyn never leaves these days and Dad just comes and goes and he seems very sad all the time. I just wish we could be a normal family and that I didn't have to go to the bridge in order to get away from them all.

I wish I could go further than the bridge right now. I would love to travel far away and let them all get on with it and I could be a vegetarian if I wanted to be a vegetarian and no one would care if I said pepperoni instead of pineapple.

So I am not listening to them any more. I will just put on my music and dance when they annoy me. I love to dance. I am not very good at it but it makes me very happy.

I don't think I have any other news except that I have a new goldfish and I feel so guilty for buying him in the first place. If I feel bored and trapped here, imagine how that poor goldfish feels. He just goes round and round and round and round and I haven't even given him a name yet. In fact he might not even be a 'he' and could well be a 'she', but whoever or whatever it is, it's more bored than I am and that is loads.

I have nothing more to report today, sorry (sorry to Simon or Henry if you are reading this and expecting juicy gossip).

I think I will just keep dancing.

Notes to Lucy Harte: *
*Don't ever stop dancing!
*Throw parties! Throw a dinner party to die for!
*Spread your wings & travel far! Don't live in a goldfish bowl!

We are travelling at high speed through the lush countryside of South Armagh and into the Republic of Ireland via County Louth and it's all very green and beautiful. It's raining lightly outside but the sun is shining through and I lean my head on the window and watch the world go by and my heart fills up with a sense of adventure.

I have done a lot of thinking on this short train ride as I

clutched Lucy's precious note book and stared out the window onto the fleeting landscapes of my homeland.

I need to keep dancing. I need to travel.

I need to breathe in and live in the moment. I need to stop dwelling on what has already happened in my life, on what is going to happen, on what might happen and what might not. I need to spread my wings. It may be just a two-hundred-mile journey but I am starting as I mean to go on, as Lucy might have meant me to. I am stepping out of the goldfish bowl. I am spreading my wings. I am going to find Tiernan Quinn.

I can't believe I am going to find Tiernan Quinn... have I totally lost the plot??

He could be anyone! He could be a screaming lunatic or a raging druggie or a serial killer, for all I know!

'What on earth are you going to say to him?' asked Flo. As excited as she was before about my forthcoming adventures in the name of Lucy Harte, I know she was rightly just more than a bit concerned.

'I have no idea if I will even say anything,' I tell her and that's the honest truth. I don't have a plan. I don't have a clue what I am doing. I am just going along with this all and hoping that in some way it turns out okay. 'I'm expecting nothing from this guy, whatsoever. Lucy sounds like she was a feisty wee girl, so I'm just going to go with the flow and see where it takes me.'

I see Roisin as soon as the train chugs into the famous Connolly Station and I stand up immediately, eager to get out of the now-stuffy carriage and greet my cousin.

She runs to me on the platform, her pink hair bouncing as she moves – it's longer than I remember it, but it says it all about her wonderfulness. She has had short hair, curly hair, long hair, shaved hair, blue hair, black hair, platinum blonde and pink. A chameleon, my mother calls her. A 'buck eejit' says my father.

'My God, you are one skinny bitch!'

She hugs me and then looks me up and down in a mixture of envy and worry.

'Really? It's not intentional.' I tell her. It really isn't.

'Ah the good old divorce diet,' she says. 'You need a good feed, missy. Are you hungry now? There's this cool sandwich bar we could stop off at en route to my place?'

'I'm mad for a glass of wine and it's only just lunchtime,' I confess, 'so I probably should eat something instead. Oh it's so, so good to see you!'

We link arms and walk through the busy early-afternoon crowds in Connolly and out into the sunshine – the rain hasn't reached Dublin yet – and Roisin stops to light up a cigarette.

'I need to give up these bastards,' she says, with the ciggie in her mouth. 'I bloody well love them, though. Don't worry, I won't smoke in the house when you are here. I know how sensitive you are to alien shit like that.'

'I'm not as sensitive to it any more,' I remind her. 'My heart is in perfect working order, apart from being smashed to smithereens, that is. Funny old organ, really, when you think about all it is responsible for.'

'Oh, you poor love,' says Roisin. 'That absolute trollop Jeff has a lot to answer for. Mum told me a bit about him and his new fancy woman, so I'm all yours for the next day or two if you need to spill your guts out. Cry on my shoulder or slap me or thump me if you need to. Whatever you want. I'm well fit for it. You need to let off some steam, my darlin'.'

I push a sandwich around my plate and make the odd attempt to nibble on it as I go through the last few weeks and months with Roisin. She is wide eyed as I drop all the revelations from the day Jeff left until the meeting at work and all about Simon and, now, why I'm here.

'So you want to go to see this band, The Madd Mollies, tonight in Temple Bar to fulfil Lucy's bucket list? Maggie, that is amazing.'

'You think I'm the mad one, don't you, never mind the Madd flippin Mollies?' I sip my hazelnut latte. It's from the Gods and the sugar rush is just what I need. 'I just feel I should do it for Lucy and there's lots of other ways her list is guiding me. I'm going to France to find the world's tallest bridge, just for her. Does that make me a bit mental?'

'I think it makes you a wonderful person and, sure, we're all a bit mental,' says Roisin. She is on some sort of green concoction that she claims will cleanse her liver and she doesn't eat bread, so it's couscous and veg on her plate. *She* needs to eat more, never mind me. 'I think it's kind of sweet and if it distracts your mind from Pillock the Prat then it can only be a good thing.'

Exactly.

'I mean, deep down, if I see this Tiernan guy then great,

but if I don't it's no big deal, really,' I say, trying to be all blasé. 'It's not as if I am here to stalk him or anything. I think it's just a good excuse to get away for a while and to see you, of course.'

'Of course,' she agrees. 'It's a fabulous idea. I love Lucy Harte!'

I try and eat another bite of my sandwich. It's actually quite good, but I'm still jittery and nervous and my stomach is in knots. 'So, if we are going to see this band tonight I'd really love a quick peep around the shops first? I need a new outfit. Would you mind?'

Roisin looks like she would rather eat her own insides than traipse after me round Grafton Street.

'I knew you were going to say that... of course I don't mind.'

I stand up before she can *change* her mind.

'Come on. I'll treat you to something nice. It's not often I get time to hang out with my favourite cousin.'

Her eyes light up, but then they drop again.

'I don't expect you to treat me at all, Maggie,' she says, lifting her handbag. 'I just tend to avoid the shops these days. I'm on a bit of a budget with no work and all. It's shit.'

I feel a sense of sadness in Roisin; something I never witnessed before. She was always the strong one, the bubbly go-getter, who was bursting with life and although she still is all of that on the outside, somehow I think she might need me as much as I need her right now.

'What's a new dress between cousins?' I say and I go and pay the bill.

Chapter 14

One little black dress (for Roisin) and a foxy petrol-blue cat suit (for me) later, a quick bite to eat at her apartment and a hello to her flatmate and we are rather pleased with ourselves as we make our way into Dublin's city centre by taxi. Roisin kindly fixed my hair into a very stylish messy bun, which shows off the nape of my neck nicely and goes with my blue cat suit, which I am very, very chuffed with.

She is looking funky and hot as hell in her little black number.

'I wish I had pink hair,' I tell her. 'You look so cool and different and I'm just ordinary and mousey.'

Roisin shoots me a dagger look and then laughs out loud.

'If you are ordinary, Maggie O'Hara, there's no hope for the rest of us! You're a head-turner, now stop fishing for compliments and believe in yourself!'

Aside from looking a bit plain beside Roisin, I am feeling great inside. In fact, I feel like I am going to see a famous Dublin band like U2 or The Script and I'm as excited as a teenager about to meet her favourite singer. It's been a while since I got dressed up and had a girly night out and maybe it's the Pinot and maybe it's the company, but I'm really going with the flow and if it happens that Jeff pops into my head it doesn't seem to sting as much. Out of sight really can be out of mind, it seems.

We arrive at the venue, a renowned live-music haunt called The Porterhouse in the Temple Bar area and I get an instant buzz from the energy of a new city. I know Belfast like the back of my hand, but Dublin is a stranger to me and it feels great. The streets are alive, heaving with tourists, and I hear all sorts of accents and languages and get a pumping vibe from the cosmopolitan atmosphere. Roisin explains that the Temple Bar area is catering exactly for visitors and that they come from all over the world to hang out here.

'In other words, when it comes to charging for drinks, the pubs know how to do it,' she giggles, paying the taxi driver at her own insistence. 'There's nothing happy about happy hour around here when you look in your purse or wallet the next day!'

'Oh, we have places like that in Belfast too,' I assure her. 'All in the name of tourism, but we're here now, so let's enjoy it and pretend we are on our holidays for the night.'

A few minutes later we are inside the warmth of the bar and it's pretty packed already. Loud music pumps through the long, narrow interior and we make our way to get our first round in. *Live Tonight – The Madd Mollies* is etched in colour on a huge chalkboard on the wall just above the small stage and I am proud of myself for getting here and making this happen in such a short space of time. It's great to go to new places, see new faces and, most of all, catch up with family. I should really do this more often.

'Choose a cocktail,' I mouth to Roisin over the music and she looks back at me like a child in a sweet shop. 'Anything you want, cousin. Pick your favourite and let's do this in style!'

'Oooh, okay then, don't mind if I do!' she says, gulping as she reads the cocktail menu from behind the bar. 'Okay, I've picked mine already. I'll be all sophisticated and go for a Cosmo. I can never afford these, so make sure and take a picture for my Facebook page!'

'Of course,' I reply and I order a Cosmo for Roisin and a Strawberry Daiquiri for me. Yum.

An Italian couple are getting hot and heavy to our left and a group of French students squeeze in to our right and we are gradually pushed out towards the middle of the little floor in front of the stage, which is a blessing in disguise as we end up quite near the front – the perfect spot for stalking.

When the band takes to the stage about half an hour later, we are on our second round and the atmosphere has really heated up.

Out they come onto the stage one by one and I have the perfect view. First comes the drummer, who strikes up a beat, then the keyboard player, the lead guitarist, who is a bit of a dude and, finally, the lead singer. Quite a pleasant-looking bunch, if a little scruffy in parts, but I find it rather cute, in a mid-thirties-bunch-of-men way.

I try to remember who's who in the band from the Facebook page to figure out which one is Tiernan and I'm guessing he is the front man, who is totally in control of the show in his white t-shirt and tight blue jeans and guitar slung across his hips. He wears a grey trilby hat over his unkempt, outgrown brown hair, has a light beard and his t-shirt creeps up as he works the mic to show a very toned and tanned midriff. He can work a crowd, for sure, and you can tell he has being doing this for quite a long time.

He is hot; the ladies love him and he knows it.

'Cead Mile Failte go Dublin!' he says into the mic in a low husky voice and it's enough to send a cluster of student types, who look like true groupies, into a spinning frenzy.

As a young teenager I'd often dreamed of fronting a band – a real girl-band who play their own instruments, like The Bangles. I could always hold a tune and my early guitar and piano lessons meant that I could fiddle about with melodies of my own, which I absolutely loved to do when my parents and my brother were out working the farm. It's one of my big regrets – not keeping up with music and writing my songs. My dad always said that being able to play music could take you anywhere in the world and now I know he was so right.

'What do you think of your man?' asks Roisin, nodding towards the stage. 'He's hot! Do you think he's the one you're looking for?'

I shrug and move along to the music. I think of Lucy. I am dancing and I hadn't even realised it.

'He looks just like I expected him to!' I shout back to her. 'He looks like a bad-boy rock star and I like it! Looks like he got some real tattoos after all!'

Tiernan Quinn, if it even is the one Lucy Harte fell for in her innocent youth, is exactly the type of man I secretly would fancy but would never have the courage to approach. He is the polar opposite of Jeff, who already feels grey and boring in comparison, with his matching jackets and trousers, his plain-white shirts and his stripy ties. Yes, Tiernan is the man a young Maggie O'Hara would have dreamed of hanging out with, but would I go for that type now?

Who knows?

The Madd Mollies play hit after hit of Celtic folk-rock-type songs and the whole audience is hopping and singing along. 'Dirty Old Town', 'Whiskey In The Jar'... all the classics that go down a treat with the various nationalities that grace the place.

Roisin is barely listening, though as she is chatted up by at least three men over the course of the next half hour while I seem to be totally ignored in comparison, perhaps because I haven't taken my eyes off the stage.

'I may as well be invisible when it comes to men these days!' I joke, but, to be honest, I'm glad of just standing here, absorbing the music and letting the warm rush of alcohol zap through my veins. I am finally beginning to really relax. I'd forgotten how much I adore live music. I've neglected this type of night out as I've always been way too tired to make it beyond dinner and a few drinks.

'I'm sure if you wanted to attract someone, you could,' says Roisin sincerely. 'It would do you no harm to have that ego of yours stroked. A few compliments from the opposite sex would do you the world of good.'

She gives me a wink and a knowing smile.

'Nah, I'm fine,' I tell her adamantly. 'But you work away, Flirty Gertie...'

The Madd Mollies end their set with a rocked-up rendition of The Undertones' classic, 'Teenage Kicks' and then make their way off stage to a huge applause and, when I lose sight of them in the crowd, I feel a slump of disappointment.

So that's it, then. They are gone.

'That was fab,' I say to Roisin, but as the applause fades and the crowd divert either outside or to the bar I can't help wondering is that really it for the big hunt for Tiernan Quinn? Is that as much as I will encounter? Though, what else was I expecting? Autographs? Photos? Best friends for life? I'm not sure why but I feel a bit empty inside now that the gig is over.

Roisin reads my mind. 'Are you going to try and find him?' she asks. 'You can't just leave now.'

'I don't know,' I reply. 'What do you think?'

'Well, at least try to talk to him!'

Roisin dances as she talks.

'I think he's gone but let's get one more drink and I'll keep my eyes peeled,' I tell her. 'Something is telling me to just leave it, but at the same time I don't feel like I have really fulfilled much for Lucy. We'll see...'

I order two gin and tonics. A DJ has taken over the decks and we find a seat at a table with high stools, which is perfect for scouring the crowd. The amount of revellers has now lessened a little since the band have finished, but there are still plenty about and enough for Tiernan and his Madd Mollies to stay out of our sight.

'Oh look, I see them!' says Roisin and she nods towards the four band members who are trying to get past a hen party with as little fuss as possible. The boys look uncomfortable and we laugh as they try to escape the clutches of several drunken lassies from Glasgow, including a rather racy hen, who is certainly making the most of her last night of freedom.

'Ah I think I'll leave him to it,' I tell her, taking a long drink through my straw. 'I don't know if I could be bothered trying to get to him. Looks like he has enough on his plate.'

'But you can't just leave it there!' Roisin scolds. 'Think about wee Lucy and her big crush on him! You could at least try and finish the job and find out if you've found the right guy. Go on! Go talk to him! There he is at the bar now with the drummer boy. You have to! Go on!'

I shake my head and watch Tiernan and his mate, who look very glad to be off duty. They have both changed clothing and Tiernan wears a light scarf around his neck with a grey blazer. The hat has gone and the jeans are the same but he has certainly freshened up after a very lively, sweaty performance.

He looks like a pretty intense guy and there is absolutely no way I am going to just walk up to him and blurt out about some teenage holiday he probably doesn't remember.

'I imagine he's the kind of man who gets a lot of attention and he would either think I'm some nutcase looking for an excuse to talk to him or else tell me where to go,' I explain to Roisin. 'Plus I don't fancy telling a complete stranger that I have someone else's heart. Plus it might not even be him.'

I have totally taken cold feet and I'm starting to feel sorry for myself, but Roisin is having none of it.

'You are no fun,' she mocks and lets out a sigh that comes from her painted toes. 'I'm not asking you to chat him up,

Maggie!' she says. 'But I thought you came here for a reason. No point chickening out now!'

'I can't...'

We look around us and I watch as Tiernan adjusts his jacket and turns his back to a few female admirers. There is absolutely no way I am going to behave like a groupie and be treated in that way. No way.

'I'm going to the bar,' says Roisin and she slips off her stool. 'Same again?'

'Jeez, Speedy Gonzales. Did you just down that?'

I look at her empty glass, which matches her glassy eyes.

'Yup. Watch and learn, cousin. Watch and learn.'

I shake my head as Roisin makes her way to the bar and stands right next to Tiernan and his band mate. You can tell she is a trained actress as it doesn't flinch her one bit to make a move. She twirls the end of her hair and casually looks around the bar and then eventually to them and, of course, they notice her, noticing them.

Tiernan says something to her and she throws her head back in a girly laugh. Boy, but she can flirt! The other guy, the drummer, looks smitten by her too and the next thing she is ordering them a drink and chatting away like she has known them forever.

The three of them look up at me and wave and I swear that my face has turned a beetroot shade of purple. So much for Dutch courage. I am shaking like a baby deer.

Roisin hands the lads two hefty pints of Guinness and grabs our gin and tonics and then makes her way back up to where I am sitting like a wallflower in comparison to Her Royal Bubbliness.

'That wasn't so hard,' she says, setting our drinks on the table. I grab mine and drink it like I've been in the Sahara for days.

'What on earth was that all about? Did you buy them a drink?'

'I did indeed and I will sorely regret it in the morning when I check my bank balance, but if it gets the ball rolling in this little mission of yours, then it will be money well spent, my dear.'

'You're an absolute scream,' I tell her.

'You're an absolute chicken,' she replies. 'They're only men. Well, thirty-something quite-hot men when you see them up close, but they're only human beings like we are. They don't bite. At least I don't think they do, anyhow. Mind you, I wouldn't mind if they did bite...'

Tiernan and the drummer keep glancing our way and I am caught out every time I do the same in their direction. The other two band members have joined them now, having been released from the clutches of the hen party and they order their own drinks from the bar.

'What did you say to them?' I ask Roisin and I swivel in my chair so that I am no longer in their eye-line.

'It's not what I said to them, it's what they said to me,' she says with a confident smile. 'He spoke to me first.'

I have no idea why but I am slightly jealous.

'Well, are you going to tell me what he said or is it a secret?'

'It's a secret,' she whispers and looks back down at him and then at me again. 'I'm kidding, you big eejit! I asked him something stupid like the time and he looked at me like I was speaking Mandarin and then he said to me that the bloody label was sticking out of the back of my dress and I laughed my head off and said I would get you to fix it. Then I bought them a drink to say thank you. Now, can you tuck that label in so I am not walking around like an advertisement for New Look?'

I laugh and fix her dress at the back and when I am done I look up to see Tiernan and company standing right beside our table. Oh fuck.

'Hi,' he says and pulls a stool out from under the table. 'I couldn't help notice you both looking our way so we thought we'd make it easier for you.'

I'm in shock. I can't speak.

'We were actually looking at the clock down there,' says Roisin, looking up at him from beneath her long lashes. 'You know the way I asked you the time?'

Tiernan looks a bit disappointed and turns around to see the invisible clock.

'I told you they weren't looking at us,' says the guy who was on lead guitar. 'We should be so lucky.'

'Well then, at least let us buy you a drink back,' says Tiernan, realising there is no clock and his dark-brown eyes go back to Roisin. 'That was a hefty enough round you were hit with. Same again?'

Roisin nods and I do too and off he goes, putting his hand in his back pocket as he walks away and pulling out a brown-leather wallet. He glances back up when he gets to the bar, but I can't tell if it's me he is looking at, or Roisin or just at the group of us in general.

'I think he likes you,' I whisper to her and Drummer Boy takes his seat.

'I'm Jack,' he says, extending a hand to me and then Roisin. We both shake his hand and say our own names courteously.

'Boy, but we're all very formal around here,' says Mr Lead Guitar, who leans on the table. 'I'm Connor and that's Mick, but he doesn't really talk. He just lets his music do the talking, isn't that right, our Mick?'

Mick nods and stays behind Connor, looking like we might bite him if he comes closer.

'And your friend at the bar?' says Roisin. 'Does he have a name?'

'He has all sorts of names,' says Connor, licking the creamy Guinness froth from his lips as he speaks. 'He answers to most things, but his mother calls him Tiernan.'

'Tiernan,' says Roisin. 'Okay...'

Oh holy shit. Oh holy *shit*. So it is him! Well, it's the right first name anyhow... Roisin looks at me and I know she is bursting to clap like a baby seal with excitement. Could it really be him?

The boys exchange glances in bewilderment just as Tiernan arrives back with our drinks. He sets them down, oblivious to our swooning over his name.

'Is it something I said?' he asks and re-joins us at the table, only this time he is sat right next to me. He leans his arms on the table and I can't help but look. I have a thing about arms. His jacket is rolled up and he wears a nice brown-leather watch and he has strong hands and tanned strong arms and he smells so good...

135

'We were just making polite introductions,' says Jack. 'That's Maggie and that's Roisin.'

I still haven't really spoken much. I am trying to get my head around the strong possibility of this being *the* Tiernan Quinn after all. He sits next to me and the smell of his musky cologne and a faint hint of sweat is making me dizzy. His arm brushes against mine and I shiver. I think I might fall off my stool. He certainly has a charisma that the leading man of any band should have and I remind myself that he is not, in fact, Bono or Chris Martin but is just a guy from somewhere in the sticks of Ireland who plays Dublin pubs and clubs and has probably chalked up quite a few notches on his bedpost because some people do believe he is Bono or Chris Martin. I will not be one of those people.

'Where are you from, Maggie?' he asks me, looking right into my eyes. Ah, Jesus. He has Bradley Cooper-shaped eyes. He is an absolute dream-boat. Lucy Harte you had good taste! I am smitten.

'Bel-Belfast,' I reply, crossing my legs under the table. I am so out of touch with this type of conversation with hot men in night clubs and I need to take a few deep breaths. Roisin keeps nudging me. I am going to kill her.

'Cool,' he says. 'A Northern girl. Nice accent.'

He smiles and takes a drink. He is sexy. Fuck.

'Thanks,' I reply and my mind goes blank. I don't know what to say. 'You're a really good singer.'

Christ the night.

'Thanks,' he says back. 'You're a really good dancer.'

I blush. Oh no. He saw me bopping along like a fan girl.

'I know the words of a lot of songs,' I tell him, and my heart rate starts to slow down a bit. I take a drink.

'You are a really good dancer and a really good singer. You sang along a lot too, I noticed.'

Shit. Crap.

'I used to make up my own songs.'

What the actual *fuck* am I saying?

He nods and smiles. 'Me too. In fact I still do, a lot.'

I swallow. I gulp. 'Cool.'

I sound like a fourteen-year-old groupie. I need to get a grip.

'So, what's Belfast like, Maggie?' asks Jack, who seems to be feeling a bit left out. Connor is quizzing Roisin and Mick is just being Mick, saying nothing.

'It's a great city,' I say with a tiny snippet of new confidence. 'Have you ever been?'

He shakes his head in apology.

'I have been there lots,' says Tiernan. 'I love it. I used to gig there every Wednesday and Thursday with my old band, but I don't get there so often now that I've joined in with this motley crew.'

'Oh, are you new to the band?' asks Roisin, who can obviously listen in on two conversations at once. She nudges me again. She is so dead if she does that again. It's really annoying and he isn't bloody well blind!

'Not any more,' he tells us. 'I joined a few years back but I used to play a lot more traditional Irish and folk stuff, so all this rocking is still a bit out of my comfort zone. Could you tell?'

Roisin and I both shake our heads.

'God no, you are a very convincing rocker,' she says and when I look at her she is doing her fluttery-eyelashes thing that she has been doing to men all night. This time *I* nudge *her*.

What am I *doing*?

He smiles at her warmly and then comes back to me.

'What type of songs did you write, Maggie? I'd love to hear some of your music.'

His arm is touching mine again. Lightly, subtly, but touching all the same and he is doing that really nice smiley, starey thing again.

Oh my God, please don't, I want to say to him. *Please don't look at me like that or be so nice to me. Please don't brush your arm against mine again. I'm a married woman. No, well, I was a married woman. Actually I am single! Am I really single? Okay, you can do it again, please do it again. I am single. I think I am…*

'I don't think I would punish you by making you listen to my songs,' I say to him and shyly stir my drink with the straw. 'I was about twelve years old and I lived on a farm. Hardly Grammy-award-winning material.'

I lived on a farm? Somebody gag me.

'I lived on a farm too,' he says to me. 'So did Connor. In fact we're all country boys at heart, isn't that right, lads?'

I'm glad he has included his friends in the conversation. I could be totally imagining it but it was getting quite hot in here for a moment.

'Yes, all from the sticks. Do you play any instruments,

Maggie?' asks Connor. Like Roisin, he seems to be able to keep up with all the conversations at one time.

'I used to,' I say. 'I've recently been challenged to learn how to play guitar, so I'll have to dust off the cobwebs and get stuck in to that soon. I'm looking forward to it.'

I think of Lucy. I wonder if she is listening to all of this? I think she would be well impressed. This has to be him! I want to ask him! I can't ask him. Sorry, Lucy.

'What song are you going to learn?' asks Tiernan.

'I have no idea yet,' I reply, trying to be dismissive. I don't even know why I mentioned that. I don't want to talk about Lucy and her list. I want him to brush against my arm again. My head is spinning. I don't want to think of Lucy. I want to get lost in Tiernan Quinn. He is bloody gorgeous.

Oh Lucy, I'm sorry if I'm doing this wrong, I think to myself. *How am I doing? I'm so nervous, Lucy, but my God, you had good taste!*

Roisin catches my eye and nods in approval. She likes him too. Whether this is Lucy's Tiernan or not, I like him. A lot.

My phone, which is sitting on the table in front of me, lights up as a message comes through. Thinking it must be a late-night check-in from Simon, who is no doubt itching to know how I am getting on, I take a quick peep at it but it's not him at all.

It's my brother, John Joe, again. What the hell does he want?

'Your boyfriend?' asks Tiernan, interrupting his song to be, well, nosey? I kind of like it...

'I don't have a boyfriend,' I tell him. I am about to say that

I have a husband, but then I remember that I don't have one of those either any more.

He smiles at my answer and my stomach does a leap. I haven't felt that in a long time, the stomach-flippy feeling and it takes me by surprise. God, I am so attracted to this stranger. Is this even possible?

It's lust, it's lust, it's lust, it's so brilliant.

'Does your *girlfriend* play music too?' I ask him.

'I don't have a girlfriend,' he tells me and he smiles again and my stomach whooshes again.

I can feel Roisin's breathing beside me becoming more and more rapid as if she is going to spontaneously combust. She is listening to every word.

'Maybe if Maggie needs some guitar lessons, she could give you a shout,' she says and does a really obvious wink.

'Yeah, or call on me,' says Connor and the rest of the boys laugh, but it sounds like Tiernan and I are inside a bubble and everything else is a blur in my ears. 'We hired him for his God's-gift good looks, not his guitar licks, so if it's lessons you're after...'

It's not lessons I'm after... I try to take my eyes off him. It just won't happen.

'Watch it!' says Tiernan to Connor and he slowly puts his hand on top of mine. 'I want to be the one to give her... guitar lessons.'

I skirt a glance at Roisin. She looks like she is watching a movie as she stares at us, mouth slightly open. She is loving this. I am too.

Back to Tiernan. His hand is still on mine. It feels good.

Then I see Jeff's face. I hear his voice. No, no it feels wrong. I shouldn't be doing this. I am not ready for this. I need to go. I take my hand away.

'I... we really should go,' I say and they all look at me like I have just sprouted a second head.

'What? Where are you going?' Tiernan asks. 'Ah, don't leave me already.'

My eyes search for Roisin, who looks like she has just been clicked out of her daze and back into real life.

'What? Go? Now?' she asks. 'Are you serious?'

'Yes, I'm serious. Yes, now,' I tell her and I lift my handbag and jacket and whisper under my breath. 'I can't do this. I need to get out of here.'

Roisin stands up and gathers her own belongings.

'Okay... well, well... bye lads,' she eventually manages, totally confused. 'It was great meeting ya. Thanks for the drinks and um... the tunes. Cheers! See ya again... I hope.'

She walks to me and links my arm.

'Bye Roisin, bye Maggie,' the band mumble incoherently and I quickly lead the way out of the bar, still feeling an incredible surge of electricity running through my entire body.

Roisin leads me out of the noisy bar and into the cool of the night, her heels clicking on the pavement as we walk to the roadside to hail a taxi.

'Would you like to slow down a bit, Maggie? Like, I need to talk to you about what just happened in there. Are you not going to jump his bones? He was so into you?'

'Am I walking fast? Just talk,' I say to her, still walking, still quite dazed. 'I have no idea what just happened in there or what the hell I thought I was going to do with that man. I am a married woman.'

'Stop!' she says. 'Just stop a minute, will you please?'

So I stop.

'What?'

'You are not a married woman any more,' she tells me. 'Your husband dumped you for a younger model months and months ago and she is having his baby.'

Ow!

'So you are well entitled to have a fucking good time with that ride of a man in there if you feel like it. Do you hear me?'

Yes, I hear her.

'But I feel so –'

'Feel so what? Don't you dare say guilty, Maggie O'Hara!' she says. 'He... Tiernan... he took your hand and was looking at you like you were some sort of Disney princess and you liked him too and you get up and walk out! How could you do that? You absolute muppet!'

'Don't be a drama queen, Roisin,' I say, but I know exactly what she means. I am a muppet. Jeff doesn't exist in my life any more. I am a prize muppet.

I breathe in deeply and wave down a cab as if on auto-pilot. I have no answers, really. Not yet, anyhow.

'Maybe I am a Disney princess,' I laugh back. 'Or maybe we're just more pissed than we think we are. Maybe there was something magic in those cocktails or in the gin. Maybe I just got scared, okay!'

'Go back in, then!' says Roisin, pointing to the bar. I start to laugh as I get a flashback of her trying to boss me around when we were little. 'Go back in and say we are going to party the night away and let's get pissed. With them. You, with him.'

'No,' I tell her. 'I don't want to get pissed. I've been pissed for the past six months and it's not helping. I don't know what to do or where to turn.'

'Oh, Maggie,' says Roisin. 'I don't know what to say.'

But she doesn't have to say anything because right behind her Tiernan Quinn has left the bar too and is coming over in our direction.

Oh shit. Oh God. Oh help.

'Maggie?' he says.

He is a little bit out of breath. He is a big bit gorgeous. I am a giant bit going to have to just fucking do this.

'Look, I'm sorry for the swift exit. It's been a while since I was out and I just got a bit –'

'Ssh,' he says and he smiles and I melt a little inside again. I am a silly bitch. He is a nice guy. 'You don't have to explain. We can start again. I'm Tiernan. Tiernan Quinn.'

He puts out his hand. I shake it.

'I was hoping you would say that was your name,' I tell him and he looks a little confused. Oh, if only he knew.

'Can I call you? Tomorrow?' he asks.

Roisin coughs, which I take as code for me to not even dare and refuse.

'Yes, you can,' she says.

He hands me his phone and I put my number in and save it.

'I don't think I've ever left a bar to run after a woman

before,' he tells me and I get a rush of warmth through my veins. 'But I think you are going to be worth it. Goodnight, Maggie.'

'Goodnight, Tiernan Quinn.'

He kisses me on the cheek and runs back into the bar and I swear Roisin is doing a Riverdance on the pavement beside me.

'Lucy Harte, you wee beauty!' she says, looking up at the stars. 'Now, any chance you can do the same for me?'

Chapter 15

I am on a beach, in a place called Malahide outside Dublin, sitting on a chequered rug, holding an acoustic guitar and Tiernan Quinn is by my side pushing my fingers onto the fret board to show me the chords I need to learn for 'Songbird' by Eva Cassidy. He played it at a wedding once and I couldn't believe he even knew it, but since it was Lucy's last favourite song it's the one I'd like to learn if I ever get round to it.

I can feel his breath on my neck against the cool breeze that comes from the Irish Sea as I strum the guitar. It squeaks a little, but I get it eventually.

'You have done this before,' he smiles. 'You said you used to play a bit, but you know a lot more than you are telling!'

'I don't remember!' I reply, but to be honest I am enjoying his teaching a lot. His left arm is resting behind my back and the guitar is just a prop that brings us physically closer without needing to make any obvious moves.

We spent the morning walking the beach and clearing the cobwebs from the night before and while I am trying to play it very cool, the urge to get physical with him is totally killing me. He is being the ultimate gentleman and is totally taking my lead, which makes me a lot more relaxed than I thought I would be.

'I'm not the stereotypical womanising musician you might think I am,' he said to me earlier as he laid out the rug he took from his car when we were finished walking.

'You can be whoever you want to be, Tiernan,' I told him. 'You don't need to explain yourself to me.'

He looked a bit hurt when I said that, but it's true. I don't care about his reputation, good, bad or indifferent. I am just enjoying his company and I think he is mine too. If he knew my past he would probably run a million miles.

With the guitar lesson coming to a natural end, it's time to talk again, or so he thinks.

'So, tell me all about you, Maggie O'Hara,' he whispers, pushing my hair off my shoulders. 'What brings you to Dublin? I'd like to think it was to see a really happening band called The Madd Mollies, but I'd seriously doubt it.'

I want to tell him the truth, the story about Lucy and how she fell for him when she was so young and how I really did track down him and his band, but I can't tell him all that. I don't want him to know about me. I just want to lie here on this beach and feel him close to me and pretend that all my troubles and baggage of the past didn't exist. I just want to be a girl with a guy showing her chords on a guitar before he kisses her in the sand and tells her how beautiful she is and how good she makes him feel, without any sad stories of heart transplants and marriage break-ups and a husband who is having a baby with someone else and who wants a divorce right now.

I don't want to be the woman with someone else's heart. I just want to feel my own heart beat when he looks at me and savour this attraction to the wonderful enigma that is Tiernan Quinn.

'I might tell you all of that one day, Tiernan,' I say to him, looking into his gorgeous eyes.

'Why won't you open up to me? You don't answer any of my questions.'

'We've only just met,' I remind him. 'Look, I have quite a story that I can't share with you today, but I probably will tell you all about it one day soon, but for now do you mind if we just –?'

And that's all I have to say for him to understand.

He takes the guitar from my hands and lays it by his side and he cups my face in his hands and kisses me so deeply that my eyes roll back in delirium. His tongue moves in my mouth and my body responds by rising towards him, and his strong, warm hand grips my waist to pull me closer. My God, I had forgotten how good this feels. He leans me back gently onto the rug and I feel the sand in my hair and he stops and looks at me with a beautiful hunger and kisses me again even more passionately than before.

'I want you, Maggie,' he whispers in my ear. 'Will you spend the day with me? Please?'

The weight of his body on top of me, the firmness of his manhood against my inner thigh means that there can only be one answer to his question.

'Yes. Yes, I will,' I reply and we lie side by side on the sand and look up at the afternoon sky and just breathe in unison as gulls circle above us and the sound of the waves crash in the near distance. I feel his hand clasp mine and we don't need to say anything else for now.

We just breathe.

'Well, hello you dirty rotten stop-out! Did you have a nice day?'

I meet Roisin back at her apartment to say my farewells before I catch the last train back to Belfast later that evening and to say I have a new spring in my step is an understatement.

'Amazing,' I tell her, unable to hide my glow.

Tiernan took me back to his home, where we spent a glorious afternoon in his back garden first of all, where we listened to music and barbecued some chicken and we couldn't keep our hands off each other for a second.

We just about managed to make it to the bedroom when it wasn't just the barbecue that was heating up and he lit a spark in me, pardon the pun, that had been out for too long.

'I feel alive again, Ro,' I tell my cousin and she gives me an almost suffocating hug in her hallway. When she finally lets go, she has tears in her eyes.

'I must be hormonal,' she tells me, 'but I am so fucking delighted for you, Mags. You need to believe in yourself more, you know that? You really need to step out of the life you've been living and go see the world instead of moping around and drinking your days and nights away in your apartment, do you hear?'

I know exactly what she is saying and I am so determined to make this day my brand-new start.

'I never thought I'd be able to enjoy myself again like I did today,' I tell her. 'He has awakened me, let's say, and it was pure heaven. Thank you, Roisin. Thank you, Lucy Harte!'

'What the hell are you thanking me for?' she replies. 'I was only a very jealous bystander. Christ, he is one hot muthafucker. Was he good?'

I blush. That gives her the answer she was looking for.

'Let's just say I am very, very, very satisfied!'

'Oh, you lucky cow! Are you seeing him again? Please say yes!'

I smile and shake my head.

'Roisin, I'm not ready for any sort of relationship with anyone right now. I need to get to know myself again, but who knows what the future holds? I know he likes me. I know I like him, but I'm going to focus on me for a while. Does that sound selfish?'

Roisin shrugs in response.

'That sounds more like the Maggie O'Hara I know and love,' she says. 'Now, don't you have a train to catch? Or are your aching loins too exhausted to travel tonight? You can stay, you know?'

My loins *are* actually aching but I want to keep riding along on this glow and get home to plan my next move as I follow Lucy's directions.

'I have a trip to France to plan,' I say and Roisin's eyes widen in admiration. 'And a few other things on her list that I need to tackle. But I'm dancing a bit inside, Roisin, and Lucy said to never stop dancing.'

'You go, girl. I've loved seeing you. I'm proud of you, cuz.'

'Thanks, Roisin,' I tell her and we hug again. 'I'm kind of proud of me too.'

I enjoy my thinking time on the train home and I close my eyes and visualise Lucy and her cheeky smile and how her list brought me such energy and excitement on my spontaneous trip to Dublin. I am spreading my wings just like she wanted to. I am travelling. I went dancing. I found a part of me that I had buried away inside – a sense of adventure and wildness that allowed me to just get up and go and follow my heart, instead of always worrying about the what-ifs and what-nots.

I feel alive inside again. Tiernan Quinn has lit a fire inside me with his music and passion and his ability to bring out an inner glow that I don't think Jeff ever did.

Was I just 'settling for' something when I met Jeff? Surely not... was I? On paper, he was the cardboard-cut-out good guy. He had a good job, a respected (if boring) family, a healthy childhood, a five-year plan (that obviously didn't involve me, after all) and he had no money worries. He was a safe bet. Or so I thought...

But did he make me dance? No. Did he make me laugh and kick my legs in hysterics on the beach and did he make me scream for mercy in bed like Tiernan Quinn just did?

No, he didn't. I deserve better. I deserve to dance. Lucy has taught me that I really do deserve to fill her heart with the best love in the world, not a one-sided plea with a man who probably never really loved me anyway. I know now what it feels like to be so enriched and I will never settle for any less.

Okay, Lucy Harte. Where are you taking me to next?

Lucy

~ *January 1999* ~

Big news, big news! Massive news! Brilliantly funny news! Are you ready?

Everyone in our house is going mental apart from me – I am in my room, as usual, trying to avoid the madness and also because if I show my face I know I will laugh at them and if I laugh at them I will be in trouble even more than Simon is now because... are you ready? Are you really ready?

SIMON GOT A TATTOO!!! A REAL tattoo! The shouting is tremendous! The reaction is priceless! He is in SO much trouble, which makes a big change as around here it's normally ME who gets into trouble, so I am LOVING it!

Mum is having a complete meltdown and is threatening to sue the tattooist for breaking the law! Dad is calling a friend, who says he knows someone who knows someone who can remove it but it will cost him loads and Marilyn is literally on her knees saying prayers that he doesn't catch some life-threatening disease from the needle that was used!

Henry, my forever loyal little gopher, is reporting back to me at regular intervals with answers to my questions from my safe haven here (if I go down I will have to give my real opinion, which will probably result in me being grounded and I have plans this weekend, so I'm not going to risk it!).

Here are the things that Henry has been able to tell me so far:

Simon told the tattooist he was eighteen. He is not eighteen, of course. He just turned seventeen. Cool!

The tattoo is still bleeding a bit, but Henry thinks it's of a star and a sun symbol and Henry says that Mum says it looks more like a chicken and an egg. This is too funny!

The tattoo is on his wrist and Mum is mortified and says at least he can cover it up with a thick watch strap when he goes to church or is out in public or when anyone comes to visit. I love my brother so much!

He says it cost £20, but Henry heard Simon tell his best friend that it was £120! That's like a full year of pocket money! He is so dead!

On the upside, our parents are totally unified in their disgust at their eldest child's decision to mark his body so carelessly at such a young age. This does not happen very often! Normally if my dad says black, my mum argues white, so every cloud has a silver lining.

Oh, I must pause… here is Henry with an update…

…

I'm back! This keeps getting better!

It's not of a star and a sun. It's not of a chicken and an egg! It's of a peace symbol and a gun! A gun! Oh! My! God! I think my mum just fainted! She says she will never, ever forgive him, which is ridiculous, but she probably won't! I think I am going to wet myself laughing! Go Simon, you absolute nut case!

*Note to Lucy Harte: Don't be a chicken! Get a tattoo!
**Note to Lucy Harte: Always forgive your friends & family. People make mistakes!

Chapter 16

I sleep a lot on the train journey home and dream that Lucy is mad at me for taking it too far with her precious Tiernan Quinn. I asked him not to text me or call and to just give me time to work out a few things in my head and I feel so bad now for being so cold and, well, for using him to stroke my own ego and make me feel better.

I text him just as we arrive at Belfast station. I hope I didn't hurt him. I really do because he did more for me than he will ever know. I haven't smiled like this in years! Yes, years!

Tiernan, I have to thank you for the most wonderful day, I write to him. *Until our paths ever cross, I will be working on sorting my crazy life out, but I do hope to see you again. I really do. Keep singing! Love, Maggie x*

I feel better for that. At least I am being honest and not flinging myself into some rebound relationship where both of us will end up getting hurt.

I think of Lucy's list again and I try to plan my next move. France is the big one, obviously, but getting a tattoo is pretty much up there too. I have always hated tattoos, but after seeing Tiernan Quinn's tastefully decorated artwork I could be convinced to get maybe a teeny-tiny one in honour of Lucy and it would also remind me of the amazing day Tiernan and I spent together, plus it would remind me at times of the need to be forever grateful for the life that Lucy gave me.

I will think about it...

As for Lucy's pledge to always forgive your friends and family? Well, all I can think of is my brother and his efforts to get in touch... it's a trickier one than most, I'm afraid, and might take me a little longer to address, but I'm working on it. I promise you, Lucy, I really am.

'How was Dublin?'

I am back in my apartment and Kevin, my neighbour, has popped in for a coffee. I left him a note to keep an eye on my place while I was away.

I burst into a giveaway smile and Kevin's eyes widen.

'You met someone! Maggie, don't tell me any different! Who was the lucky man?!'

I try to hide it, but a smile keeps bursting through. I can't deny it. I have to tell someone about Tiernan or I will explode! I reach for Lucy's notebook, which is never far from my side and hand it to him.

'I got this from my donor family just last week,' I explain to him. 'It's Lucy Harte's diary and in it she wanted to meet a guy called Tiernan Quinn, who was her first crush as a young teenager. I tracked him down and, well, it was never my intention, but my God, Kevin, I couldn't resist! It was out-of-this-world amazing!'

Kevin looks like his head is spinning with all this information. He flicks through the notebook in awe.

'This is the best news ever,' he says. 'I knew there was something different about you. Your clothes, your skin, you have a new spring in your step – and it's all because of this? I love it!'

I put the kettle on. I have no wine in the house and I don't even feel the need to have any. This time last week I would have been nursing a bottle and having panic attacks if there wasn't a second one in the fridge to prop me up, or knock me out, by bedtime.

'It has really got me thinking of how precious my life is, Kevin,' I tell my trusty neighbour. 'I was given a massive gift from this little girl and I have been taking it for granted, going into self-destruct mode all because of that worthless git I married and sinking booze like it was going out of fashion. I nearly lost my job too. She is saving me. She is really saving me again.'

Kevin looks elated.

'So you're going to do the rest of these things? Find the world's tallest bridge... get a tattoo? Are you seriously going to get a tattoo?'

He frowns and I don't blame him. Kevin is a clean-cut health freak and I am not the tattoo type at all.

'Tiernan has tattoos,' I tell him, and my eyes go all misty and dreamy at the thought. 'I could get a nice henna one, you know, take the girly way out?'

'This just keeps getting better! You're a legend, Lucy Harte!'

He closes the book and looks up to the heavens and then

155

pretends to cough, but I know he is choked up at the change in me.

'Do you think she is watching you, Maggie? It must be such a connection to have someone else's heart beat inside you.'

'I feel her with me every day,' I explain to him. 'But I know I don't have forever. I have had Lucy's heart for seventeen years now. Some day soon she is going to want it back.'

Kevin looks down at the floor.

'Don't say that,' he tells me. 'I hate it when you talk like that.'

'I'm sorry,' I whisper. 'Come here, you big softie, give me a hug.'

Kevin wraps his bulky arms around me and gives me a tight squeeze. He's a super-fit gym junkie who begged me for months to stop drinking so I know how much this change in me means to him.

'It has really got me thinking of where I want to go in life, Kevin, and it's not back to Jeff. I have closed the door on that possibility and I feel free already. It's made me think of some of the things I'd like to do with my own life, as well as doing those that Lucy never got to do.'

'Tell me more,' says Kevin, sitting down at the table. 'I'd love to hear of all your plans.'

I hand him a coffee.

'Well, when I had my operation all those years ago, there were certain things I couldn't do for a long, long time. I couldn't eat properly for months, I was on heavy medication and I never thought I would walk or run again as I was so weak from the whole experience, both physically and emotionally.'

'I bet,' he says, stirring his drink. 'To owe your life to another person, to another family, must be a huge thing to deal with on so many levels.'

'Have you ever run a marathon?' I ask him and he drops his spoon.

'A *marathon?* Well, that is a big fat change of subject.' Then his eyes light up. 'Are you thinking of running a marathon, Maggie? Are you sure you could do it?'

'No, I am not thinking of running a marathon, silly,' I explain to him. 'Something shorter, yes. I'd like to do something physical, just for me.'

'That's a great idea!' he tells me, straightening up in his chair. 'I've run marathons, yes. What are you thinking? Ten K? Five K? Are you sure you're up for it, Maggie?'

'I'd like to do something really, really challenging for Lucy, and well, for me. Would you do it with me?'

Kevin is already there in his head, I can tell. He takes out his phone and scrolls through a search engine for information.

'Of course I will!' he says. 'My friend is organising a mini marathon, thirteen miles for charity in June. You could start with that? What do you think?'

Kevin is already on his phone, texting his friend.

'The most I have ever done is five K in a charity run,' I tell him. 'I mean, I don't even know if I could do any more than that, but it would kind of fit in with some of these challenges I am setting myself and the mini marathon would be a great start. I'd love to do it. Really love to.'

'Say no more. I will sign us both up,' he says. 'I've got the online registration here and, believe me, if you can do five K now, you can do a half marathon in a few months' time. Easy.'

'I didn't say I could do five K *now*,' I say, shuddering at the thought. 'I'm kind of out of practice lately. It was quite a while ago, the five K... in fact it was probably ten years ago...'

'Well, you know what to do about that, my dear!' says Kevin, getting up and putting his cup by the sink. 'You have a big fat Dublin hangover to nurse,' he says. 'And a half marathon to train for. Great to see you smiling, kid. You've just made my day.'

He tilts my chin back and kisses me on the cheek.

'Now... training? Don't overdo it, do you hear?'

I know what he is thinking. He glances at my chest and not in a luring way. He looks at my heart.

'I will start off very gently,' I tell him and he playfully jogs on the spot on the other side of the door, exactly in the spot where I punched Jeff. I still can't believe I did that.

'See, I'm training already,' he says. 'I never miss an opportunity.'

'Well, before you get to your own front door I will be doing laps of the apartment,' I tell him. 'I mean it. I will.'

'That's my girl! Get on it!' he replies and I laugh as he runs and shadow boxes his way down the corridor to his own apartment. 'We can do this, Maggie! Operation Mini Marathon is on!'

'It's on!' I call and I watch him as he goes.

That's it. I'm going for a run.

A flurry of images go through my mind as I jog through Botanic Gardens, my head down, my earphones in and I am lost in a train of thought of what the next few months of my life will bring.

I am going to run the mini marathon with Kevin all in Lucy's memory. Yes... I will use that date as my official way of letting her go and moving on with the rest of my life, whatever that means.

Everything else on her list, I am going to fit in between.

It feels so liberating to be out in fresh air with music beating in my ears and a faint line of sweat across my back and on my brow. I think about Lucy and the weight and worry she had on her shoulders and how she couldn't wait to run away from it all.

Her childhood was a far cry from my own on the farm at Loch Tara with my doting parents, where we really did not have a care in the world apart from whose turn it was to clean out the chicken coop or who would go to the corner shop for some freshly baked buns from Mrs Taylor's parlour.

My brother John Joe loved those buns. I used to marvel at how he cherished every bite of the soft cake and fresh cream and how his eyes lit up when he saw Mum had been to Mrs Taylor on her way back from the Mart on a Saturday.

I stop running to catch my breath and notice that my heart is beating really fast. Like, really fast. Maybe I'm not as fit as I thought I was. Or maybe it's the thought of John Joe and the knowledge that he wants to talk to me about something and I haven't replied that is making me all a-fluster.

I find a park bench and take a long drink from my water bottle and focus on my breathing, then I check my stepometer, which tells me I've done over 7,000 steps so far. I'm happy with that. I check my phone. No messages. Good. And then I scroll back to find the one from my brother and I stare at it and I don't notice I am crying until my tears fall onto my phone screen.

I need to talk to you, it says.

I need to breathe. I just need to breathe and get re-focused and then I can continue with my training. I have stuff to do in my life. Stuff for Lucy, like running the marathon and going to France to the bridge...

But what does John Joe want from me? Is it good news or bad news or has he finally realised how shit he has treated me down the years? Is he feeling sorry for me over Jeff or does he just want to gloat and rub it in that my marriage failed.

On auto-pilot, I find myself messaging my brother back. I don't even know what part of the States he is in any more. I have totally lost track, as well as having lost interest in his whereabouts.

What do you want? I ask him. Blunt as it may seem, it's all I need to know and he doesn't deserve any formalities, plus by the time he gets it over there I will probably have forgotten that I even sent it. It's gone. Sent. Done.

I stand up and fix myself for the last lap of my run. I will do the same route again and then call it a day. I might even pop in to see Flo on my way home and see Billie for a cuddle, plus I am desperate to tell her about Tiernan Quinn!

My phone bleeps. It is him. Already! So much for time difference between here and America...

Can you talk now? he asks me. *Can I call you now?*

I sit back down on the bench and my fingers shake as I send him a reply.

I can talk, I tell him. *You can call me now.*

Shit.

Chapter 17

So here I am, sitting on a park bench in my navy sports leggings and fluorescent-pink running vest on a warm evening in April, staring at my phone and not knowing what the hell to expect from my long-lost brother.

I have butterflies in my tummy like a teenager on a first date and when the phone rings I let out a light yelp and then answer it like I have been given an electric shock.

'At last!' he says and I gulp at the sound of his voice. 'You really do like to make me sweat it out, don't you?'

Oh, my God, there is so much I could say to that but I bite my tongue and I put on a radiant smile as if he can see me, as if no matter what he says right now won't have the slightest effect on me like it used to.

'I've been busy,' are the first words I say to him. 'Really busy. What's up?'

I want to ask are you sick? Are you dying? Are you pregnant? (Well, you never bloody know with Mr Casanova Yankee Doodle Doo!) Nothing would surprise me.

'I just wanted to see how you are,' he says and my mood lightens.

'You... you *what?*'

He has floored me for sure with that statement!

'I've been worried about you. Are you okay, Maggie? I know you can't be exactly on top of the world right now and I've been thinking about you and worrying.'

I am utterly confused. So much so that I start to laugh.

'Is this a joke?' I ask him. 'You want to know how I *am?* Are you for real?'

I can hear a woman in the background, speaking in some sort of foreign accent and I roll my eyes in a mixture of pity for her and disgust at him for using women like they go out of fashion. It must be Vivienne, the French girl who Mum told me about. Actually, it probably isn't Vivienne. That was two weeks ago. He has probably moved on to someone like her sister or her mother, knowing his high moral standards.

'I don't expect you to believe me, but Mum told me about you and Jeff breaking up and I just wanted to say I'm sorry that it didn't work out,' he says. 'Do you want me to break his face?'

He laughs but I put my hand on my forehead and shake my head in disbelief. I am lost for words.

'That was a joke, Maggie. I have no intention of laying a finger on him, plus it would be pretty hard to break his face with the Atlantic Ocean in the way.'

'You don't need to break his face!' I say down the phone. 'I already did that all by myself, if you really want to know, and I'm not proud of it!'

I am proud of it, actually, but I will never admit that to anyone.

'So, is that it?' I ask. 'Is that all you want?'

'Maggie, please!' he replies in a tone of voice I barely recognise. 'I totally get where you are coming from, but I'm your
brother. I do care about you, no matter what you might think
of me. You know you can talk to me anytime. Don't go through
this on your own. You don't have to.'

'I am not on my own!' I shout and an elderly couple shoot
me a disgusted look as they shuffle past on their evening
walk. I mouth sorry, but they are too busy tut-tutting to notice.

'I wish you would stop shutting me out, Mags,' he says and
my eyes fill up when he calls me that. Of all the memories I
have with my brother, when he called me Mags... those were
the good times. I can't take this. I don't need this emotion.

'John Joe,' I say to him. 'I have moved on from you and
from all of that and I don't want to go back there again, so
you can stuff your concern right up your arse because I don't
ever want to hear from you again unless it's life or death, do
you hear me?'

'But Maggie!'

'Goodbye John Joe!'

I am about to hang up dramatically but the woman in the
background is saying something again in her stupid accent.
Actually, she is *shouting* something and the nosey part of me
wants to know what she is talking about. What's any of this
got to do with her? She will probably be dumped by the time
the phone call is over, knowing my brother's romantic history.

But she sounds desperate to talk to me.

'Your brother is sick, Maggie!' she is saying. 'Please talk to
him! He is very sick!'

He is sick. I drop the phone onto my lap. I bloody knew it. I fucking knew it. Christ!

I lift the phone to my ear. Pins and needles run right down my arms to my fingertips. He is sick. Fuck.

'Are you still there, Maggie?'

'I'm here,' I tell the woman I have never met, and who I probably never will.

'I am Vivienne, your brother's wife.'

His *wife*? Oh great, so he got married and never told any of us! I try to speak to her. My *sister-in-law*. I try again. I shake my head as tears stream down my face. No words will come out. I am too upset. I don't even know what I am. I don't know how much more I can take from this conversation.

I hang up the phone and I start running like I never want to come back.

'This is all very immature,' says Flo when I tell her about John Joe. 'You need to stop letting childhood memories strain your entire relationship with your brother, Maggie.'

Well, it's okay for her to say that, isn't it? She wasn't the one left for dead! I know I am being childish. I can't help it. My counsellor told me the same, that when it came to my brother and I, that I was stuck emotionally but no matter how hard I try, I cannot bring myself to get over it.

'You have no idea what I went through,' I say. I am sulking. I am actually sulking.

'Tell me about Dublin,' says Flo, trying to lighten the mood. 'Did you find your mystery man? Was he hot?'

I lift my car keys and purse and put on my coat, much to Flo's surprise.

'I'm not in the mood,' I tell her. 'I'll fill you in some other time. I feel like getting pissed and forgetting all about John Joe, Tiernan Quinn, Jeff and my whole stupid life right now.'

'Come on!' says Flo. 'You can't leave me hanging like this! I have been waiting very impatiently for all the goss. What's next on the list, then? Don't leave like this, Maggie. And please don't get pissed. You are doing so well.'

I bite my lip and then I bite my tongue. John Joe has upset me, just as he always does, only this time it's a different feeling from usual. It's guilt. It's pure, rotten guilt seeping through my veins and into my bones and I hate it. I actually hate it. I want to hug him and adore him like I used to. Why can I not just do that instead of bringing on all of this pain? He's my brother... I am a failure.

'I am not doing well, Flo!' I say to my best friend. 'I can kid myself that I am but I'm a long way off doing well! A quick shag in Dublin isn't going to change my life, is it? My brother gets under my skin and right now all I can think of is him dying and it scares the bloody life out of me! I miss him, Flo! I miss what he used to be to me when we were really young, before this stupid heart transplant took over our whole lives and made me so different. Lucy says to forgive my friends and family but I can't even forgive myself for how I have blamed him for so long!'

'Is that what Lucy said on her list? Really? Well, then that's your next move,' says Flo. 'Call him up. Arrange to visit. Do something, because right now you're only torturing yourself and it's not what you need right now. What do you think Lucy would do? What would she say if she saw you right now?'

'She would say to go see him.'

I know that she would, but I am exhausted with this all. I am tired and weary and right now, I want to forget about Lucy Harte. I just want to forget about it all.

I am drunk, just as I had planned to be. Well, 'pleasantly pissed' would be the proper term and the numbness I feel right now from all my real life is just what I needed. I'm on a high, a rush, and if anyone stands in my way I will give them a piece of my mind.

'Another vodka please,' I ask the bar man, who serves me immediately, totally oblivious to the emotional car crash he is witnessing. I am in a bar I have never been in before in the city centre and I chose it carefully because there is a tattoo parlour next door and as soon as I get this next drink down me, I am going to get a tattoo, but not for the reasons I should be. I am doing it because I know that when sober I never, ever will.

You were doing so well. Please don't get pissed.

Flo's words keep echoing in my ear. What does she know about how well I am doing? She lives in her little bubble with Billie and moping about over her ex and she drinks too! Everyone drinks to forget. It's just for some reason any time I actually do it, there's alarm bells as far as America, where my sick brother still finds time to be concerned.

I down the vodka and step out into the evening sun as

ordinary people who don't need to numb their emotions with alcohol go about their daily lives, shopping and chatting and going for coffee and dinner and doing ordinary things like I used to do when I had a husband and a life of my own.

The tattoo parlour is dark inside and another woman is in the waiting area, flicking through a magazine. I plonk down beside her.

'Don't get a tattoo when you're drunk,' she tells me and I want to tell her to mind her own business. 'I mean it. I did it before and it cost me a fortune to have it fixed.'

She rolls up her sleeve and shows me the evidence, but I barely notice. I'm not going to let a stranger influence me on what I am about to do.

'Is this your first?'

Oh would she just shut up already?!

'Yes,' I answer. 'First and last.'

She sniggers.

'We all say that,' she says and goes back to her magazine. 'I still say that, twenty-one inks later.'

The tattooist shows his face for the first time and asks me 'what I'm after'. I hadn't actually thought of that bit. I think of Lucy. I don't want to think of Lucy. I want to do this for me, just me. I am sick already of everything being about Lucy.

'A heart on my wrist,' I tell him and the woman bursts out laughing.

'What's so funny?' I ask her. She is really not helping right now.

'A heart! On your wrist! It's just so...'

'There's nothing wrong with love,' says the tattooist, who rolls up his sleeves and calls me into the back, where he will work his magic. 'We all need a little bit of romance in our lives.'

'This is nothing to do with love or romance,' I tell him. 'Nothing at all.'

By the look on his face, I know he believes me.

Lucy

8th April 1999

I am in the midst of a domestic with my mother.

I mean, it's not like we really get on at the best of times, but today was a particularly bad day because it started out over a simple request (from her) for me to have my hair cut and a simple reply (from me) stating that I did not want to have it done.

Here are the reasons I do not want to have my hair cut:

1) I don't see anything wrong with how it is at the minute.

2) Having it cut means going to the hairdressers and I don't have the patience to sit while someone talks to me about holidays and how I am getting on at school and do I have a boyfriend yet? (The answer to that is no, but I am working on it.)

3) *I am a wee bit afraid of how it might change me. My hair is very long and I am used to it. I don't want to let it go.*

So , for now, I have won the argument and avoided having my hair cut, but I know this is only the beginning of this discussion and that my mother will win in the end because, let's face it, mothers always do. All she has to do is:

a) *Ban me from going to the youth club and that would be a disaster because my best friend Amy is going and so is George Bleeks and he is even more important than Amy, but don't tell her I said that.*

b) *Make me wear a dress out in public. I am still not over my intolerance to frilly dresses.*

c) *Hide my CD collection or take down the posters from my bedroom wall, which would be the end of the world for me. I have to wake up with Take That looking over me. I just have to.*

Anyhow, I need not fear of any of the above for now because I have discovered (when my mum isn't in a really bad mood, i.e. drinking) that there are three ways to get round her or distract her from persisting with her hair-cut plans and these are:

1) *Suggest we get a new puppy – she goes into a spin when we even mention the 'P' word, as she calls it, and no matter if a bomb went off she wouldn't notice because she would*

be too busy letting us know there would not be a new dog, ever, in our house.

2) *Tell her she looks a bit like Celine Dion. My mum LOVES Celine Dion and it is her favourite subject of all time. It's also an idea to have Celine music playing when you say this, to make sure she stays distracted.*

3) *Make her food of some sort, preferably sweet, and surprise her with it! This is my favourite method of all because it means that I get some too!*

So, basically, all is well that ends well because I mentioned all three! I asked for a puppy, threw in the Celine compliment and then... then I baked my mum a chocolate cake all from scratch and she was over the moon!

She genuinely was touched and despite the intention (to distract her) it gave me a fuzzy, warm feeling inside when she said how much it meant to her that I had gone to such an effort.

We actually had 'a moment'. You know, one of those rare moments when the world stops just for like a millisecond and you feel full up inside.

I should do it more often, really. It's not that difficult and it really can let someone know you care. Maybe we should all do that more often and we wouldn't argue as much in our house. If we all just took time to show the people we love that we do actually know how to use our hearts and not always just our hot, steaming heads, I think the world would be a much nicer place, but then I am only fourteen so what do I know?

I should bake my mum a cake more often. It's nice to surprise someone you love.

Note to Lucy Harte: Surprise someone you love and watch their face when you do!

Note to Lucy Harte: Don't be afraid of change. Get yourself a haircut!

PS… I feel bad now for not having a haircut when my mum thinks it's for the best. I will go downstairs now and tell her she is right and we will go to town and I will talk nonsense to the hairdresser about school, holidays and imaginary boyfriends. Simon is having his new girlfriend around so I think he wants us to disappear for a while, so I'd be doing him a favour too.

Okay, here goes! Watch out world, the new-look Lucy Harte is coming to you very soon! Over and out! Goodbye!

Chapter 18

Simon calls me later that night when I am back at home in my pyjamas in front of the TV with a bottle of wine, a thumping headache and a very sore wrist. The tattooed heart stares at me and I can't decide if I like it or if I've just done something I will sorely regret in the morning.

I have just read Lucy's very last diary entry and it has pained me deeply. All of my gratitude to her is now riddled with guilt as to how her life was cut short and I have been given a second chance, which I seem to only make a mess of.

I contemplate not answering the phone. I am not in the mood for jolly bucket lists right now and I can't do any heavy, sentimental chat when I am so low in myself.

Sod it, I'll answer.

'Hello, stranger!' Simon says in his usual upbeat tone.

I just can't rise above this. It's like I'm on an emotional rollercoaster, up, down, up, down, elation, grief, delight, guilt, joy, anger... it just goes on and on and on.

'Hi, Simon,' I reply and my words come out in stark contrast to his greeting, like a tired slur. 'How are you?'

'I'm excellent, actually,' he tells me. Oh, wonderful. 'I visited my parents' grave today, and I had this really strange experience, strange in a good way, so I thought I'd ring and tell you. That's if you don't mind. Maybe you're busy. Are you?'

I take another mouthful of wine. My head is nodding involuntarily. I am really busy... really busy hating the world and getting drunk and getting tattoos on my wrist. That's how busy I am. I try to concentrate.

'I'd love to hear it. Go.'

Simon speaks with great animation as he explains how he and Andrea had a scan appointment that morning and how emotional it was to see their baby again on screen.

'We have only ten weeks to go to meet our little one,' he says and the joy in his voice should really snap me out of my drunken bitterness, but it doesn't. 'I guess I am on some sort of dad-to-be high, so sorry if I seem hyper.'

'You're very entitled to be,' I reply. 'You and Jeff should team up and swap stories.'

Woops. I didn't mean to say that, but it just came out. Simon stalls.

'What? God, I'm sorry. Are you okay, Maggie?'

'I'm sorry, I'm sorry,' I retort. 'I'm... I'm having a bad day. It can't all be roses and bucket lists and happily-ever-afters unfortunately. I'm not the one having the baby, am I?'

I shouldn't have said that.

'Oh...'

'I'm sorry, Simon. Don't mind me. Please go on.'

'If it's a bad time I can call you later in the week,' he says, his tone dampened by my negativity. 'I just thought you'd like to know about it, that's all. No big deal if you don't.'

'I do! I do want to know! I can imagine how thrilled you all must be,' I say to him, but it's not really what I am thinking.

I am delighted, over the moon for you, Simon, and for your beautiful wife, but I can't help it. Right now I am so lonely and empty inside…

'Are you still there, Maggie?'

'Yes, yes, I'm still here. Go on.'

'Well, you'll have to tell me all about Dublin in a second, but anyhow, gosh I feel silly saying this but…'

I close my eyes and try to focus on what he is trying to tell me.

'I heard the most beautiful morning springtime sound,' he says, 'and the next thing, right by the grave, a tiny yellow-and-grey songbird sat right between us and chirped and sang for what seemed like minutes.'

What the hell is he on about?

'Like, it sat there right between Andrea and I with no fear and it just sang. It was so beautiful. It was like a message, a sign. Do you believe in all that, Maggie?'

I should really say goodbye. I am not in the right frame of mind to hear about fucking songbirds. The man is grieving. He would take anything as a sign from Lucy or his mother or his father.

'Yes, yes, I suppose I do,' I lie. 'That's a really beautiful… thing to happen.'

I feel really, really sick. The room starts to spin. I wish he would just hurry up and go because I am drunk and selfish and don't deserve to hear this.

'Andrea and I, we just sat there in awe and then we were

both saying how amazing it is that you are carrying out Lucy's wishes,' he continues. 'It's like you are keeping her memory alive and I am so grateful. It's like Lucy is alive in you, Maggie. It's like I have found my little sister again. It's amazing.'

I need him to stop talking. I feel hot and claustrophobic, slightly breathless when I hear his words. His elation is suffocating me. I wasn't expecting to feel like this. I can't keep Lucy alive. I can't talk to Simon right now. I can't listen to his voice any longer, but he keeps going.

'So, Dublin, then? Did you find our guy?' he continues. 'Did you say hello from Lucy? I know it was a long shot, but I hope it was fun. How weird if you found him and he remembered –'

'I'm sorry, but I can't do this any more, Simon!' I tell him and I sit up on the sofa. I am really going to be sick. I lean forward and hold my forehead in my hands and beads of cold sweat roll on to my fingers.

'What? What do you mean you can't? But you said you would. You have to.'

'I don't *have* to! I don't *have* to, Simon! This is ridiculous!' I shout. 'I am not Lucy, Simon! I am not your sister! I am Maggie and I need to focus on my own life, you know! You and Andrea have your life and I have mine. My brother is sick. My marriage is over. My job is potentially on the line. I can't do it any more. I'm sorry! I can't do it!'

I am sobbing now. Sobbing like the drunken, pathetic loser that I am.

'But – but I thought you wanted to?'

'I don't want to,' I say emphatically. 'I don't want to any

more. Focus on your wife and baby, Simon. Just forget about me. Focus on your present, not your past. Let Lucy go and let me go! I can't do this any more! Goodbye.'

I slump back onto the sofa and drop my phone on the floor, then get up and clumsily put Lucy's bits and pieces into the navy biscuit tin they came in. Her photos, her notes, her diary, her list. I take the box and shove it in a bottom cupboard in the kitchen and close the door, and then I lean up against the door, crying and howling like a mad woman.

Find Tiernan Quinn; go to the world's tallest bridge; forgive your friends and family; spread your wings and travel far; learn to play guitar, throw a dinner party, surprise someone you love, have a haircut, get a tattoo, never stop dancing...

The list is going round and round and round in my head and I can't block it out! I close my eyes and block my ears, but I can still hear her young voice and see her with her long hair and freckled nose.

'Go away!' I shout out loud. 'Go away, Lucy Harte! Leave me alone! Please!'

And then it dawns on me... the bird that visited her grave. The songbird, just like in the song I said I would learn in her memory.

It's all too much. I can't do this any more. I need my own life back.

I find myself on the steps of Powers Enterprises early the next morning, in my work attire, and I wait in the foyer, much to the shock and delight on Bridget's face. I am not saying she is delighted to see me, more that she is delighted that there may be a bit of reaction around the team since I am not due back for another three weeks.

Melanie from Finance is first to arrive in the building and I can almost see gossipy speech bubbles above her head as she scuttles past me and says a surprised hello.

'Aren't you supposed to still be off, erm, sick?' she comes back to ask me, unable to resist some titbits of information straight from the horse's mouth.

'Sick? Who said I was sick?' I ask her. 'I am not, and never was, sick.'

'I heard...' she leans in and whispers, looking at the floor when she speaks. 'I heard you were having some sort of breakdown after, you know, your husband leaving and all that.'

I want to punch her, but instead I smile.

'Davey the porter was glad to see me back,' I tell her. 'I thought the rest of you might be too.'

'Oh we are, I mean, I am. Like no one else knows yet. Does Mr Powers know? You should really have told him. He's out of the country at the minute. He should really know you are coming back early.'

Sylvia Madden, one of the CEO's who was at my meeting a few weeks ago, is next on the scene. Thankfully, she handles my grand reappearance with a bit more tact.

'Maggie! I wasn't expecting to see you this morning. How are you?'

'I'm wonderful,' I tell her. 'On top of the world and ready to get stuck into my job. You know, my job that you all said I could come back to when I wanted.'

She remains calm and then whispers softly.

'Of course. Yes, we did say that, but can we go and chat about it over coffee? Somewhere away from prying eyes and ears?'

She looks at Melanie in distaste.

I follow her out of the building like a lost puppy. I have no idea what else to do.

We sit by the window in the coffee shop across the road from Powers and I stare outside as Sylvia orders for us both. I feel like a child who has turned up in school uniform on a non-uniform day, embarrassed and out of place. I want to go home. I shouldn't have come here.

'Tell me, how have you been getting on?' asks Sylvia, now that the waitress has gone. 'And you can be totally honest with me. Are you really feeling better? Are you really ready to get back into the nine-to-five rat race?'

I nod slowly and then bite my lip. Better? I thought I was better. I don't even know where to start. I don't know if I will ever feel better.

'It's... it's hard,' I tell Sylvia. 'I need to get back to work. Is it okay if I just come back and get on with things?'

To my surprise, Sylvia reaches out her hand onto mine.

'You know, Maggie, it was my idea to give you some time out,' she says, a sincere warmth in her eyes.

'It was? Why?'

She looks around the café and then fixes her sleek grey bob behind her right ear. For the first time ever, as long as I have worked for Powers Enterprises, Sylvia Madden is showing a human side. She was always known as a tough nut, the only woman to have reached the very top of Team Powers and everyone both admires and fears her at the same time.

I didn't know she was so kind inside, but then I remember her passing me a tissue on the day of our meeting and then I remember the day I really messed up an appointment and she should have let rip at me but didn't. Maybe this isn't the first time she has shown some humanity to me. It's funny how we don't see the wood for the trees sometimes...

'Can I tell you something, Maggie? Something about me?' she asks.

'Of course you can.'

She looks around nervously again and then back to me.

'About fifteen years ago, Maggie, I went through the most humiliating, painful experience of my life,' she tells me in a soft whisper.

The waitress arrives with our coffees and we both mumble a hurried thank you, then Sylvia continues as soon as she has gone.

'My husband left me for one of my own friends,' she says. 'My very best friend.'

'Oh God, Sylvia. I'm sorry.'

'I came home from work one day with a migraine. My father had just died and my husband, Michael, had been nursing me through the grief that comes with losing a parent. He was the most adoring husband, the apple of my eye and we were trying for a baby.'

'Sounds familiar... Jeff was so attentive and loving to me too.'

'Well, exactly,' says Sylvia. 'I saw my life-long friend Christine in my kitchen as I pulled into my driveway and I will never forget the look on her face when I caught her eye through the window. At first I thought she had popped round to do some chores or shopping as she was so worried about me, but I knew she had no key to get inside.'

'My God...'

'I walked into my own home and my husband came down the stairs in his bathrobe. His look and her look said it all. I ran out of the house and I never went back. Will Powers Sr was a friend of Michael's and he took me under his wing and gave me a new start, a fresh start. A chance to find the new me. But first I had to take some time out and rest my heart and mind.'

I take a sip of my coffee but it tastes bitter. Sylvia just stares at hers. I take a deep breath.

'You are not the same person who worked for us a few months ago, Maggie, and you never will be,' she says. 'I see so much of myself in you. You need to take this time to read-just and decide what you want to do next with your life.'

'Okay...'

'Do it for you, just you,' she says. 'Don't rush back and try and slot in to how it used to be. It is not how it used to be. Sure, your job can help distract you and get you by, but from my own experience, I think after such a shock and life-changing thing to happen, you should have a rest, have a holiday, go away and do something that's just for you, some-thing that will help you know if it's here that you really even want to come back to. You might find that it isn't, and you might find that it is, but give yourself a chance to find out.'

We sit in silence for a few moments.

Sylvia has said what she has had to say and I can't really argue with her since she actually does know what I am going through.

'I wanted to have a family,' I tell her, and here we go with the waterworks. 'I was trying to have a baby too and now she is having his baby. He was my husband.'

Sylvia nods in empathy and then smiles.

'Lift that chin up, Maggie O'Hara,' she says. 'Look at you! You are beautiful, you are intelligent, you are funny. You have so much going for you. Don't let one man kill your soul. Don't give him that power.'

'Please don't say there are plenty of fish in the sea,' I joke with her. 'I never want to go fishing again.'

'Well, I did go fishing again, eventually,' Sylvia tells me with a shy giggle. 'Sooner than you would have thought, actually, but then life has a funny way of leading us in different directions. Sean and I have been married now for ten years and our twins were born a year after we met.'

I want to tell Sylvia about Lucy Harte. I want to tell her about my brother, John Joe, and his grand entrance back into my life. I want to tell her about the bucket list and how I chickened out last night with Simon because I am so, so afraid of where it is going to take me.

But I don't need to tell her anything more because she has already helped me more than she will ever know. I need to wise up and get back to Lucy's list and let it take me forwards instead of going backwards.

The Legacy of Lucy Harte

I'm so sorry, Lucy, I say as I walk down the city street after our coffee. *I am sorry for leaving you and for being such a self-centred asshole. I am taking your advice. I am not afraid of change and I am going to start with a mighty-fine new haircut.*

Chapter 19

I am giddy with excitement as I check in for my flight at Belfast International Airport, especially when I don't recognise my own reflection in the mirrored wall as I pass it.

I did what Lucy never got to do. I had a damn good haircut and it feels like a weight has been, quite literally, lifted off my shoulders. For the first time in years, I went to a strange salon in the city instead of going to Flo because I was so afraid of changing my mind.

'I like your tattoo,' the hairdresser told me and I held my thumb over the little heart and rubbed it gently as I breathed in and out in preparation for my new look.

I love the new tattoo, now that I am sober enough to appreciate it. I have made my peace with Lucy again but I am more determined than ever to see this list through in a bid to find a new direction for me. I need her. I need her more than I thought I did and to let her go now would be foolish and would make me drift back in time to a life of misery and never-ending hangovers and returning to a job I am no longer sure that I really want to do.

'Any luggage to check in?' the stewardess on the desk asks

me and I am delighted to tell her no. For this trip I am deliberately travelling one way, totally alone, with no baggage, not even in the most literal sense. I have a light rucksack that can hold my passport and a few pairs of shorts and vest tops and a light jacket, my make-up and that's it.

She does a double-take when she looks at my passport photo. In it I am blonde and my hair goes down past my shoulders. In real life now I have a short, funky bob and I'm a feisty red head. Not ginger, not auburn – but red and I love it!

'That's you all checked in, then,' says the lady with her lipstick smile and she hands me back my passport and boarding pass. 'You will do a self-connection at New York for your connecting flight to Nashville. Have a nice trip, ma'am.'

It was like I handed my mother a million pounds when I arrived at her door last night. After my hair cut, I went to Tesco and bought the makings of a jam-and-cream sponge cake. I haven't baked in years and had no equipment in the apartment, so I'd to start literally from scratch, but just like Lucy said, the feeling of doing something for someone when they aren't expecting it was so rewarding and it felt so good inside.

I whipped the cream and I spread the jam and marvelled at the whole thing coming together, then I boxed it up and drove out into the countryside to deliver it personally to the two people who mean the most in the world to me.

Dad was on the tractor when I tooted the horn on the way past and he stood up and gave me the biggest wave. I could have cried at the joy on his face and how he hurried to climb down and come and greet me properly.

'Jesus, Mary and St Joseph!' my mother said, coming out to meet me on the driveway. 'I hardly recognised you with that hair-do! I thought you were our Roisin from Dublin! Did she tell you to do it?'

I shake my head and it feels so different without the long, blonde locks. It feels young and wild and free and I love it!

'No, another little girl told me to do it, what do you think?'

I do a twirl. We always do a twirl in our house to show off a new hair-do or a new outfit. It kind of goes without saying.

'It suits you,' said my darling mother. 'It will take some getting used to, but it does suit you.'

My father's opinion was, as ever, glowing. I think if I turned up with my nose, tongue and eyebrows pierced he would still tell me I was beautiful.

'It will be the making of you!' he said, putting his big strong arm around my shoulder. 'And you're well mended too. You must be on the way up. Didn't I tell you you'd be fine? Look at Marilyn Monroe! You didn't see her moping after men! They moped after her and they will after you one day soon too!'

I giggled at his latest dead-celebrity reference as we made our way into the farmhouse kitchen, where every smell and sound and sight holds a memory for me.

'It's good to be home,' I said, inhaling the aroma of my mother's home cooking. 'Is my name in the pot? I brought dessert.'

'It's always in the pot,' said my mum and she set a place at the table for me. 'Wait a minute, did you bake this for me?'

I nodded my head and watched them both admire it, like it was some award-winning masterpiece and I felt my heart swell inside.

'I love you Mum. And you too, Dad. Thanks for being there for me always. I should show it more. I do love you.'

My father put his arms out and embraced us both, hugging us so tight that I feared for the cake's future.

When he managed to let go, I sat down and looked across at the empty chair opposite, where my brother used to sit when we were little. I feel my stomach flip.

'What part of America is John Joe in?' I asked my parents.

'He's in Nashville with Vivienne,' my mother told me. 'I can give you his address if you want to write to him?'

It's a very loaded question and we all knew it. Me, write to John Joe? To see both their children happy again would be the greatest gift I could ever give my parents and I have been too selfish to ever see past my own anger and remorse. They have no idea of his marriage and, more importantly, no idea of his illness. I owe it to them to follow Lucy's advice.

'I plan to do better than that,' I replied. 'I'm going to visit him.'

'You're what? Oh my God, Robert, she's going to visit him!' said my mother, just in case my dad didn't hear me the first time.

And that was enough to set them off again. It was like they had won the lottery.

I seem to spend a lot of my time these days travelling and thinking and doing so has given me a great insight into how much I owe to Lucy Harte and her family. Big things like this – like going to America at the drop of a hat to surprise my brother. Little things like getting a new hair cut or baking a cake, and it's not just from Lucy's list, it's all the things I got to do before that, in the seventeen years of life she has given me so far.

I passed all my school exams; I had such fun at university; I graduated; I learned to ride a motorcycle; I went skiing; I worked at many things including in an ice-cream parlour, a dog-groomers, a restaurant, as an au pair, in a local stable, in the florists and I spent many years meeting people in many walks of life in my job in real estate. I have travelled, I have loved, I have lost, I have won, and it's all because of you, Lucy.

I write this down and tuck it in along with my other notes to Lucy in the back of her notebook. I can feel her pushing me along, guiding me, making me strong again and I owe her so much.

Forgive your friends and family, she said. Surprise someone you love, she said. I actually can't believe I am doing what I am about to do.

Please don't leave me, Lucy, I chant to the heavens. *I need you more than ever right now.*

Chapter 20

Here I am, on my own, with just an address on a piece of paper, a small bag of luggage, my wallet and my phone in the country-music capital of the world and I am absolutely bricking it.

'Where ya'll off to, ma'am,' asks the taxi driver at the airport and I read out John Joe's address.

'Is it far?' I ask him. I am like a fish out of water and anyone who looks at me knows I am not supposed to be here. I keep getting overwhelming waves of doubt, an urge to turn and go back and forget it all but Lucy's words to forgive, to surprise someone you love, to never be afraid of change all ring in my head and keep me going with each step forward.

The taxi driver mumbles something in response that I don't understand and weaves through traffic until, just under an hour later, with a heavy heart and a much lighter wallet, I am outside my brother's home and it feels like I'm meeting a stranger for the first time.

I stand at the gate and look up the pathway onto the white porch of the little pale-grey wooden house. The heat is stifling, it cuts my throat as I stand and stare at the place he calls home. The house is set on a neat boulevard of similar build-ings and, to my surprise, a For Sale sign hangs in the garden. John Joe and his wife must be moving on already.

So this is his life. This is where he gets up every morning, goes to work – I realise I do not even know what he does for a living any more – kisses his wife, eats his dinner. I am like a snooping stranger looking in on a life I do not know.

'Excuse me, ma'am? Can I help you?'

I jump and put my hand to my chest at a lady's tart voice, which seemed to have come out of nowhere. She puts her hand on my brother's gate as if to prevent my entry.

'Vivienne?'

'Oh my... are you Maggie?'

I nod and smile and shrug and she drops the grocery bags she is carrying and opens her arms out to embrace me like I'm some long-lost relative – well, I am a long-lost relative now, I suppose.

'Come in! Come in and see your brother! This is just the best surprise ever!'

She picks up her bags and I automatically take one from her, despite her resistance, and we walk up the pathway towards the pretty little house. I'm not sure I have been this nervous ever in my whole life.

Seconds later, I am in my brother's living room and Vivienne has gone to let him know I am here.

Oh, please God, let him be nice to me. Please, Lucy, tell me this is the right thing to do!

I use the time to try and focus on my breathing and as I breathe in and out I take in my surroundings. It's a very cosy home and Vivienne certainly has decorative style. Or perhaps it's John Joe's taste? What would I know? The wooden floors are rustic and strewn with multi-coloured rugs, guitars hang on the wall and floating shelves show photos of the two of them in a variety of happy-couple poses. He looks so content with her and she looks... well, she doesn't look like anyone I ever imagined him to be with. I want to get up and take a closer look around the walls but I'm a bit afraid to, to tell the truth. I don't want to take anything for granted and be too familiar.

Maybe I'm just jet-lagged. I still can't believe I'm here.

I want to go back. I want to go back and envelope myself in the comfort of Lucy's words and write to her that I tried to find him and lie that he was on 'vacation', but at least I tried, right?

Give me a sign, Lucy. Give me a sign that I am doing the right thing.

I look around and see another photo on one of the shelves. *Is that... is that me?*

I get up to take a closer look. It is a photo of me in my teenage years, about two years after my operation, and it was the first day I got back on our family pony. It was such a big moment for me, and here it is, on the other side of the world, staring back at me like a ghost from my past.

There is another of us all as a family beside it which shows me, John Joe, Mum and Dad on my graduation day and I take it down and look at it closely, biting my lip as the memories come flooding back. I remember being so jealous that John Joe had turned up that morning, back from Switzerland,

I think, and I realise how utterly selfish I have been for so many years against my own brother. Instead of being thankful that he made the effort to come home for my big day, I was always too wrapped up in him stealing my thunder. I feel very sad. And very, very sorry.

'I'm so sorry,' I whisper and slowly put the photo back in its place.

Have I been living in a selfish bubble all this time? The photo was the sign I needed that I am doing the right thing. Yes. I *want* to see him and tell him I'm sorry and ask him can we please start again? Can he please give me one more chance?

My insides are riddled with the most horrid guilt and there is no room for anything else.

I would die to lie down somewhere, anywhere, right now. It's so hot and my eyes are dropping with exhaustion.

'Hello?' I hear him call from the top of the stairs and the room closes in on me. 'Maggie?'

I hear his footsteps across the little hallway and then I turn and see him and I think my heart might collapse when I look into his eyes.

'Maggie!' he says, 'My God, Maggie, come here till I see you! This is... this is just the best surprise in the whole wide world!'

I go towards him until I fall, quite literally, into my big brother's arms and I hold him so tight and I feel like I am home.

'I think I've covered you in snot,' I say when we finally let go of each other. 'I didn't mean to just call unannounced. It was a very last-minute decision.'

I take a deep breath and look directly at him, into his big, soft brown eyes.

'It wouldn't be the first time you did that!' he says, wiping wet from under his eyes. 'My eyes are sweating. Remember you used to say that when you didn't want to admit you'd been crying?'

I nod my head and sniff back the emotion.

'I believe you have just met my wife,' he says and puts his arm around me, then leads me to the sofa, where I sit down beside him.

Vivienne comes into the living room behind him, protectively watching his every move.

'Maggie! It really is so good to have you here!' she says in that glorious accent I last heard on the phone but was too stubborn to appreciate. 'You have made your brother very, very happy! And that makes me happy too.'

I stand up again and she gives me a warm hug and I am very conscious of getting tears and snot on her nice silken blouse.

'I'm sorry to land on you like this,' I explain, 'but I was so afraid I'd chicken out if I didn't just go for it.'

'Sit down, Mags, and don't dare apologise,' says John Joe. 'Do Mum and Dad know you're here? You look really tired. Are you okay? Are you sure you're okay?'

He sounds like Dad, he fusses like Mum, but he looks like me. I am not sure which question to answer first, but I know he means well.

'Can I get you a hot drink?' asks Vivienne. 'You have had quite a journey.'

'No, no please, I'm fine,' I tell her. 'Thank you so much."

'I'll get you some tea, then,' she says. 'You look like you need some tea.'

Vivienne already knows me through my brother, it seems. We O'Haras always did love our cup of tea and no always means yes.

'Mum and Dad know I'm here, yes,' I tell my brother. 'And I know I look like shit; you don't have to say I look tired or pale or anything. I just look like crap.'

'How have you been?' he asks me. 'Are you looking after yourself through all this change?'

Change... well, that's one way of putting it...

'I'm good, I'm going to be fine,' I tell him and for the first time in a long time I actually mean it. 'I'm doing really well. Going to new places, meeting new people, spreading my wings, all good. I'm more concerned about you, though, which is why I am here. Are you going to be okay, John Joe? Please tell me the truth.'

I look forlornly at my big brother. We really do look alike. We have the same eyes and the same Roman nose and when he smiles his dimple on his right cheek is in the same place as mine. He looks gaunt and off-colour but doesn't look as sick as I imagined he would. I just hope I am not too late.

'I've been through a lot,' he tells me. 'We both have, but it looks like they may have got it on time.'

'It meaning... is it cancer? Is it terminal? Oh my God –'

I am shaking with what I am about to hear and I hate myself for holding onto such unnecessary, childish resentment for so long.

'Yes, it is cancer, but I had a kidney whipped out within a matter of days and we just spent the past week doing absolutely nothing in a place very close to our hearts, so I'm well on the mend.'

I cannot look him in the eye. All those times he has tried to get in touch with me and I was so wrapped up in my own selfish life... I want to look in the mirror and scream at my own reflection for being so bloody self-centred. He needed to tell me and I couldn't have it in my own heart to answer his calls because I was too focused on me.

'John Joe, I am so, so sorry,' I whisper to the floor. 'I should have been here sooner. I should have at least taken your calls. I should have –'

'Life is too short for should-haves,' he replies. 'Look at me, Maggie.'

'I can't.'

He laughs lightly.

'I bet you can.'

I turn to him and see how his features have changed over time and through his recent illness, but his smile is the same. He is my only brother.

'It has made me realise a lot of things, believe me,' he says. 'When you reach the point that your life could be over, it really does separate the shit from reality and I have had a few lessons come my way too. You have experienced what I am going through – only you were just a kid. I need to apologise to you too for not understanding how frightened you must have been all those years ago.'

I let a deep breath out.

'It's not a nice place to be,' I tell him with a shrug. 'But we are both still here. I hope it's not too late.'

He shakes his head and takes my hand.

'It's not too late,' he says. 'I've a few more appointments to attend and I've got great medical care in place, so everything is going to be okay. Oh, Maggie, I can't tell you how good it is to see you. Now, enough of the sad stories! We have much more important things to catch up on, I'm sure!'

Vivienne arrives with our tea and I am so glad of it. She was right. I do need a cup so badly.

'You do look very pale, Maggie,' says Vivienne. 'Maybe you're just tired after your journey?'

'Yes, she does look like she has seen a ghost,' laughs John Joe. 'I hope you weren't regretting coming here. You are always welcome. Anytime.'

'I'm absolutely fine, It's probably just my new red hair,' I assure them and then do my best to shift the subject from me. 'Tell me about your life here. I thought you still lived in New York, but that's my fault...'

My eyes drop to the floor again with embarrassment.

'We've been here a while,' says Vivienne softly. 'And we'll be here for a long, long time, won't we, darling?'

I look up at the two of them as they nod to each other in a mix of hope and relief. Despite John Joe's best efforts to be all happy-clappy and positive, we can't escape the obvious. He has cancer. Had cancer. Whatever. But he keeps trying to stay in the now.

'Vivienne works for one of the big publishing houses here, so it's going to be our base for the foreseeable future,' he says.

'A publishing house? Cool,' I reply, trying to match his efforts to shift the mood. 'So you get to know all the big stars? I know I sound like a teenager, but that's pretty impressive.'

'Yes, she has discovered some pretty big stars,' says John Joe proudly. 'Vivienne is an amazing talent. I always knew she'd be a phenomenon.'

The way he looks at her, well, it makes me want what they have. Did Jeff and I ever have that connection? I honestly can't say we did.

'So don't tell me, you work over in Graceland or somewhere equally exotic too?' I say to John Joe. 'I feel so ordinary and boring in comparison to your life here.'

'Not quite so exotic for me,' he says and his eyes crinkle softly, showing his age. When did my brother get so grown up? 'Vivienne gets to hang out with the greats; I get to mow their lawns. I have a landscaping business.'

Vivienne pats him playfully on the leg.

'Don't be so modest, honey!' she says. 'Maggie, your brother is in massive demand all over the city. He is wonderful at his job and is very creative. You two have so much to catch up on.'

We do. I have been such a moron.

'I'm sure you saw the For Sale sign, but that's not our choice, really, and we'll be sad to leave this house,' Vivienne continues. 'We've rented it for a while and the landlord is selling up so we have a decision to make. Do we stay here in the city and buy somewhere, or do we go and retire in the Maldives and live off the life insurance?'

For a moment I think she is serious but then they both burst out laughing at the reaction on my face.

'We couldn't leave Nashville,' says John Joe. 'It's our home now and we hope to start a family soon, so no, the Maldives will have to wait.'

I can't believe the change in my brother. I wonder just how much of his warmth and endearing side have I chosen to bitterly ignore for far too long now.

There is so much to talk about, so many lost years, so many questions to ask and answers to seek. But my eyes are heavy and I stifle a yawn, then Vivienne does the same, and so does John Joe.

'It's getting late,' I state the obvious, and look at the clock to see it's just gone 1am, but my body clock is all over the place. I don't even know if I could sleep now, but I should definitely try.

'I hate to ask,' says John Joe, 'but how long are you here for? I'd love to show you around and hang out for as long as you are here.'

I actually don't know the answer to that question, but I don't want to overstay my welcome either. My brother has just had a huge operation and I get the impression he and Vivienne want him to get over it quickly so they can get on with the rest of their lives.

'I'll be here for just a few days,' I tell him. 'But I can't wait to hear all about everything you have been up to, and I mean everything.'

'I bet you have a lot to tell me too, Mags,' says John Joe.

'You'd better believe it,' I reply. 'I won't know where to start.'

John Joe and I spend the next afternoon together and he shows me the sights of his home town, which makes me fall in love with it by the second. I marvel at places I had only ever heard of – The Grand Ole Opry, The Bluebird Café, Tootsie's Bar, which he promises me a drink in later and we dine out at his favourite quick stop for lunch, which he reckons has the best sandwiches in the city. And there is live music. There is live music everywhere – on the streets, in the cafés, in the bars – in every corner there is room for music you will find it.

'What's the name of that bridge?' I ask him as we emerge from the deli with full bellies past a busker singing 'American Pie'. We are beginning to relax in each other's company, though there is still that elephant in the room that I need to address.

'That's called the John Siegenthaler,' he tells me. 'It's named after a famous journalist and civil-rights activist who once saved a guy from jumping off it, so they changed the name of it to his. Fancy a walk across it?'

'Sure,' I tell him.

I want to tell him about Lucy. I want to tell him about the list and how she loved bridges and how I can feel her right now as we walk towards the longest pedestrian bridge I have ever seen. She would love this. She would so love it.

But I also need to apologise to him wholeheartedly for shutting him out, for blaming him for all these years. I can see now that it has been entirely my loss and I know that he wants to clear the air as much as I do.

We make our way to the mighty Cumberland River that runs through the city of Nashville. I realise how little I actually know about this place, yet it has already seeped into my bones and I can see why my brother and his wife adore it so much.

As we walk towards the river I decide it's time to bite the bullet.

'I met Simon Harte,' I blurt out and John Joe stops in his tracks.

'You met who?'

'Simon Harte, Lucy's brother. You know, the little girl –'

'Yes, yes I know who Lucy Harte is. Of course I know who Lucy Harte is,' he says. 'My God, Maggie. How on earth did you find him? What... are you okay with that?'

I nod my head and my brother pulls me towards him instantly. I realise now that only he would really know how much this means to me, how long I have waited to get in touch with Lucy's family and thank them for my life.

'I'm okay,' I tell him. 'I'm really okay. It's kind of thanks to Lucy Harte I'm here.'

'Here on earth or here in Nashville?'

'Both,' I tell him and we both manage a smile. 'Simon gave me her diary and a list of things she wanted to do when she grew up, which of course she never got to do and it has really made me think a lot about my life and well... that made me think of how I've treated you.'

We are near the river and he leads us onto the John Siegenthaler footbridge until he finds a stop that overlooks the city and we pause.

'I didn't hear you that day, Maggie,' he says, looking over the water and then he looks at me. 'I have tried to explain this to you so many times but you never wanted to believe me. You had it in your head and I know you needed someone to blame, but that someone wasn't me.'

I look down onto the water now and then I close my eyes.

'I called for you,' I tell him and I feel my eyes fill up as the horrible pain of that day comes flooding back. 'I called for you as loudly as I could but you didn't come to me. I was so alone and so scared. I nearly died, John Joe. I was so afraid that I was going to die on my own.'

I can hear him inhale and exhale as he stares out onto the river.

'You have no idea how much that has haunted me all through my life, Maggie,' he tells me and I can sense anger in his voice – not towards me, but to himself. 'I had been left in charge and I didn't look out for you, but I wasn't near enough to hear you call. If you'd just told me you were ill, I'd have stopped everything and called a doctor – or found Mum and Dad, or called a neighbour, or –'

He is crying now. We are both standing in broad daylight reliving the most traumatic moment that has created a wedge between us throughout our adult lives.

'I've always believed you hated me for it,' I tell him. I can't look at him right now. I need to get this out, no matter how wrong or right I may be. 'I thought you were jealous of all the attention I got when I was sick. How you were no longer the blue-eyed boy. I might not have lost my life that day, but I lost you.'

He turns to face me now and I look at him and the pain in his eyes is so deep. He shakes his head. He touches my shoulder. He tries to speak, but the words won't come.

'I have missed you so much,' I tell him. 'I always just wanted my brother back.'

He holds me close to him and we both sob into each other's arms, squeezing all the pain and misunderstanding away and the healing power of his hug fills me up so much that I don't want to let go.

'I never hated you, Maggie. I hated myself,' he says under muffled sobs. 'It's why I ran away from it all. I wanted to get as far away from that day and never look back. But I have missed you too, so much. I missed my little sister.'

We let go and I look up at him and wipe away his tears.

'Even the annoying parts like when I used to steal your CDs?'

He smiles and glances away, then looks back.

'Even the annoying parts, yes,' he smiles. 'I miss our family. I've always felt like I had done you wrong, but I didn't hear you... I swear to you I didn't...'

It dawns on me at last that all of this resentment, all of this distance and such cruel misunderstanding has caused my brother just as much pain as it has me. He has regrets, he has guilt, he has run away from it all and it has taken ill health to finally make both of us finally get it all out in the open.

'I believe you,' I tell him. 'What I can't believe is that we waited so long to address it. I have run away from it too, I suppose, and I should know more than anyone that life is really too precious to hold silly, misinformed grudges. We've been a bit stupid, haven't we?'

'I wouldn't say stupid,' he says with a smile. 'More stubborn, but I think we get that from Mum's side of the family.'

I roll my eyes in agreement. 'We don't need to talk about it again, then, do we?'

I glance up at him and he is smiling.

'No, we don't,' he says. 'We have a future to talk about and I suppose it's all down to Lucy Harte?'

'Well, on my part, yes. Just another thing I have to thank her for. My God, I never could have predicted her little list of things she wanted to do would have such a huge impact on my life. She is helping me through everything, John Joe. It's like she's my little guardian angel. I'll be sad to let her go.'

'You don't have to ever let her go,' he tells me. 'Keep her close, if that's what helps you through this crazy thing called life.'

'I wish I could. I don't know why but I always feel that Lucy and I are on borrowed time,' I reply. 'Like, she is only mine for a little while longer. Does that make sense?'

He doesn't answer. I don't expect him to either.

'She loved bridges,' I whisper, watching the current below again.

'Lucy did? Really?'

'Yes, she said they made her feel on top of the world,' I tell him. 'They were an escape to her, a place to feel free and I can see what she means. There's something magical about standing here, looking down on the water below and seeing for miles around us.'

He puts his arm around my shoulder and we stare out ahead, both feeling the weight of resentment and misunderstanding leaving us at last. Here, on a bridge, miles from home, we are feeling the power of forgiveness.

'I would never do anything to harm or hurt you, Maggie,' he whispers into my red hair. 'Never. You're my baby sister, my pride and joy and I am so proud of the beautiful woman you have turned out to be.'

'You? Proud of me? What on earth are you proud of me for?'

He turns towards me and the pain in his face is so tangible.

'Your beauty, your talent, your wit, most of all, your strength for what you have been through. I could go on and on. You're one of the strongest people I know.'

'Stop, you're embarrassing me,' I say, unable to take his compliments. 'I don't deserve them, especially not lately. Like you said to me in one of your messages, I was on some sort of death wish after Jeff left. I could kick myself now for getting so low.'

'You were just dealing with rejection,' he says. 'Rejection sucks.'

'You sound American,' I tell him and we both laugh.

'You know, if you had stuck at song-writing you could have ended up in Nashville too, for sure,' he tells me. 'I used to listen to you sing with your guitar or on the piano and well, if there was one thing I was slightly jealous of, that was it. You were always so talented in everything you set your mind to.'

I burst out laughing for real now.

'I hardly think that strumming a few chords and writing about the boy next door would have changed the music world, but thanks, bro,' I reply.

'I'm serious. Have you ever done anything like that since?'

I shake my head, still in denial.

'Song-writing? No way. Though music is on Lucy's list,

believe it or not. She wanted to play guitar and learn some songs, but only because she wanted to impress her teenage crush. It has got me started, a little. I should really do more.'

'Yes, you should! That's the type of thing you need to keep doing!' he tells me. 'Look, no harm intended, but when I heard you were marrying that Pillock guy and getting all cosy and settled with him and his straight-laced life, I thought, that's not my sister. That's not Maggie. You are bigger than his small-town ways. The world is out there waiting for you, Maggie. Don't let him, or anything you have been through, hold you back any more. Do you hear me?'

He is lecturing me and I love it. I have my big brother back.

'Loud and clear, brother,' I say to him and I wonder what on earth I have done to deserve this. 'I'm going to be a better sister to you from now on. I've been shit, but there's still time.'

'Well, I'm not going anywhere, are you?' he says with a smile, referring of course to his recent dice with death.

We both pause, knowing that with me, it's not just as straightforward as that.

'I'm not going anywhere until Lucy needs her heart back,' I tell him and I see a flash of fear in his eyes. 'Don't worry, though. I talk to her every day now so I'll make sure she gives me another while to make up for lost time with you.'

'Please do,' says John Joe and I link his arm. 'Now, let's get back to mine and hear you strum on some of Viv's guitars. You can't be in Music City and not play some music.'

'Sounds good to me,' I reply and as we walk back across the famous bridge. 'I'll give you a squealy rendition of 'Songbird'.'

'Since when did you like soppy love songs?'

'Since never,' I reply with a giggle. 'But this one is growing on me. It brings back special memories.'

Tiernan Quinn and our day of passion runs through my mind and my stomach whooshes at the thought. I beam a huge smile and I can feel Lucy smile down on me too. Or maybe it's just her heart smiling from inside me. Maybe it's the unconditional love between a brother and a sister that has lain dormant for too long.

Whatever it is, it feels as good as I have felt in a very long, long time.

Chapter 21

'Are you sure you are up for this?' I shout over the honky-tonk music in a downtown bar later that night. 'You have been host with the most for long enough today! You must be exhausted!'

John Joe is sipping on water while Vivienne and I slurp on beers and we can barely hear ourselves think over the music, but the atmosphere in Nashville by night is so absorbing, I want to come back here already.

'You two girls go and dance and leave this sick guy to people-watch,' my brother tells me, and before I know it, Vivienne and I are on the sawdust dance floor and a stranger puts a cowboy hat on my head and twirls me round the floor.

'Ever danced with a cowboy before?' he asks in an authentic Southern tone. At least, I think that's what he is saying! I am being spun around like a rag doll by a six-foot- something all-American hunk of burning love and if I wasn't laughing so hard at my attempt to keep up, I would probably chicken out and run for cover.

'This is my first time!' I shout back, over the steel guitar and drums. 'But it's fun!'

'What's your name, princess?' he asks and I catch a glimpse of Vivienne, who is clapping along from back at her seat beside John Joe. They seem to be enjoying this as much as I am.

'It's not 'Princess', anyhow!' I reply and I'm not sure he gets my humour. 'I'm Maggie! What's yours?'

'Justin,' he tells me, still twirling me, still dancing. 'But they call me Big J.'

The song ends and I thank him and go back to my family, who are whooping with delight.

'That must be one for the bucket list,' says John Joe. 'You can now say you were danced by an all-American cowboy!'

'And not just any cowboy!' I reply. 'They call him Big J!'

We almost choke on our drinks laughing.

'You could have had the night of your life with him,' says Vivienne with a wink. 'Big J!'

'Oh stop! He's probably a tourist from England or somewhere but I'll note it down as an achievement anyhow!' I reply over the music.

It's hot in the bar and I know that both Vivienne and John Joe would much rather be tucked up in bed than being my tour guide for the evening. John Joe takes a gulp of water and Vivienne and I exchange knowing glances.

'I think we'd better get this big guy home,' says Vivienne and I totally agree.

'Yes, of course,' I reply. 'Thanks so much. That was so much fun.'

'It's so good to see you smiling and laughing like that,' says John Joe. 'I hope you do that a lot.'

'Not as much as I should,' I tell him. 'But I will from now on, that's for sure.'

We take a taxi back to their little wooden house and I fall asleep on the way, feeling so full up and content and so grateful for making amends with my own flesh and blood. I will go home tomorrow a very different person. Plus, I have one more destination to see for Lucy Harte and I can't wait to see what adventures it brings.

John Joe and I share a late brunch as I wait for my taxi to the airport for my connecting flight to Belfast via New York City.

'You better come back really soon,' he keeps saying between munching croissants and cheese on toast: a craving he apparently developed when he was sick.

'I actually want to come back here forever!' I tell him. 'I have had such a great time, even though it was a flying visit, but I have to pack in as much as I can before I go back to work.'

'Are you really going back there? To the real-estate place?' he asks and I sense his disapproval.

'It's a job, John Joe. I can't live on fresh air. These few months are flying by, but some day I will have to be back in the real world of bills and routine and work.'

He shrugs and pours more coffee.

'I just think you are much more creative than what you do there,' he tells me. 'But if it makes you happy... does it make you happy?'

I feel like I am wearing a tight collar around my neck or a tie that needs loosening when he asks me that.

'I wouldn't say happy, no, but it's fine. They are nice people and it's... yes, it's fine.'

John Joe raises an eyebrow and chews and then he speaks.

'Maggie O'Hara, fine is fine, yes,' he tells me. 'But fine ain't good enough for *you*. You're too special for fine, do you hear me?'

'You're only saying that because you're my brother. You're becoming so like Dad.'

'Maybe I am, but I want you to promise me something,' he says emphatically and I dare not agree. 'This list you are working from. Add your own things to it. Make the most of it. I don't want to see you wasting these precious years of yours just doing *fine*.'

By precious years... my final years is what he means. It's no secret that my heart is really not my own and that one day it will stop beating, content in the work it has done to give me a longer life than I should have had. Fifteen years, they told us back then. After that, every year is a bonus. I'm on borrowed time with a borrowed heart and I should be living every day like it's my last.

'I'm already doing that,' I tell my brother with a smile. 'I'm doing a mini marathon with my neighbour Kevin and I've always wanted to do more song-writing and you have encouraged me to do that, so that's a start. Plus I've this trip to France to see Lucy's favourite bridge, and who knows what that will bring.'

'Great,' he says with a look of sorrow and he reaches over and takes my hand. 'You have no idea what your visit has done for me. I am all the better for seeing you. I really am. I worry about you, but only like any big brother should and I want you to be okay. You are okay, aren't you?'

'I am absolutely fine,' I tell him and he has to laugh. 'You know what I mean. I'm doing good and a lot better now having seen you too.'

I feel like apologising again but we've already crossed that bridge, pardon the pun.

'Now can you do something for me?' I ask him.

'Shoot,' he says.

'Please tell Mum and Dad you've been sick but that you're on the mend,' I say to him. 'And introduce them to your wife. They will be so hurt if they hear from someone else that you are married. You don't need to run away any more.'

He laughs and squeezes my hand.

'I fully intend to, don't worry,' he replies. 'In fact, Vivienne and I are planning a good-old Irish knees-up with a blessing back home, so that's something for them to look forward to. I just need a wee while to mend and to get my head around what I've just been through, is that okay?'

My eyes widen with excitement. I love a good wedding celebration, even though I'm almost officially a divorcee.

'That is the best news ever!' I tell him. 'Make sure you tell them soon because I'm not sure I will be able to keep that to myself!'

'I will,' he assures me. 'Now, I think that's your taxi. You look after yourself, Maggie O'Hara. You mean the world to me – I hope you know that now.'

We stand up and he gives me the tightest squeeze I've ever had. Sick or not, he is still as strong as an ox, my big brother.

'I do. You're my hero,' I tell him and he loosens his grip.

'Get outta here,' he says and ruffles my hair just like he used to when we were little.

'And, by the way, your eyes are sweating,' I tell him as I take one last good look at him.

'So are yours. I'll see you real soon back home at Loch Tara, Maggie.'

'You will, John Joe. I love you.'

'I love you more, little sister.'

I walk out the door, down the pathway and out through the gate of my brother's American home and I feel a rush of blood pumping through my veins and filling my heart so much I could scream with joy.

I give him a final wave and get into the taxi and we keep waving until he disappears.

'You had a good visit?' asks the taxi driver and I recognise him as the one who brought me here. What are the chances?

'The best,' I tell him and I take out Lucy's diary and write a short note at the back. I love to give her little updates on the progress of our list.

I danced again Lucy and I am going to keep on dancing, I tell her in my neatest handwriting. *I danced and I sang and I laughed and I travelled and I even crossed a bridge, in more ways than one, but most of all, I have forgiven, and doing that has allowed me to feel real unconditional love again.*

Thank you, once again, my dear little friend. You'll be pleased to know that your big heart, which I really thought was broken for good – well, you have helped me fix it.

And it still works just fine.

Chapter 22

I spend the next few days resting after my impromptu trip to Nashville and as I rest I reminisce on the wonderful time I had, however brief it was, with my brother. I tell Flo over endless coffees, I tell Kevin as we train for our run, I tell anyone who will listen to me how glad I am to have him back in my life and how much I am going to make up for lost time by being a much more attentive, loving and caring sister to the one sibling that I have been blessed with in my complicated, second-hand life.

And then I think of Simon and of Lucy and how she was his only sister, just like John Joe is my only brother, and for the first time I truly understand just how painful it must have been to lose her and never get her back. I lost John Joe but I got him back. Simon never had the chance.

I open my laptop and start to write him an email.

Dear Simon
I'd like to say I'm sorry.
I'm sorry for being a self-centred cow to you when we last spoke. I could use all sorts of excuses, like wine or a

bad day or feeling sorry for myself, that other people are happy in relationships and having babies, or that the world is turning and mine had stopped, but none of them would be good enough.

That bubble of self-pity has well and truly burst, Simon, and I hope you can forgive my teenage, or should I say toddler, fit of throwing my toys out of the pram and saying I'm not playing any more.

I did what Lucy said. I took a big step, one I thought I never would do and I went to visit my brother in the States and, boy oh boy, you were right. Everyone was right. He didn't hear me that day, he couldn't have. He is not jealous or bitter or any of the things I have accused him of being in my clouded head and he is not just womanising his way around America.

He is a sweet, caring, loving person and it's my loss that I had chosen to ignore that for so long.

So, really, I just wanted to let you know that as much as I denied it the last time we spoke, Lucy's legacy is very much living on in me and will always do so as long as her heart keeps me taking one step forward at a time in this thing we call life.

I know that as long as I have her on my side, I can keep going in the right direction. The songbird is still singing...

Please give my regards to your beautiful wife and her precious growing baby bump – I truly wish you both all the love and light from my heart to yours and I hope we can still keep in touch.

Your friend,
Maggie.

I press 'send' and feel that itch again, but I won't scratch it. I will not give in to using alcohol as a crutch every time I have to apologise, or feel lonely or feel like the world is against me. I have so much to look forward to. I go to France in just two days and my brother has asked me to help with some logistics for his forthcoming celebrations, which we will have at Loch Tara in late June. I will use the next two days to make a start with a marquee, some catering, a jazz band, the works. My mum is insisting the parish priest gives a blessing, which nearly gave my dad a coronary, but he gave in because he knows he will never win that argument.

There are lots of fun times ahead.

The mini marathon with Kevin is just around the corner and I will keep up the training regime we have both worked out for me when I'm in France and then when I come back we will really get stuck in until the big day comes. When I say 'stuck in', I mean stuck in as far as I am allowed to because any heavy stress on my seventeen-year-old heart could do me serious damage and I owe it to Lucy to stick within our limits.

I focus on the future, on France and all the avenues that she has opened for me with her little list of dreams. I wonder about Tiernan Quinn and his whereabouts and even the thought of his name makes me smile. We really did click and maybe some day I will pick up the courage to get in touch with him again and see how it goes. I could be too late by then, but I will find out if the time ever comes.

Then, just as if it's the most natural thing in the world, I do something that I haven't done without forced thinking or someone asking me to do.

I pick up my old guitar and I start to strum and sing and I feel alive from the very tips of my toes.

'The Boy Next Door', that song I wrote when I was just a spotty teenager, might not be as bad as I thought it was. And if it is, I have lots of material for some new ideas. I might even buy a new notebook.

In fact, I just will.

I don't hear from Simon Harte until the morning I am due to fly out to France and it has greatly worried me that he might have decided he wanted nothing more to do with me after our last conversation, but I couldn't have been more wrong.

Dear Maggie,

Andrea and I send you lots of love right back! The bump is growing beautifully and we are very excited indeed as the weeks pass by and the sleepless nights begin, so we are trying to take it easy as much as we can for now.

It was so good to hear from you and I am thrilled that you have made peace with your brother and now have some wonderful times ahead with him. That was a brave step for you and it's great that you have your family on your side. I bet you feel like a different person for it!

On the other hand, I think I should probably say sorry too for being so caught up in my own feelings with this all and not thinking of what you are going through as much as I should have.

Perhaps I am grasping at everything I can just to keep

some part of my immediate family alive, but if I am I hope you can forgive me.

Andrea thinks, or rather hopes if she admitted it, that when our baby comes in just a few weeks, that I will be able to move on in a new direction and maybe she is right. I'm told a new baby kind of does that to its parents, so you may only have to bear with me a little longer! Soon I will be drowning in nappies and baby-talk and won't have as much time to think about the things that Lucy wanted to do and how you are out there doing them.

However I have a feeling that we will always be friends. You're a great person, Maggie.

Have a ball in France, or should I say 'bon voyage' and thank you from the bottom of my own heart for keeping Lucy's wishes alive.

Only a very special person would do that and you are very, very special to me.

With love from my heart to yours and Lucy's,
Simon x

Hearing from Simon at this moment, when I am about to make this final big journey on his sister's list feels even more right than before.

Let's do this, Lucy. Let's go and see if this bridge is as big as you hoped it would be.

Chapter 23

The flight and its connections in London are uneventful, with a long wait in between, but I feel relaxed and the evening Mediterranean heats my bones when I step out of the plane at Montpellier, near the southern French coast, a grand total of nine hours later.

'*Au revoir et merci*,' I say to the stewardess, whose name is Brenda and who lives in inner-city Birmingham, but she smiles at my enthusiasm. I won't be so smartly bilingual when an actual French person speaks to me, but I plan to make an effort even if I haven't a clue what they are saying. It's only manners to attempt the native language when in a foreign country, so I will do my best.

Je m'appelle Maggie.

My old school lessons come back to me and I like it.

I find my credit card in my purse and my driving license and swiftly and smoothly I arrange my car, which will be my only definite companion for the next few days. It's both exciting and scary to be here on a one-way ticket with no idea really where I am going (apart from the bridge), what I am going to do (apart from see the bridge) and where I will be staying (definitely not on the bridge!).

I am suddenly quite exhausted and I yawn as the car-hire people get me all sorted with a groovy little cream-coloured Fiat 500, which is ideal for just me on my travels. It is 9pm and I haven't arranged anywhere to stay yet. Somewhere near the airport will do for now and I will set off on my travels in the morning.

I start the ignition in the car and wobble a bit at first when French radio blasts in my ears and I hear a horn beep while I try and get my head around driving on the right side of the road. I park just a short drive away, much to my relief, at the Aeroport Hotel and to my luck they have a room available for the night.

A milky hot chocolate, a quick look on Facebook later and I am tucked up in bed, relaxed, eager and ready for what the next day will bring.

But the next morning I wake up in the sparse hotel room with an entirely opposite mind set.

What the hell am I doing here? Where the actual hell am I? There is no John Joe to seek out, no familiar face to make me feel welcome, no one to show me the sights or take me for lunch or tell me I'm doing the right thing.

I am frightened and disorientated and unfamiliar with the sounds of aeroplanes zooming overhead and I wonder if I should just go right back and forget all about this trip. I'm sure Lucy wouldn't mind. I've done almost everything else on her list, haven't I? Okay, I still need to throw a dinner party, but that's easy peasy. This is... well this is a little bit scary right now and I'm not sure I like it.

I check my phone, hoping for some sort of comfort and familiarity and I'm glad to see a message from Flo waiting for me.

'Call me!' is all she has written, so I do so straight away and turn around on the smooth white pillow and look out the window onto the blue French sky, feeling a tiny bit less lonely when I see her name on the screen.

'So, is he hot?' she asks over the usual background noise of her son pretending to be his latest animal craze.

'Who?'

'The French guy you have picked up and fallen madly in love with, that's who!' she says. 'I just know they are going to be all over you like a rash, especially with that funky new hair-do and don't-fuck-with-me attitude. Billie, will you get down before you fall! He's on the kitchen table.'

'Jeez, Flo give me time to taste my first croissant, never mind tasting a French man! I only arrived last night and... well, oh God, what am I doing here Flo? I just woke up and –'

'And what? And what? What happened, Maggie?'

'Nothing happened! I just kind of panicked, that's all.'

Why did I even tell her? I forgot she is a mother now so it is programmed in her brain to worry more than before.

'Are you safe?' she asks. 'Do you feel safe?'

'Of course I feel safe,' I say and I sit up and stretch. She is making me laugh now. 'I am very sober and I am safe in a very nice airport hotel and I have hired a car to go and see some of the locality. I just... well, I just got a bit freaked when I woke up, but I'm a big girl, Flo. I can do this.'

'Okay... but don't force it,' she goes on to say. 'You don't have to force it, but I just know you are going to have a great time, just like you did in Dublin, just like you did in Nashville. Lucy is with you and she won't lead you wrong.'

She is right. This is going to be great. If I can just get out of this hotel room and on the road I will be fine. Oh, I'm not meant to use that word, am I? I will be great! Really great!

'It's like this, Flo,' I say just to reassure myself. 'I've had my world totally tipped upside down – my whole present and future ripped apart, and I need to know that when I manage to tip it back up the right way again, I put everything back in the proper place this time, which is not necessarily going to be the same place. Does that make sense?'

I get up and open a window and let some fresh air into my room. It feels so good and my tummy rumbles, so I lift a room-service menu from the side table.

'That makes perfect sense,' says Flo. 'Billie, will you please stop climbing! You will break your leg!'

'How is he?' I ask with a smile. My godson never fails to cheer me up.

'Hyper,' says Flo. 'His dad is home.'

'Oh,' is all I can muster. His 'dad' just seems to fly in and out when it suits him.

'He is taking him swimming soon and you'd think to hear Billie he was going to Disneyland,' says Flo. 'He is so excited. Oh Maggie, it does my heart good to see them together, it really does.'

I scan the menu in front of me. Smoked salmon on a bagel with cream cheese... and freshly brewed coffee. I think that's what I will have for breakfast. Al fresco. My room has a balcony. I look outside again and then open the sliding door that leads outside.

'And what about you and Damian?' I ask her. 'Are you getting on okay?'

I hope for Flo's sake they are and that it's not all mummy and daddy role-play with Billie.

'Well, he stayed over last night,' says Flo and I can feel her energy all the way from here.

'What??'

'Don't be cross at me, Maggie!'

'I'm not cross! It's your life and he's the father of your child. It's your business, buddy. Sometimes we just gotta do what we gotta do.'

'Oh thanks, Maggie! It was awesome to have him back home. He hasn't changed a bit. Sorry if it's too much information, but we just, um, fitted together as well as we always did.'

She sighs with glee and I sit down on the edge of the bed and feel sorry for myself again. I look down at my flowery pyjamas. Hardly a sexy beast, me.

'I'm insanely jealous,' I admit to my best friend.

'Of what? The sex?'

I shrug, wearing a very sad and lonely face.

'Well, yes,' I admit. 'You know exactly what I mean. The physical touch. A hug, a kiss and yes, sex. I miss it. I have been so tempted many times to text Tiernan Quinn and bag a quickie off him. I feel like a desperate slut.'

'Well, go get it, Maggie!' squeals Flo. 'You're in a place where no one knows you and the French men are renowned for their passion between the sheets! Va va voom! Go have a one-night stand and get it all out of your system with Jean Claude or Pierre or... what other French names are there?'

'The guy in reception was called Patric,' I laugh back, putting on my best *Français* accent. 'He had a twinkle in his eye when he heard I was from Ireland.'

Flo lets out a raspy laugh.

'Oh Patric,' she says loudly. 'Let me show you a lee-tle someth-eeng *dans ma chambre*! Go get him, Mags! Go and do stuff to him that he will never forget! Show him the Emerald Isle! Your Garden of Eden!'

I am laughing my head off at the idea. What I didn't tell her is that Patric is about sixty- three years old with hairy ears, a hairier nose and a body-odour problem. But I get what she is saying. No one would ever know.

'I will keep you fully up to date with any such encounters,' I promise her. 'Now, I need food so I will speak to you later tonight, okay? *Au revoir, mon amie!*'

'*Au revoir* you lucky bitch!' says Flo. 'And make sure he wears a condom! You don't need any illegitimate French babies in your belly, or worse, a disease!'

'*Au revoir!*' I say again and I hang up with a smile. Flo always makes me feel better. She is like the sister I never had and I love her dearly.

I take out Lucy's notebook as I wait for my room service and the world feels exciting again. I am over my nervous blip and I am ready for this! I am ready and I am going to make this work! I scan through her little list of things she planned to do and it feels good to mentally tick them off:

1) *Find the world's tallest bridge – I'm on my way to it, I hope!*
2) *Find Tiernan Quinn and kiss him – I did that one in style!*
3) *Learn to play guitar – I'm getting there…*
4) *Never stop dancing – I am on it!*
5) *Get a tattoo – Did it, love it!*
6) *Forgive friends and family – the best thing ever…*
7) *Spread your wings and travel far – you bet I will! And I am!*
8) *Throw a dinner party to die for – not yet…*
9) *Get a new haircut – uh huh! Feels amazing, thanks Lucy!*
10) *Surprise someone you love – done!*

Every single thing on her list has driven me on, taken me on a new direction and I read it often to remind myself how far I have come and how I need to keep on going. The Maggie of a few months ago is like a stranger to me now. I was literally clutching a bottle, staring into space in an apartment that felt clinical and isolated and I was letting Jeff and his rejection lead me down a very unhealthy path of self-destruction.

I had nowhere to turn, I was avoiding everyone who loved me and my own self-loathing and low self-esteem was dragging me deeper and deeper into the gutter.

And then I was reminded of a gift I had once been blessed with – the gift of life from a little girl who lost hers and there I was abusing it. I was allowing her precious heart to be battered and bruised and walked all over, but those days are gone. Every day is a new opportunity to me now, thanks to Lucy's guidance and I won't ever take it for granted again.

I pencil in my own entry – to run the mini marathon with Kevin – on to the end of Lucy's list, which reminds me to get into exercise mode during my French vacation and I feel rejuvenated and excited, just as I do every time I achieve something for her that in turn becomes something positive for me.

I will keep adding to our list so that my journey with Lucy doesn't have to end as I tick off the final few things. We have much more to see and do before this journey of ours is over, but right now it begins with breakfast, which has just arrived at the door. Moments later, I am indulging in my first taste of French cuisine and my taste buds dance with every bite.

Ooh la la, Lucy, ma cherie! Let our French adventure begin!

With a full belly and all the time in the world, I enter the coordinates for the Millau Viaduct bridge into my phone and the clever sat nav tells me it will take just over an hour to get there. I have done some research on the place and since you can't walk across it on foot, I plan to cruise across it in the car and see where it takes me. Then I set off north towards the Tarn Valley with the radio blasting and no one to tell me to turn it down.

Jeff hated loud music in the car. He said it distracted him and even if I was driving, it made him nervous. He never, ever went over the speed limit, which I know is not essentially a bad thing, but what I am trying to say is – he never really broke the rules in life.

Up early, work all day, bed early, tick tock, tick tock, tick tock. It was safe, it was reliable and at the time I went along with it, but now, as I drive along this strange road in a strange country with the sun beating down on my hired car and French cheesy pop tunes belting out, I realise we really didn't have an awful lot in common.

Okay, he liked live music, I'll give him that. He liked to travel, but only at certain times of the year. He was a package-holiday type of guy – no risks, no chances, just A to B to C and back again.

He also had trouble relaxing when he did have down-time, which really irritated me. I could find time slipping away with a paint brush, restoring old furniture or writing in a journal yet he always had to be busier, more practical and everything was urgent. He was just like his father in that way. Everything by the book. Everything the opposite of me.

I am very proud of how I am managing this whole right-side-of-the-road business and I find peace in my heart and mind that he is not here dictating to me to *indicate now* or *brake now* or *Jesus, Maggie are you blind? You're going to kill us!*

In fact, it's actually blissful here without him. I never, ever thought I would say such a thing, but I am in a state of heaven as I take in the sights around me without him chirping in my ear and it's like my life with him is a world away.

I think of him and Saffron and their baby and, to my surprise and great delight, I don't feel sick any more. I feel numb to it. I feel free from it. I actually feel like I have had a lucky escape and it's bloody well brilliant!

After my visit to Nashville, the power of forgiveness has changed my whole outlook entirely and has strengthened me from the inside out. Holding on to such resentment and pain from the past is damaging to the heart and soul, I now realise. Perhaps that's what Lucy was trying to remind herself of when she said to forgive your friends and family – not always perhaps because they deserve it, but sometimes because it is better for you to release the pain in a form of forgiveness?

The peace in my heart that I now have with my brother has helped me see how nourishing it is to forgive and let go and it's how I am slowly healing from Jeff's rejection. I can see now the imperfections in our relationship. I can see now how he wasn't the person I believed him to be. He wasn't a loyal or committed husband and he certainly didn't love me like he said he did.

I need to constantly remind myself that he doesn't deserve me and that I deserve better.

Someone else will love me, I remind myself now. Someone else will treat my heart like it deserves to be treated, but in order to let that someone else in, I needed to forgive Jeff and set him free from my mind. I needed to heal and I am healing every day and it feels so good.

'Woo hoo!' I shout into the open road and I long to beep the horn, but I'm not that cocky at this driving malarkey just yet. I need to stay focused on the route ahead.

Montpellier itself is a delicious mix of old and new, from the ancient Opera House and myriad narrow streets to dazzling modern architecture, which gives the impression of two very different worlds.

I will explore it more on my way back to the airport, whenever that will be, but for now my sights are set on the Tarn Valley, which in no time at all I am approaching – I am moving into wild scenery and colours of regal purples and greens so lush that I feel like I am travelling through a French rainbow.

With its thick-walled stone houses, steep emerald valleys and deep gorges, this is France at its most beautiful, from what I have seen so far in my lifetime. I inhale the scenery and drive at a pace at which I can take it all in, feeling no sense of time or rush and the wonderful knowledge that I can go where I want in this area when I want and don't have to please Jeff – with his moaning and need for an itinerary.

The town of Millau – pronounced *Mee-yo*, which I have decided is where I am going to put down some roots for a few days, is truly magnificent in a picture-postcard way. I resist the urge to drive straight to the bridge and instead park up in a bid to find some accommodation. It's impossible to ignore the bridge's magnificent structure in the distance and from where I am, it looks every bit worth the journey.

Je suis ici, I text Flo. *C'est magnifique!*

Cool! She replies. *I knew you'd find one! And how is the place itself?*

Dirty bitch! I reply back. *That's what I meant and you know it.*

The mood in the air in Millau, *une ville d'art et d'histoire,* spells authentic French food, the finest of wines and easy, laid-back living and when I find a place to park up, I step out of the car into the morning sun and stretch and smile at the new world that awaits me.

I find a quaint little shaded seat outside a café bar, feeling very Audrey Hepburn (okay, Audrey Hepburn with red hair) in my oversized hat and sunglasses and I order a *vin rouge* and sit back on my seat and take it all in.

'Are you staying here or just passing through?' the waitress asks politely, with a smile, as she takes my order.

'I'm hoping to stay for a few days,' I reply. 'It's more of a short break, I think, but I'm not sure yet. I've just arrived this minute and my main aim is to check out the bridge for a friend.'

'Ah, the bridge,' she says. 'Everyone comes to see the bridge. I came to see the bridge three years ago and I am still here! I'm Starling. You are very welcome to Millau.'

'Why, thank you, Starling!' I reply. If everyone in Millau is as friendly as she is, I can see why she stayed. 'I'm Maggie.'

'I warn you, Maggie,' she laughs. 'It can be very addictive here – the food, the wine, the countryside and the sunshine – especially at this time of year. Not to mention the charming men...'

I give her a knowing smile. 'So that's really what keeps you here?'

She nods and gives me a wink.

'This is my fiancé's family restaurant. His dad, Anton, is my boss, but it's cool.'

'Well, it certainly is a delightful town, from what I see so far,' I agree with her. 'I look forward to sampling the hospitality and, I have to say, you are a fine example of what to expect.'

'Ah, thank you,' says Starling. 'You like wine, yes?'

Me? Wine? If she only knew just how much I like it sometimes...

'I do like wine. Don't we all?'

I hold up my glass.

'Good. There is a wine bar, *Le Bouchon,* which I really love a few streets away,' she says. 'There is a piano and guitars and a wonderful atmosphere, where lots of tourists, locals, couples, families and single people go. Nice *single* people. It will help you settle in. That's where I met my man.'

She gives me a nod and a clever smile.

'I am not here for romance,' I assure her. 'No, really, I am not!'

Despite my conversation with Flo earlier, romance and men really are the furthest things from my mind. I am more than happy to enjoy my surroundings without any complications, thank you very much. I am here to complete the final parts of Lucy Harte's list and I trust in her to take me in the right direction, whatever that may bring.

Starling rolls her eyes dramatically.

'But *Mademoiselle* –'

'Just Maggie is fine,' I smile.

'Oh, Maggie! You simply cannot come to France and not experience a bit of light romance,' she exclaims. 'You could meet the man of your dreams. At least, the man of your dreams for one night, anyhow!'

She laughs and then leaves me with a hand-scribbled note of the name of her piano bar. *Le Bouchon.* I might check it out. It's nice to have a recommendation from someone who knows the locality.

'Oh, Starling?' I call out to her.

'Oui, *Mademoiselle?*' She looks pleased to be of assistance again.

'Sorry, I don't mean to be a pain, but I don't have anywhere to stay as yet. Perhaps you might know of somewhere? A hotel, or even an apartment or a cottage – anything?'

She pauses and thinks for a moment.

'I think, to look at you, that you would like something, can I say, quirky?'

I raise an eyebrow. 'Yes, but I'm really not too fussy.'

'I will find you somewhere nice,' says Starling, and I have no doubt that she will. 'I will ask Anton about a great idea I have.'

Starling comes back moments later with a complementary glass of red for me and I realise that if I accept it, which it would be incredibly rude not to, I will have no choice but to park up for the night and stay within walking distance. Sod it... I decide to go with the flow.

'*Merci beaucoup,*' I say to her when she tells me the wine is courtesy of Anton.

'Anton agrees with me that we have the perfect place for you,' says Starling with a bright smile.

Great. I like Anton already.

'It is a *gîte* belonging to his brother Gerard, a little cottage down by the river with the most spectacular views of the great bridge you have come to visit,' she tells me. 'It is private and homely and it is available at the moment, so if you like it, you can have it.'

A *gîte*... a real French cottage by the river? This is too good to be true.

'Gosh, Starling, that sounds absolutely perfect. Is it close by?'

She nods enthusiastically.

'Just a short walk from the town centre, but Anton is on his way to speak to you directly with all the details,' she says. 'He is on the phone to Gerard now, though he won't be long. Enjoy your wine, *Mademoiselle*. And once again, welcome to Millau.'

Chapter 24

'You must be Mademoiselle Maggie?'

I look up moments later and then stand up and remove my sunglasses to greet Anton, the owner of the café-bar. He is not what I expected, though what I did expect I cannot really explain.

'*Bonjour Monsieur,*' I reply and he kisses me on each cheek.

He is a tall, tanned, bald man of around fifty, I am guessing, and he is a bit rougher around the edges than I thought he would be, though handsome all the same. He wears a bottle-green apron over his working whites, which look like they are in need of a wash and he has a dark stubble on his chubby face.

'Have a seat, please,' he tells me in word-perfect English and once again I kick myself for not being more fluent in his language. 'So you are interested in our *gîte*? I can give you keys – you can check it out and, if you like it, it's yours for your stay.'

'Yes, yes it sounds perfect,' I respond with gratitude. 'And *merci* for the *vino* as well.'

I know I sound ridiculous mixing up my French and

English. I should really stop trying and just stick to one, which will be English, of course, seeing as my French doesn't stretch to a full conversation.

'It is warm, it is clean, but I have to say, please don't mind my brother who lives nearby,' says Anton. 'He is turning into a grumpy old man and doesn't like to be disturbed, but he has agreed to let you stay for as long as you need it.'

'I am here to see the bridge,' I tell him, as if it's the most important thing in the world to me – well, it is right now, I suppose. 'Is it near?'

The man chuckles as though he has heard it all before.

'You can see the bridge from the *gîte*,' he assures me and I gasp with excitement.

'Really?'

He nods his head.

'You can look out on it every single day when you wake up, or last thing at night, or stare at it all day, if you must!' he says. 'Stay as long as you need to. Starling will show you the way.'

I smile from the inside out. This is more than I could have dreamed of. I want to pinch myself to see if it's all for real? A view of the bridge from my own little *gîte*!

Well, Lucy Harte, it looks as if everything is falling into place. I feel at home with these people already, almost like a sense of familiarity with their warm welcome and willingness to help out a stranger to their town. I know you are near me, making sure everything goes according to plan. Thank you!

The old Maggie would have been petrified of making this trip alone, but now I am not afraid at all despite the language barrier and the distance from home. I am not alone, you see. I have Lucy and I also have a strange feeling that all of this is meant to be and I can't wait to see the bridge and where our adventures will take us next.

We fetch my bag from my hire car and then walk through the streets, further into the town, past boulangeries, patisseries, the piano-bar that Starling loves so much, a range of restaurants of various themes and then down a side street and onto a rocky, secluded path that takes us down a stepping-stoned hill towards the river bank. Two canoeists race up towards the majestic bridge in the foreground and the evening sun is beginning to set. The scene is truly breathtaking.

'This is a shortcut for when on foot, but when you get your car in the morning you can drive along the road,' says Starling, 'and avoid the risk of breaking your ankle like we are doing now.'

'It's okay, I am fairly fit these days,' I assure her. 'I can't wait to go running along the river bank tomorrow, when I get my bearings.'

'Ah you are a runner? Then you will fit very well in. Millau is a very sporting town,' Starling tells me. 'Canoeing, rafting, paragliding... you see it all here and it just adds to the visual beauty of the place.'

'I can see that already. It's to die for.'

We reach the bottom of the steps and she stops to point out the bridge in the distance. Birds swoop below it, just above the canoeists and the sun sits perfectly, like a big orange ball, right behind it. If this was a movie, there would be a big classical soundtrack now reaching a magnificent crescendo as I see the full bridge in all its glory for the first time.

It is perfect.

'Wow!' I exclaim and I am sure my jaw has literally dropped. 'Holy flippin' wow!'

I wish Simon could see me now. I lift my phone and take a photo and I send it to him and he messages me right back a photo of him smiling and I just know he is as proud of this moment as I am.

I'm here, Lucy Harte. I'm really here. Can you see it? That's your bridge, Lucy! That's your dream, right there!

I forget totally that Starling is standing, waiting, beside me.

'I... I'm sorry, Starling, but do you mind if I just take a moment. This is what I came here for and I want to just –'

'Of course,' says Starling and she moves towards the pathway. 'I'll just go inside. Take your time. I'm in no hurry at all.'

I look to my right and briefly watch her disappear into a light-stone cottage, which is built into the hilly river bank, only its rooftop and half of its back wall visible from where we stand, but for now I need to take this all in. I need to focus on Lucy.

I stand there and breathe right to the pit of my stomach and stretch my arms out as far as they go and I throw my head back and close my eyes and I move round and round in circles and stop before I get dizzy.

'I hope you are here, Lucy! I really hope you can see what I can see!' I tell her out loud. 'That's your place, right up there! The tallest bridge in the whole wide world! I found it for you, Lucy! We found it! We are here!'

My heart is beating faster than it has in any training session with Kevin, in any moment with Tiernan Quinn, in any fit of bad temper at Jeff's antics with Saffron, in any anticipation of seeing John Joe – this is the big one. This is the one that was top of Lucy's list and the one that she wanted, I imagine, to experience the most.

'Let's see where I am staying,' I whisper to her and I walk down the hilly pathway to the front of the *gîte*, already in love with what I see before we even go inside. Lilac bushes line the way to the stone porch, where a potted green ash tree grows right up over to frame the doorway, which is painted a cool pale blue. It is wonderfully inviting and I cannot wait to see more.

'Who is the lucky owner of this paradise? Did Anton say it belongs to his brother?' I ask Starling as I step into the open-plan terracotta-tiled floor that covers the living and dining area, with a step up into a cute compact pale-blue kitchen, fully equipped with all the mod-cons I will need for my stay.

'It's Gerard's, yes,' she tells me. 'But lately Anton and I have been making sure it is kept well as Gerard is really busy right now. Isn't it heavenly?'

'It really, really is. It's so perfect.'

Starling shows me how to work the cooker and small washing machine and then leads me through a Venetian-style white door, which leads to the bedroom and en-suite. The walls inside the bedroom are rough stone like on the outside of the cottage and voile cream curtains hang from a window that looks out onto the lush green of the Tarn Valley. This is exceptional. How on earth did I manage to get so lucky?

A patchwork quilt, which Starling explains was made by her fiancé Bernard's grandmother, who used to own the cottage, covers a cosy-looking double bed and I want to jump into it already.

'There is a heating system, if you need it,' she lets me know, then shows me how to use it, 'or there is always the open fire in the living area. It can get quite chilly at night here, so don't be afraid to switch it on. We won't mind at all. Oh, and if you need to stock up on wine and food, there is a *supermarché* open until ten most nights on Boulevard George Brassans. You won't miss it.'

I start to laugh with nerves and Starling looks at me as if she has said something wrong.

'What's so funny?' she asks. 'It really can get cold at night. Don't be fooled by the day-time sun.'

'No, no I believe you! I... I just can't believe all of *this*!' I tell her and I fan my face as I feel myself overcome with emotion. 'I mean, here I am in the most beautifully spectacular place I have ever seen in my whole life and I have no idea how it happened. Well, I do know how, and that makes it even more wondrous. I am so, so grateful.'

Starling shrugs and smiles like she is very used to such a reaction.

'I must confess that we don't advertise this place, ever,' she tells me. 'We just let it out to people who we think might make good use of it. It's a special place where special things happen, and it's not for just anyone.'

Her eyes dance as she speaks and I become more in awe of my new friend.

'I am so, so grateful,' I repeat and I follow her outside through a side door off the bedroom that leads to an enclosed patio, which is overlooking the river. Two coloured chairs, one purple and one lime green are perfectly placed at a little white table.

'So would you like to stay here?'

I nod and I am not sure if I should hug her to show my gratitude. I don't know if that would be too familiar, since it's essentially a business transaction. Or is it? I don't think I know what is going on any more, nor do I want to.

'I told Anton earlier you have a good heart and he said okay,' says Starling and she holds my hand for a second when handing over the keys.

'What makes you think I have a good heart?' I ask her, a cool breeze washing over me and shivers rising on my skin. 'You only just met me a few hours ago.'

'Oh, I could tell the moment I saw you,' says Starling. 'Now I better go and meet my darling Bernard for dinner. If you need anything, just call me.'

She hands me a business card and I stare at it and then look back at her.

'Thank you so much, Starling,' I say. 'I am so grateful for all your help today.'

'*Au revoir*, Maggie,' says Starling, her dark hair swishing as she walks. 'Call me if you need me! Don't be a stranger!'

And then she is gone, leaving me to my own devices under the shadow of the world's tallest bridge, just as Lucy dreamed of visiting one day.

I sit down on the brown-leather sofa in the living room

and take in my surroundings, which will be my home for a whole week, then I look at the business card in my hand and I see the official name of the *gîte* for the first time – it is called *Maison d'Henri*.

The gîte is called *Henry's House*.

Henry is Simon and Lucy's little brother, who survived the accident. Henry is who Lucy wanted to take to the bridge one day. I feel a shiver run over my skin and I rub the goose bumps from my arms. Perhaps I am like Simon now, looking for constant signs of reassurance to keep Lucy with me. Perhaps they are merely coincidences. But whatever they are, they keep showing up and I can't ignore them.

I go to the window and look out onto the Millau Viaduct in the distance, thinking of Lucy and Simon's little brother whose body is trapped in the mind of a child back in Glasgow and whose dreams were killed off on the day that Lucy went to heaven.

I couldn't take Henry with me, not this time anyhow, but it looks like part of Henry might be here with me in spirit after all.

Chapter 25

As the evening sun drops down behind the bridge, I wander out from the cottage and up the stone steps that lead back into the town to grab a few essentials from the *super-marché*. I have no idea, of course, where Boulevard George Brassans is but I am confident I will find it.

It's closer by than I think and I take a shopping basket and explore all the goods it has to offer, picking up some fresh bread, cheese, a few cold meats and two bottles of delicious red wine.

'You are staying at the *gîte* by the river?'

I am at the till when I hear a gruff, heavily accented voice behind me and it makes me jump.

'Excuse me?'

I look up at a tall, bearded, dark-haired man who is clutching a six-pack of beer under one arm and a baguette under the other.

'You are staying at the *gîte*? I saw you earlier, with Starling. You're the Irish girl, *oui*?'

He is blunt, his tone slightly rude and I am totally flustered as I unload my groceries from the basket, feeling totally exposed as this strange man watches my every move. And then it clicks with me.

'Ah, yes. You must be Gerard?' I say, finally putting two and two together, though he is much younger than the old, greying man I had imagined. I almost say *grumpy Gerard,* but thankfully I don't. 'It's your place, right? It's very beautiful.'

He nods and then looks away. Then he looks back. He smells like tobacco and methylated spirits and looks like he hasn't washed properly for weeks and his clothes are splattered in paint of all sorts of colours.

'Yes, I suppose you could say that it is my place, but my brother likes to think otherwise sometimes. I am not as grumpy as he may have told you. I am just younger and busier and much more interesting than he is and sometimes he gets jealous.'

He looks so grumpy and moody as he says it, which makes me laugh and then he smiles, looking embarrassed and his green eyes meet mine for the first time.

'You don't want to know my family problems or my grumpiness, right?' he says, laughing now. 'I am sorry. Can I start again? I am Gerard.'

This time he extends a hand and I greet him back with a handshake. Boy, he is strong and his hands are that of a physical working man.

'You are a painter, yes?' I ask, stating the very obvious.

'Oui, an *artiste.* How could you tell?'

'Your clothes?'

'Ah, my clothes! Of course! Sorry. That was my attempt at a joke,' he says, looking down at the very obvious. 'Perhaps I am not very funny. I'm much better at being grumpy.'

He brushes his wavy dark hair off his face and I notice that underneath the beard and the paint and grime is a very handsome man. He is in his early forties, I'd imagine, and in great shape; big and strong and very, dare I say, manly.

'Are you any good at painting while being grumpy?' I ask him, bagging my groceries as his turn comes to pay the cashier.

'*Oui*,' he says with a smile curling on his lips. 'I am 'so, so' at painting. Is that what you say in Ireland? So, so?'

'Monsieur Gerard is being very modest,' says the cashier, speaking to him under fluttering eyelashes. 'He is our local celebrity. He is quite famous in our region and his paintings are everywhere you go. They are very... amazing.'

He smiles. She swoons.

'So you *are* good, then,' I say, lifting my bags. 'Maybe some-time I will get to see you at work before I go home?'

Now he looks grumpy again now. Not as smug or even playful but more grumpy than before.

'I am sorry, but no, you cannot see me. I am very, very busy working for a grand exhibition,' he tells me, as the cashier watches on, still slightly star-struck. 'I only come out once a day for essentials. You won't see me again, probably. I am too busy. Nice to meet with you, Mademoiselle.'

He holds up the bread and beer and I nod in mock under-standing, suitably rejected and totally cut to the bone.

'Oh okay. May-maybe on my next visit,' I suggest. 'Nice to meet you and good luck with your work.'

Asshole.

I cannot wait to get away from him.

'*Merci*,' he says and the cashier strikes up a conversation, thankfully distracting him as I walk outside.

Perhaps I am over-sensitive but his words have really pierced me deep.

It's just rejection, I hear John Joe's voice in my ear. *Nothing more, nothing less, just rejection and it will pass.*

It's just downright rudeness, actually! I was just being polite! I don't really give a shit about his artwork! I continue to lick my wounds as I walk through the winding streets across to the stepping stone walkway that leads to *Maison d'Henri* and try not to take his rejection so personally, like it's not as if he knows me. If he wants to be so rude to people he has just met, then that is his problem. Not like he is Vincent van bloody well Gogh!

'Mademoiselle! Mademoiselle, please, can you wait?'

I am halfway down the little steps that lead to the riverbank cottages when I see Gerard hurrying behind me, following me down, carrying his beer and bread like they are precious cargo, which I suppose to him in his hibernation state, they kind of are.

'*Oui?*'

Oh, how I wish I could speak some more French! There is so much I would love to shout at him, the arrogant 'so and so', in his own native language, which sounds much more angry and passionate than English right now.

'Please wait on me,' he pleads.

I walk on defiantly and then I change my mind and stop. Just because he is rude doesn't mean I have to be too.

'Thank you, please,' he says as he comes closer.

It is getting dark now and I realise that I am standing by a river in a place I have only arrived in, with a man I just met in a supermarket and I have no idea if I am safe or not. If Flo saw me now she would be worried sick.

'I hope I wasn't nasty to you back there,' he says and a new kindness in his voice puts me at ease, erasing the bite of his words in the supermarket. 'I think it came out all wrong. I haven't spoken English so fluently in a while and perhaps my words and tone were more aggressive than I intended. Please accept my apology.'

He looks at me with puppy-dog eyes beneath his floppy, dark fringe, which really could do with a trim.

'I fully understand you are a very busy man, but it did seem a bit rude. Apology accepted,' I tell him and I start to walk towards the *gîte* again as he follows me.

'I really didn't mean it. It's just I am so busy and my work is unfinished.'

'Yes, your brother mentioned you live near here but that you are a very private person,' I tell him. 'I understand. It may have been cheeky of me to ask when we had only just met.'

'No, no, you were not cheeky,' he says so earnestly. 'I think it is nice that you are interested. And yes, I live just a bit further up the river, in a studio with a bed and a small kitchen. I live in my workspace. I live and breathe my art at the moment. Pretty sad, perhaps.'

I shrug.

'Not really. Each to their own. I have met artistic types like you before. I get it totally.'

He looks defensive and rubs his beard.

'I am truly not a boring or a nasty person, Maggie,' he says. 'Nor am I always this, how you say, scruffy? I am just so, so busy right now. Time is ticking on me. I feel the pressure. It makes me mad.'

I look down onto my place, or his place, or whoever's place and then back at him to see a sadness in his eyes, a loneliness and I am tempted to invite him onto the deck for a beer and some wine and a chat about art, but then I don't because if he said no, I would dread ever bumping into him again, as unlikely as that may be.

He lingers, as if he wants to say something too, but then he doesn't, so it's up to me to end the conversation.

'Well, it's nice to put a face to the name and I look forward to seeing some of your work around town,' I tell him, realising that I am speaking very fast but he seems to be able to keep up. 'I am fascinated by art of all sorts. Really fascinated.'

'You are? Really?'

'Yes, very much so. I studied it many years ago,' I say proudly. 'Back in Ireland.'

'Ahaa, so you are *artiste* also?'

'No, no, I wish I was.' I shake my head. 'No, I am not an *artiste*. In my dreams I am many things, but in reality I work in real estate. I can be pretty boring too. And sometimes selfish and grumpy. We are all only human.'

Gerard looks out towards the bridge and changes the subject entirely.

'You are here to see the bridge, my brother tells me? It is quite spectacular, yes?'

'It sure is,' I reply and we both stand and stare for what seems like minutes. 'Anyhow, I'd better let you get back to work. I need to get some sleep so I can be a proper tourist tomorrow and not sleep my time away here in Millau. Seeing the bridge and reading some trashy novels are about all I have planned so far. I need to try and plan some more.'

He looks a little disappointed and I sense he doesn't talk to a lot of people very often, or not lately, anyhow.

'Perhaps... yes, I better get back to work then also. Work, and a few beers and snacks is what I have planned. As well as being boring and trying not to be grumpy. *Bon nuit,* Maggie.'

'*Bon nuit,* Gerard.'

He leaves and I wave back at him as I make my way into the cottage with a smile.

'Oh, and happy painting!' I shout at him as he walks along the pathway.

'Ha! Happy painting,' he repeats and laughs as he waves back.

I wasn't meaning that to be so funny...

I go inside the cottage and close the door, and then I bolt the lock and pull all of the curtains. Gerard seems like a deep, gentle soul behind his initial tone, but as friendly and vulnerable and pleasantly charming as he seems to be, I cannot afford to be complacent on my first night here.

I put a match to the fire, put on my pyjamas and find my new novel. Then I pour myself a glass of wine and relax under lamplight and the blaze of the fire. This is cosy. This is peaceful. This is just what the doctor ordered.

I spend the next few days in blissful solitude, not moving too far from the *gîte* apart from taking my car down and parking it outside, going to pick up some groceries when I need them and I've stocked up on another two particularly 'so bad they are good' novels, which I read in the sunshine in the blissful haven of the patio with its spectacular views.

I eat baguettes with cold meats and salad, warm crepes with *chocolat*, fresh fruit from a little market stall I have discovered accidentally, sparkling water and, of course, the odd obligatory *vino*.

I am at ease. I am totally at ease and it is pure heaven.

Flo sends me the odd text but says she doesn't want to distract me from my time out, as does Kevin, who I totally forgot to tell I was leaving and who was afraid I had been kidnapped or locked myself in the apartment for good.

'I hope you are training!' he messages and then follows up with another to say that I have officially his permission to take it easy until I get back, but to be prepared as then he is going to kick my butt into shape for our run.

I enjoy the silence and when the silence gets a little lonely, I listen to classical music on a radio in the little kitchen or watch the rowers glide up and down the River Tarn or the hang-gliders sail across the sky. I look out onto the bridge and see the chains of traffic whirr across – it is by no means just an ornamental masterpiece but a very practical and busy four-lane motorway up there and as yet I have no desire to venture onto it, but I will do it before I go, just for Lucy.

As the days drift by, I allow myself to wallow in self-pity over Jeff, when the notion surfaces, and there have been times when I have sporadically burst out crying when I think of him with Saffron that day in Tesco, his hand resting on her hip. On her fertile, child-bearing hips...

Then at other times I deliberately give my mind a reality check, where I remember other elements of life with Jeff and how, for example, I could have never experienced this current feeling of empowerment and independence and dare I say, contentment, when I was with him.

He would be climbing the walls by now, demanding we draw up an itinerary, rating restaurants and taxis and any service providers for his obsessive reviews on TripAdvisor and complaining about the price of everything.

He would be looking for dust on the mantelpiece, complaining about the weather, which would be either too hot or too cold and looking up reasons as to why the cottage might get a bit chilly at night. I can just hear him...

'It must be damp, Maggie. I will have a word with that Gerard guy. He should really clean up his act a bit instead of hibernating with his art and go get a real job. Artist, my ass!'

Despite the very odd minor slip, my rose-tinted glasses are totally off when I look back on our relationship and I can now acknowledge some of the finer detail that I perhaps ignored at the time. I am finally moving forward in my new life without Jeff. I am doing it. It is real, and I am dealing with it. Go me.

The doorbell of the cottage rings for the first time in three days and its loud shrill goes right to my core, taking me out of my list-making exercise, which I realise I have spent over an hour on. I haven't heard from Starling or Anton since my arrival, so perhaps this is a routine mid-week check to see if all is okay at *Maison d'Henri*. They are either very relaxed or else very busy, as I really thought I might have heard from Starling by now since she was so friendly when we first met.

I scrunch up the shreds of paper and throw them in the bin, check my hair in the mirror which is more birds' nest than 'bohemian chic'. Oh dear. I push back the loose strands and go to the door, but there is no one there.

'Hello?' I call out into the balmy afternoon. 'Hello?'

I look up and down the riverbank, but there is no sign of anyone I know and then I see a package propped alongside the pot of the ash tree that sits by the front door.

Mademoiselle Maggie is written in chunky black marker on a rather large box wrapped in brown paper and tied with string. I am totally intrigued.

I go back inside, set the box on the dining table and untie the string, and then I carefully tear back the brown paper and lift the lid off the box to find a set of oil paints, a palette knife and three blank canvasses. There is a small white envelope stuck to the side of the box which I open and read.

Just in case you get bored reading your trashy novels, I thought you might like this. There is an easel behind the bathroom door. Happy painting. Your fellow artist, G.

Well, that has floored me.

Gerard left me all of this? I am so moved and touched, not to mention thoroughly delighted to have some paintings to work on in this idyllic landscape. *Happy painting.* So he does have a sense of humour after all. I am flummoxed at his generosity and I go back outside and up onto the walkway to see if I can catch up with him to say thank you, but there is no sign.

I go back inside and carry the box through the cottage and then further through the bedroom onto the patio and I prop up a canvas on one of the chairs while I go and fetch the easel. Sure enough, there it is and I wonder how I have never noticed it before.

It is two in the afternoon and I am feeling sleepy but I can't resist the urge to get stuck in and paint the beauty that lies before me. I decide to have some coffee to perk me up and soon I am perched in my own little outdoor studio, a palette knife in my hand and a new wind in my sails.

This truly is the life. I could get very, very used to this.

Chapter 26

Later in the evening, I am slightly tipsy and I truly believe, in my little haze, that I have created an artistic masterpiece on my first canvas painting, courtesy of Gerard. I have used almost a rainbow of colour – greens, blues, purples, yellows and pinks – to depict the rolling valleys that cushion the Tarn River and I am totally delighted with myself.

So delighted in fact, that I think I deserve some chocolate to celebrate, so I go inside and check my stash in the kitchen, but one chunk from the last bar in the cupboard is not going to satisfy my craving.

I check the time and to my surprise it is only 9.30pm, so I still have time to pop to the *supermarché* for more supplies. Excellent.

I pull on a cardigan over my shorts and vest and grab my purse and keys, then make my way up the bank and into the town, feeling quite the local now that I have been here almost four days and know my way around so well.

I have only three days left and it saddens me greatly to even think of leaving the Tarn Valley. I could stay longer, that I know, but my brother is making plans to come home to

Loch Tara and I want to be back and settled into my own real life before then.

I enjoy the cool breeze of the air conditioning in the store and go straight to the confectionary, knowing if I browse at all I will end up buying more food that I don't really need.

'You just missed your friend,' says the cashier and I recognise her as the same girl who served me on the night I met Gerard in here. It seems like an eternity ago.

'Ah, Monsieur Gerard?' I ask her. 'He's a kind man. He gave me some paints to make use of my time here.'

'*Oui*,' she nods. 'I think he likes you. I think he likes you a lot. There was chemistry.'

'Chemistry?' I can't help but laugh. All I can remember is his rudeness and how I walked away so hurt, but he was quite friendly until I mentioned seeing his work. Then our second conversation when he caught up with me, well, that was sweet, not to mention the box of art materials he left for me on the doorstep. But chemistry? Nah!

'I am renting one his properties,' I tell Cilla Black, the matchmaker behind the counter. 'I think it was just conversation.'

'I don't,' she tells me emphatically. 'A lot of girls would wish to be you. He doesn't talk much to anyone. He is a very beautiful creature, inside and out. So creative and talented and so, so handsome.'

Her eyes widen and she swoons as she speaks, then swallows when she finishes and I am entranced by her observations.

'Well... well, that's interesting,' is about all I can muster and I open the chocolate bar and put a chunk into my mouth right there in front of her. '*Au revoir, et merci.*'

'*Au revoir!*' says the cashier, which I take as my cue to leave and I wander out onto the streets, contemplating whether to go back to the cottage, as I always do, or to check out Starling's favourite piano bar, *Le Bouchon,* to see if it's as good as he made it out to be.

I am hardly dressed for socialising and, come to think of it, I don't have a lot of clothes with me to do such a thing, so I decide to go back to my corner and admire my painting, then have an early night. Perhaps I will take the car up to the bridge tomorrow and do what it is I first meant to do when I came here.

I step down the stones to the cottage a little more cautiously than normal, feeling ever- so-slightly wobbly and giggly and I inwardly congratulate myself for finding this little state of happiness all by myself. I am not depending on anyone while I am here. No Jeff to please, no Mum and Dad to depend on, no cocoon of work for routine, no Kevin to keep an eye on things, no Flo to call on when I tremble, just me. Just me, myself and I, and aren't I doing so well?

'Just me,' I say aloud and smile to myself, bobbing along down the steps until I reach the bottom.

'It's a sign of insanity when you talk to yourself, you do know that, Mademoiselle Maggie.'

Oh, well! If it isn't Mr Artiste Extraordinaire himself standing on the pathway with his bags of groceries! The one I probably wouldn't see again as he was so busy! *Quelle surprise…*

'Hello, I mean, *bonjour Monsieur Gerard*. Thank you for the paints. I was pretty blown away by that, I have to admit. Really, really blown away. You are much kinder than you pretend to be.'

He kicks the stones and shrugs with a smile.

'I thought it might keep you, what can I say, entertained.'

'It did. It is still keeping me very entertained. How's your work going? Are you nearly done?'

He shakes his head.

'Alas, no I am not yet. I wish I was,' he says. 'But the good news is that they have given me an extension, so I can breathe a little bit easier now. And take it easier. Take some proper breaks instead of staying up all day and night.'

He takes a big deep breath in and then out again, just to make sure I know what he means.

'Well, that's good news. So, are you painting tonight or are you on a break?' I ask him. It sounds suggestive and I don't mean it to be. Shit.

'Actually, no, I am not painting tonight,' he tells me. 'I am finished for the evening and I was just stopping by on my way back from the store to see if you fancied a walk.'

What?

'Me?'

'Yes, Mademoiselle... you. I still feel so bad about our first encounter, so I thought I'd try and show you the real me. Perhaps you don't care to see that, though.'

The cashier is right. He is *very* handsome, but I am *very* not interested.

'I am here for a very specific reason,' I try to explain to him.

'You don't have to make an effort with me. You really don't.'

'You are here to see the bridge?'

'Yes.'

'But not for you, it's to see it for a friend?'

'*Oui.*'

Word sure travels fast around here!

'That's very intriguing,' he says and he licks his top lip. I shouldn't notice that, but I do. 'So, can I show you the bridge from where I like to see it?'

'You mean not from the top? I kind of have to see it from the top.'

'My way is nicer.'

'My way is more important.'

'To your friend, right?'

'Yes, to my friend.'

'So, can I show this much nicer way to you, for you?' he asks and I don't know how I am supposed to refuse. I think of what John Joe told me to do. He said to do some things for myself as well as for Lucy.

'Okay, let's go, then,' I tell him and we walk towards the direction of the bridge, which is still about a mile away. We both barely speak until we come to a wooden building with a little walkway that leads out onto the river.

'Your studio?' I ask and he nods.

'My home,' he says. 'Have a seat here and I will be right back. Please don't go anywhere. I will be back in a second.'

He guides me to a chair that sits outside the studio and, just as he promised, he is back within seconds, having left his own bags indoors.

'Come,' he says, reaching for my hand and he pulls me up from the chair. I stumble and bump into his chest, much to my utter embarrassment, and we begin to walk again, this time a little bit more relaxed than before.

'Where did you learn such good English?' I ask him as we walk along the wooden walkway across the water in the dusky air. 'You Europeans really do put us Irish to shame when it comes to learning languages.'

He seems chuffed at the compliment.

'I went to a boarding school in South London,' says Gerard. 'A very posh boys' school and then university outside of the city which taught me a lot about art, education and, of course, a whole lot about life.'

He is very serious and I am very intrigued. A posh boys school in South London? And a London university... and a lot about life too... I don't doubt it for a second. I wish he would shave off his beard so I could get a proper look at him. I'm all for beards and freedom of expression and the *au natural* look, for sure, but his is kind of hiding his face a bit too much. I bet he has a lovely face underneath his beard.

'I went to a convent school in Ireland,' I tell him. 'But you probably could have guessed that already. You can sometimes see my halo in the moonlight.'

He laughs and stops for a look.

'Yes, I knew that for sure. And there is the halo shining bright. An angel in disguise.'

He tilts my chin back and holds my gaze and I feel a surge of electricity, or is it lust, run through me. He is a very handsome man and I cannot deny that his kindness has made him very attractive, but I must be careful not to get carried away just because he touches me on my chin.

Yes, I really must keep it cool. Gerard is just a friendly soul who fancied some company for the evening with someone who enjoys art as much as he does. It's very simple. Not to be misread under any circumstances.

I look up at him when he takes his hand from my face and then I close my eyes and inhale his closeness. He doesn't smell of tobacco or methylated spirits tonight. He is fresh and clean in his jeans and pale-blue shirt and his floppy dark hair and even his beard looks soft and very touchable. Very soft and welcoming and...

'So, this is how I like to see the bridge,' he says in a low voice and bringing me back to the present. 'Take my hand.'

I put my hand into his and he leads me to the edge of the walkway to a raft-type jetty, which is tied to two posts and which bobs along in the river. He steps onto it, still holding my hand and expertly balances himself, then leads me on beside him. I am petrified inside, yet feel very safe as he doesn't take his eyes off me for a second.

Beside the raft is a rowing boat, a pretty little old-fashioned blue rowing boat with two oars, and he steps onto it next.

'Can you swim?' he asks me.

'Of course I can,' I tell him. 'I grew up beside a lake. Are we going for a swim? Now?'

'No, no I'm joking,' he says. 'Here, sit down in the boat and keep warm.'

He reaches for a blanket beneath one of the little bench seats in the boat and puts it around my shoulders and I clasp it with my hand at my chest. Then he climbs over and sits across from me, his feet touching mine.

'I've never been on a rowing boat like this before. Not at night, anyhow.'

'It's the best way to see the Millau Viaduct, believe me, I know,' Gerard tells me as he rows us away from the jetty and out onto the black of the river. 'I have a feeling you have not got close to it yet.'

'I haven't, but I look at it from a distance every day.'

I think of Lucy. I want to tell him all about her, but I don't. How she would have loved this place never leaves my mind and I think of her every time I look across at it, but this... this is nothing I expected at all.

We start to move along the water.

'I'm here for very sentimental reasons, so forgive me if I get emotional,' I tell him.

He raises an eyebrow as he rows the boat with ease.

'Does it remind you of someone in happier times?' he asks.

'No... it's deeper than that,' I say, looking up at the bridge. 'It really is spectacular. Have you ever painted it?

'No, I have not painted the bridge, much to everyone's surprise,' he says emphatically. 'Many other artists have, though. I prefer to paint the stories behind the bridge. The little things that visitors, or those who cross it, do not see.'

He is a man who knows what he likes, that's for sure.

'I have painted some of the people who live and work by the river, but you are not allowed to see it, before you ask,' he says with a smile. 'I have not finished it.'

We both laugh at the acknowledgement of our first conversation.

'I understand totally. No pressure at all,' I reply. 'What is your exhibition about? Or is that top secret too?'

'I cannot tell you,' he says and then he laughs. 'I am joking. I had a lot of themes running through my head, but then I settled on one I have wanted to explore for many years now. It is a simple theme that reflects everyday life here on the river and in this valley I call home. The theme is *Les Personnes*.'

'*Les Personnes*... doesn't that just mean people?' I ask, afraid of digging too deeply into his privacy.

'Yes, people. You know, human beings.'

He laughs again.

'Okay... well that's a pretty wide subject,' I say. 'What type of people?'

He seems to be enjoying the conversation now, so I allow myself to explore it with him a bit further.

'All sorts of people, of whom I have way too many to choose from,' he explains.' People who mean something to me in all sorts of ways. Heroes, villains, family, friends, lovers...'

His arms move rhythmically, back and forward, back and forward and I can see now where he gets his toned physique from. He must exercise like this... a lot.

'You are a great rower,' I say, stating the obvious and making me sound like an idiot. A great rower! Why on earth did I say that?

'I have had plenty of practice. I used to compete when at university in England,' Gerard explains and the penny drops with me.

'Oxford?' I ask him, imagining him in his younger days in his shorts and vest and big muscly thighs and...

'Ten out of ten,' he says with a smile. 'I have very fond memories of competitive rowing and I like to de-stress from the art world by getting out on the water and just forgetting the world.'

I can see exactly what he means. The water is serene and we glide across it, watching the lights of Millau on one side and the distant town of Peyre on the other, with the almighty Viaduct on our path. *Oh, Lucy Harte, if you could only see this now.*

'So, did you study art at Oxford?' I enquire, not knowing if you can even study art at Oxford. I always imagined it as home of upper-class business and law and economics, and the like, but then it's not something I have ever checked out.

'I wanted to,' says Gerard. 'I wanted to study fine art but my father would not hear of it. He pushed me into a business degree, which I completed much against my will and then I tried several ventures in London before life took me back here. Instead of joining Anton in the family business, I began selling my art, much to everyone's surprise – and the rest is history.'

He smiles with great pride at how he has proven his family wrong and used his creative talent to earn his living.

He looks directly into my eyes and I can feel the energy rise between us. The mood is slowing down, the atmosphere is calming and his leg is touching my inner leg and it feels so, so nice that I don't want to move.

He holds my gaze with such intensity as he builds up to

a steady speed and the bridge is coming closer and closer, its majestic lights glittering in the night sky.

'You can lie back now, Maggie,' he instructs me. 'Lie back and relax, but don't close your eyes. I don't want you to miss a thing tonight.'

His voice is soothing and seductive and I do exactly what he says. If he said to jump in the water, I probably would at this stage, I am so under his spell, so I lean back, balancing myself by holding on to the side of the boat and I look up at the multi-coloured sky above.

'Lean back further and let go of the boat,' says Gerard softly. 'There is a cushion behind you. Please trust me. You will enjoy this.'

I lie back and feel the soft cushion meet the back of my head, then I let go of the sides of the boat. I see now what he means. It feels like I am floating. I am truly floating on air.

'This is amazing,' I whisper, up into the night sky. 'So, so beautiful.'

I think of Lucy, up there somewhere, looking down on all of this and taking it all in. I want to call out her name, to make sure she is with me, but, most of all, I don't want to miss a thing.

'We will be going under the bridge really soon,' Gerard whispers. 'Take it all in, Maggie. Focus, relax and breathe. Breathe in the night sky. Breathe in the moon and the stars. Breathe in the river. Are you ready?'

We soar beneath the sky, skimming across the black water at quite a speed, looking up into the navy skies and the stars and moon that twinkles above us, sailing between valleys that loom over us and close in like imposing shadows in the darkness.

'I'm ready, Gerard.' I really feel like I am flying or floating on air.

'Enjoy it, Maggie. Relax and enjoy.'

I take a long, deep breath in and then a long breath out and I feel ripples of tension leave my body as I tingle from head to toe. I feel every hair on my head rise, light prickles on my skin and a warm rush running through my veins, gushing in waves through my entire body.

Holy God in heavens, Lucy Harte, you should actually look away if you are watching from above because I swear this man is doing things to me inside and he hasn't even laid a finger on me. Forget what I said earlier. Look away. I don't know what is going on right now but it's not for your eyes, not this time.

I feel the breeze of air on my face and through my hair and listen to Gerard's heavy-breath panting as he rows faster and faster and faster and faster and then wow!

There it is above me! The most magnificent sight I have ever seen. The lights are a dazzling mix of pinks and blues and yellows and they colour the water as we ripple through, so tiny in comparison to this Goliath-style structure that dominates the sky above.

'Woo hoo!' I shout at the top of my lungs. 'We're under the bridge! Lucy Harte, you can look again! This is your bridge! Woooooooo!'

We slide underneath its dizzy height, which is taller than the Eiffel Tower, and I shout and scream and laugh and laugh and Gerard puts the oar across the boat and leans forward to me before taking both my hands and pulling me up towards him.

I sit up and my head spins slightly.

'That was...' I cannot find the words. 'That was just... oh my God, that was amazing!'

My face is pink and I am so breathless and totally exhilarated and just when I think I have felt it all he hooks his arm around my waist and pulls me right up against him, with the oar lying across his lap.

He lifts my legs in a swift move and wraps them around his waist, under the oar and I think I am going to explode, but all I can do is nod at him in approval. His body is warm and he moves me closer, then just when I can take no more he puts his mouth on mine and kisses me hard and firm and I swear I am so dizzy I think I am going to faint.

He kisses me deeply. He kisses me so tenderly as the boat sails down the river all by itself, slowing down, but he doesn't slow down at all. I am totally gasping for air when he eventually does and it feels so, so good.

'I have wanted to do that for a few days now,' he says in his glorious accent and I try to focus on catching my breath. This is so intense, so magical and so, so perfect.

'I'm glad you did,' I tell him, utterly breathless, and he lifts the oar again. I move back to my seat and he steers the boat around until we are drifting back towards his art studio, the place he calls home, silent in mutual exhilaration.

Chapter 27

Gerard walks me to the door of the *gîte* and neither of us mentions what just happened on the boat. For some reason, there are no words, no explanation. To discuss it and analyse it would take away from it and our smiles and inner glow says it all.

It was an experience that took me to a much higher level than if we had rolled around naked on a bed and did what most other consenting adults might do in such a situation.

I am so energised, so full up within my soul and truly satisfied with what was a perfect evening with him.

'How many days do you have left with us here in Millau?' he asks me as we stand under the ash tree at the *gîte*.

I have the key in the door but I don't want to end this yet. Should I ask him in or should I leave us both wanting more, as we so evidently do?

'Three days,' I tell him. 'Two nights, but three days.'

He nods but says nothing. Instead, he does that thing again where he softly tilts back my chin and looks into my eyes.

'You are exceptionally beautiful and your halo is still shining,' he whispers and then he kisses me, wet and hard and then softly until our lips part. 'Don't ever stop shining, Maggie. See the world. You are too pretty and smart to be hidden away. You deserve to shine.'

I want him to stay. I want him to stay so badly and lie with me in the cosy cottage, where we can talk more and explore more, but he has to... he has to work. Damn. I have to let him go.

'Thank you for an amazing time,' I say and I hug him tightly. His body is so firm and strong and safe. I want him so much, but I have to let him go. 'Good night, Gerard. Thank you.'

'And thank you, Maggie. Enjoy the rest of your stay.'

I lie in bed beneath the patchwork quilt, naked and reliving the magical evening I have just spent with the most intriguing, charismatic and sexual man I have ever come across. There is no need for extra heating tonight in the cottage because I am burning up inside still as I remember every move, every way he made me feel and every word he said.

I can't sleep.

I wrap the patchwork quilt around me and go outside to the patio, where my easel and painting and my empty glass of wine sits from before. It is going to break my heart to leave this place. I didn't ever believe that an actual place could get inside someone as much as this part of France has done to me. I don't want to go back to my goldfish bowl and look out at people like Flo with Damian and their rekindled love, or the gossips at work in a job that I am not even sure I like any more, or dinners for one in my city apartment.

I sit outside with my thoughts and I look into the midnight sky and the stars that sparkle down on me.

The bridge stands tall in the far distance, keeping me company into the late evening and I bring my knees up to my chest and hug them with my eyes now closed, taking in the wonder of where Lucy has brought me to. I do this until my eyes get heavy and then I stumble through the French doors and fall onto the bed into a blissful sleep.

I step out onto the patio again the following morning with a coffee and a warm croissant to the sound of birdsong and the now-familiar chatter of people in the distance on the river. It is a heavenly way to wake up and begin your day and the warmth of the sun envelopes me and I sit down to absorb it all, where I have come from and what has brought me here.

Lucy has made me unrecognisable. I am totally brand new. I know I am still me but I am a shiny new version and I feel cleansed inside, almost repaired and I am so, so grateful. I don't think I have ever felt so content or enriched in all my life and it is exhilarating.

I want to hold on to this positivity, this inner glow and build on the heightened pleasures I am now taking time to experience. Things that passed me by before now make me appreciate every single moment of the life Lucy gave me – the taste of a warm croissant with home-made blueberry jam; the sound of birds as they circle above me every morning; the warmth of a hug from my brother or, indeed, a welcoming stranger like Gerard; the glow and passion of a kiss that came from nowhere but which ignited me from my very toes and filled my soul, leaving me wanting more.

I would love to see him again, I really would, but I will not force anything on this final part of my journey with Lucy's list. I will stay cool and calm and let things unfold just as they were meant to be.

I don't have to wait for long before I do see him again.

I am running along the river bank, in the opposite direction from where Gerard brought me last night when I see him in the distance, standing at his easel painting a fisherman at work in front of him. I slow down my pace, wipe the sweat off my brow and lean my hands on my knees to get my breath back and compose myself before he notices me.

I don't want him to notice me – not yet anyhow. I want to do what he has deprived me of since I first met him a few days ago. I want to watch him work.

So I stand there, taking it all in, in awe of his poise, of his stature, of how the muscles in his back move as he tilts and sways with the brush in his hand, totally engrossed in his subject and totally unaware that I am anywhere near him. He looks a lot more contented than he did that first time at the supermarket, but then again, he is no longer so stressed and is doing what he loves to do.

His eyes skirt around him and I freeze, fearful now that he may think I am snooping on him, but it's too late. He has seen me. He waves. I wave back. He smiles. I smile back. I turn to walk away but he calls me and then walks towards me.

'You found me,' he says with a cheeky grin. 'I just can't hide from you, Maggie, no matter where I go.'

Huh! What? I was not looking for him!

'Find a better hiding place, then!' I respond, feeling a rush of adrenaline as he makes his way towards me. 'I would never have dreamed you would be up here. Never in a million years.'

I am protesting, but he laughs in response.

'I am joking with you,' he says, 'I am finishing a portrait of Pierre, one of our oldest residents here in Millau and he really is not happy with me watching him as he fishes out on his boat. I know exactly why. Perhaps I am a hypocrite.'

His eyes crinkle in the sun as he speaks to me and his paint-splattered arms and t-shirt look very welcoming indeed.

'I'll go back in the other direction, then, so as I don't run past your work – in case I see your unfinished business,' I tell him. 'Sorry if I broke your flow of concentration.'

'Perhaps you and I have unfinished business also, Maggie?' he suggests and my stomach does a leap. 'We can't keep bumping into each other like this for no reason. Perhaps it is fate?'

At the suggestion of fate, I can't help but imagine Lucy, up there in the heavens, orchestrating her magic and leading me into his path at every turnaround, but I don't need to let him know that.

'It can't all be fate,' I tell him, not wanting to totally fall for his charms. 'You made a deliberate effort by taking me to the bridge and by leaving me some paints, so perhaps the unfinished business is all entirely planned on your behalf?'

He looks away, then back to me and shrugs. We both can't help but smile.

'I won't say it hasn't crossed my mind,' he says. 'I have thought of you a lot, Maggie. You are distracting me from my work, but I like it. You break my concentration more than you will ever know.'

I roll my eyes and laugh in response.

'Oh, Gerard, you do know how to flatter me,' I tell him. 'Well, it's about time you got back to your work and I'll leave you to it. Happy painting.'

He grabs my hand.

'Please don't run,' he says. 'Please don't run away.'

I feel a tingle shoot up my arm as he holds my hand and pulls me in a step closer to him.

'But I am distracting you,' I whisper.

My God, I am flirting so much but I can't help it.

'Don't ever stop distracting me. I don't want you to,' he says. 'Can I take you to dinner? Tonight?'

I look away shyly. My heart is racing and I am hot and sweaty and pink from my run and he is asking me out for dinner. How the hell could I possibly refuse?

'Pick me up at eight,' I tell him. 'We'll know then if we have unfinished business or if I'm just nothing more than an idle distraction.'

'I look forward to it,' he says and when he lets go of me, I think I might fall at his feet.

I watch him walk away and then, as his back is turned, I quickly change direction and run again back to the *gîte*, where I find myself at a loose end and full of va va voom.

I have a date, Lucy! An actual, proper date with a hunky French man!

I also have a whole day to kill before that and I also have nothing to wear, so with a deep breath I get into the car and decide to do what Lucy wanted me to.

I need to see the view from the top of the bridge and see how it feels to be on top of the world, because, right now, I am feeling as high as I ever did in my whole entire life.

I am excited about tonight with Gerard more than I could have expected. He is unlike anyone I have ever met before. He is deep and moody and exceptionally talented and he has a charm that is making me like him as if I am in some sort of out of control-free fall. I need to use up some of my new-found energy and finally biting the bullet and driving across the bridge is a perfect way to do so.

I grab Lucy's diary on my way out of the house and I set it on my knee as I pull the car out of the driveway, into the town and onto the main road that leads to the tallest bridge in the world.

The drive to the bridge is much shorter than I expected and when I get up there, driving through four lanes of manic traffic as though I am sailing through the French countryside at more than 1,000 feet above ground level, I look down onto the valleys and rivers below and I let the tears flow and flow and flow until I reach the viewing point that allows me to park up and see it in all its glory.

I step out of the car and feel a gush of wind through my hair and I close my eyes and inhale the feeling of being higher than the clouds.

This is more than breath-taking. This is more than magnificent. It is more than words could ever describe.

We are here, Lucy! Please look with me, Lucy! It's like a movie, Lucy Harte. It's like I'm flying. It's like all my cares and troubles are left behind, just like you used to feel on your little stone bridge in Scotland. I hope that it's all you had hoped it would be, but I think it is even more than that! We are on top of the world now, Lucy, I tell her as I stand tall over the rolling hills and valleys against a crystal-clear blue sky with the wind in my face and the sun on my shoulders.

You and I are finally here. I can never thank you enough for this moment, for all the wonderful opportunities that I can still experience. I know you are here – I know you can see what I see and feel what I feel because you are part of me and you always will be. You have made the heart we share beat again, only this time it beats faster and it is fuller than I could ever imagined. I am smiling again, Lucy, and it's all because of you. We did it! We found it! Take it all in and enjoy every moment, Lucy Harte! We are on top of the world!'

I take a teary-eyed selfie with the view behind me, which I plan to print off and put in Lucy's diary as a memory and I send the pic to Flo, Simon and one to Sylvia from Power's Enterprises, which may be a bit too familiar but I have a feeling she may appreciate it. She replies in an instant with a message that reminds me just how important this trip has been for me.

'You are glowing,' she says. 'Keep going, girl! Keep spreading your wings!'

I have a spring in my step and a new energy that makes

me want to keep experiencing more and more for Lucy, so I get into the car and I drive and drive away from the Tarn Valley to see what lies on the other side. Lucy always thought of how bridges could take you from one place to another, so I owe it to her to explore more and I soon find myself in the direction of the city of Toulouse, which is just over two hours away.

La Ville Rose, as it is known, due to its dusky-pink buildings, is simply beautiful and I am delighted to browse in the shops, where I pick up an off-white lace-and-linen strappy dress and a pair of cute wedged sandals to match it for my dinner date tonight.

As I eat a light prawn salad washed down with sparkling lemon water, I think of Gerard and the way he lit a fire inside of me. A fire that I feared had been dampened, smouldered and then extinguished by Jeff's rejection and public humiliation. I feel awakened again on a deeper level than the instant gratification I felt that night with Tiernan Quinn, so I know it is not just sexual – hell, the man barely touched me, but I feel like he has opened up my mind and has led me closer to discovering where I want to go next in this life.

I treat myself to a pink ice-cream with fresh strawberries and sit on the bonnet of the car watching the colourful, vibrant southern city life and drinking it all in like the fascinated tourist that I am before making my way back to the Tarn Valley, where I will get ready for my dinner date with the very intriguing Gerard Florvel.

Life, Lucy Harte, is very, very fine indeed.

Chapter 28

Ispray on some perfume and inhale its light floral scent deep into my lungs as I wait for Gerard to come for me. I slip in some dainty earrings and put on my new shoes, rather pleased with how my shorter hairstyle sits on my shoulders against the light tan I have managed to pick up here in France.

Gerard doesn't disappoint and arrives just a few minutes before eight and when I answer the door, he is barely recognisable but even more beautiful than before.

'You look like a young Elizabeth Taylor,' he says in admiration before I can even say hello.

'You sound like my father,' I reply, and he looks at me puzzled. 'It's a joke. My father always compares me to her, but not necessarily for my looks.'

He steps into the *gîte* and I notice him looking around at how I have made it my home for the past few days.

'You look very handsome without your beard,' I tell him, and he nods his head in agreement.

'It's a better look, I do admit,' he says, stroking his naked chin. 'I normally don't shave until I finish my exhibition, but since I keep on being interrupted by this beautiful Irish girl, I made an exception this time.'

'Interrupted?' I laugh. 'You –'

'I know, I know,' he says. '*I* am very much chasing *you*. You smell very nice too. Are you hungry?'

'I am very hungry,' I reply, feeling the innuendo linger in the air. 'We should probably go and eat?'

'Yes, yes,' he says in agreement but the electricity between us is mighty. 'I have a very special place to take you to. I think you might like it. Do you have swimwear?'

'Swimwear for dinner?' I am truly puzzled now.

'No, not for dinner. But for after,' he says with a smile. 'Trust me.'

Well, this is a first... I quickly pack a bag and soon we are in his car and he is driving with the windows down and music turned up and I feel like I am not in the real world right now. I do feel like Elizabeth Taylor and for the first time in years I am actually experiencing life and it has awakened me and brought me to a place where I finally belong.

I lean my head back and listen to the beat of the music as the warm evening French sunshine warms my face and fills my soul.

'Are you okay, Maggie?' he asks me. 'You are smiling. Are you happy?'

I raise an eyebrow and look towards him.

'I am very happy, thank you, Gerard.'

What feels like only minutes later, we arrive at our destination and my jaw drops as we go in through the gates of an ivy-clad twelfth-century castle hotel, which the sign tells me is called *Château de Creissels*. I gasp at its grandeur and Gerard laughs.

'*C'est bien, oui?*'

I can only nod in response, but when we go inside I am even more impressed than before. The medieval-style restaurant has stone walls with matching stone arches as ceilings and low lighting and is truly enigmatic, but the waiter leads us out onto a balcony which overlooks an outdoor heated swimming pool and an almighty view of the Millau Viaduct bridge in the distance.

The waiter pulls out my chair and invites me to sit and I am too overwhelmed to speak.

'I thought you would like the view,' says Gerard as he takes his seat opposite me. 'For your friend.'

Wow. I feel my eyes well up at his effort and the thought he has put into our evening together.

'I'm... I'm pretty speechless right now,' I say to him. 'Lucy would love this. Oh my God, this is just perfect, Gerard. It's so, so perfect.'

'And now you know why I said to bring swimwear,' he laughs, referring to the pool in the grounds below. 'Hardly something we will do straight after dinner, but it is nice under moonlight later if you feel like hanging around. It's the most romantic location I could think of that has a view of the bridge for you.'

'This is the most romantic place I have ever been to in my whole life,' I tell him and he takes my hand across the table. 'I'm totally blown away. You are pretty amazing.'

'You deserve only the very best,' says Gerard. 'I am determined to show you the best before you leave me in two days, when I shall be weeping onto my canvas and nursing a very broken heart.'

I can't help but giggle at the idea of him doing so but at the same time, the thought of leaving here hits my stomach like a heavy weight.

'Let's not talk about that just yet,' I say to him. 'I don't want to think about leaving. I just want to savour every single moment of your company tonight.'

'And me yours, Mademoiselle,' he replies and he lightly kisses my fingertips, making my insides flutter. 'Now let's eat.'

'So, tell me more about you, Maggie,' says Gerard as we eat together comfortably later. The impeccable menu is almost impossible to choose from but with Gerard's help, I go for a mouth-watering duck dish with roast potatoes and salad and every bite is like an orchestra playing in my mouth.

'Well,' I reply, scooping up another forkful of food, 'I am here for a very special reason and you have made it even more special by bringing me here tonight.'

He looks intrigued.

'Go on,' he says.

'It's a long story and I really don't tell it very often,' I try to explain, 'but back when I was just a teenager, a little girl called Lucy Harte died and she gave me the gift of life, so my trip here is a way of trying to give her something back, strange as that may sound.'

I don't want to go into any big detail of organ transplants as we eat dinner but I know he wants to know more.

'I can explain in greater detail how she gave me life but will save it for after dinner,' I assure him and he nods in understanding, 'but recently I was given her diaries by her brother and one of her wishes in life was to find the tallest bridge in the world, so I thought I'd come here to see it – for her.'

Gerard hangs on my every word and he looks behind him onto the bridge that stands far away in the distance.

'That's a pretty powerful reason to be here, Maggie,' he says. 'Are you okay with it all? It must be a very emotional experience for you.'

'It is,' I reply, biting my lip. 'Every time I look at it I feel a flurry of emotions that range from happiness to sorrow to guilt to delight. The past few months have been the most challenging and rewarding times I have ever lived through as I worked through a series of things she wanted to do, or little pieces of advice she wanted to leave for herself in her later life.'

I see that Gerard is experiencing a range of emotions as he listens to my recent life with Lucy.

'I'd always hoped that someday I could portray my thanks to her family for keeping me alive and this is the only way I feel I can do so,' I try to explain. 'Her brother, Simon, has found my journey a great source of comfort, but I get the feeling that I am also gaining from it in many more ways than I ever thought possible.'

Gerard dabs his mouth with a napkin and takes a sip of his wine. I do the same. When I hear myself say aloud why I am here it reminds me of just how surreal this all really has been.

'So, when you showed me the bridge the other night, forgive me if I seemed like an emotional wreck,' I laugh, trying to lighten the mood. 'I drove across it today and I stopped and had a moment for Lucy, meaning my work here now is done.'

Gerard nods in understanding.

'And then what?' he asks. 'Where do you go from here?'

He looks a little bit hurt, like I am wasting his time by leading him on or something.

'I don't honestly know,' I tell him and it's the truth. 'I don't have any children back home, I don't have a job I love, I don't even have my dog any more... I just have an empty apartment that I just moved into but which feels like the coldest place on earth to me, so I don't know what happens next. I guess I will just have to wait and see.'

For the first time I am realising that I don't have an awful lot to go back to. There is nothing to pull me there. Yes, I have my brother's wedding at the farm to look forward to and I love my friends and my darling parents, but what is there for me? I honestly don't know.

'Stay,' he says. 'Stay here for as long as you want and think about what it is you want to do with your life.'

'Are you serious? I have no income here,' I remind him. 'I'm on a career break with a minimal salary that my boss granted me out of pity, but I can't take that forever. I would love to stay here, I really would, but I need to do the usual things like get a job and pay my way.'

He nods and looks away again towards the bridge.

'I don't think you will ever leave here, really,' he says and he looks me right in the eye. 'No one ever does. You'll see.'

'I know one thing,' I tell him. 'After all of my recent discoveries, thanks to Lucy and her list, I will never look at life in the same way again. I won't settle for anything that doesn't fulfil my purpose for being given a second chance at life. I won't think the world revolves around me either.'

Gerard seems to enjoy my confession of having been a little bit selfish.

'We can all be guilty of that sometimes,' he says. 'And you obviously had been through a lot at such a young age, so maybe you hung onto the attention.'

'I should have passed on my gratitude to others instead of always playing the victim,' I explain to Gerard. 'You know, in a pay-it-forward way? I think that might be my plan for the future, no matter where it takes me. To give a little more, you know. Does that make sense?'

'You have given me great joy and great... inspiration,' says Gerard and I laugh off the compliment.

'Well, that's a good start, then,' I tell him. 'To the future and to paying it forward.'

I raise my glass and he does the same.

'To the future!' he says. 'And I wish you only the very best, Maggie, whatever life brings you after this. Now, speaking of moving forward, do you have room for dessert?'

Fine food, delicious wine, the most picturesque of evenings under French moonlight and surroundings and the company of an amazing man... can this all be real?

I am dying to tell someone about all this – someone like Flo or my brother or even my own mother, but I don't want to leave Gerard's side, not even for a moment to do so. I want to savour every single part of this perfect evening as we sit under the night sky by the pool sipping cocktails and laughing at each other's jokes and touching ever so seductively when we are both gasping for more.

We have laughed and chatted and flirted for a couple of hours now but it feels like only minutes and I don't think I have ever felt so attracted to anyone without even trying.

'So do you fancy a dip in the pool?' he asks eventually and, I must admit, now that the food has settled, it does seem like a very romantic thing to do.

There is light background music, a few other couples and a group of single girls, who are in and out of the water as they enjoy cocktails – and with a merry glow through my veins from the few drinks I have been sipping I think the time is just about right.

'*Oui, Monsieur.* I'll just go and find the changing area,' I tell him and when I stand up, he takes my hand and looks up into my eyes.

'You are beautiful,' he says to me. 'I am sure you have heard that many times.'

'You are drunk,' I say back to him. 'How are we going to get back to Millau, by the way?'

'I assure you I am not drunk,' he says, standing up to meet me. 'I am over the limit, though, so we'll get a taxi. But the night is only beginning, I feel. Come on. Let's go and get changed and let me see how good you are at swimming, Miss O'Hara.'

I am certainly up for that challenge.

In the changing area, which is just off the hotel lobby, I slip into my favourite aqua-blue swimsuit, which always shows off my figure, though nowhere near perfect, to the best it can be. I have put on some weight during this trip and I am glad as I see it as a good sign of health – away from the dreaded 'divorce diet'.

I am just about to go when I notice for the first time in a long time my scar, which is now fully exposed on my chest. It is just a long slither down my breast bone, nothing revolting or scary, just something I always hide with high-cut tops or scarves to avoid questions from strangers who don't know my history. Besides that, I don't normally notice as it has become just a part of me that belongs there. But now it glares at me, lightened in colour against my tan, and I try to adjust the top of my swimming costume to hide it as much as I can, but of course it can't be done.

I put my hand to my chest and take a deep breath. It is not ugly, I remind myself. It is a mark of life, a mark of Lucy's gift to me and I will not be ashamed to show it. Without dwelling on it any further I go out to the pool area, where Gerard is waiting for me in the water.

He gets out and walks to me, his wet, strong body glistening under the moonlight and I can't help but give a shy smile at the sight of him in his shorts, which cling to him in all the right places. He is noticing me too and he shows his appreciation by taking my two hands and kissing me full on the mouth as we stand by the poolside. His kisses are electric. My head starts to spin.

'It's beautiful,' he whispers into my ear and then runs his

finger down the line of my faint scar and kisses me again, lightly this time. His eyes widen when he looks into mine.

'Come and swim with me.'

I step into the water and I glide my body into the warm water and make my way through the smooth ripples in a breast stroke with Gerard by my side.

We glance at each other every now and then and I feel the sexual energy vibrate through the water and into my very bones as we move in synchronised glory until we reach the other side. I push my damp hair off my eyes, realising for the first time that it will no doubt look a frizzy mess by the time we are going home, but with Gerard it doesn't feel like I should care about such things. He rubs his eyes and then kicks back and floats along the water in a backstroke, which I silently mirror, and as I look up into the stars, gliding along the surface of the water, I know that I will never feel so full up inside for as long as I live.

'Thank you for all of this,' I say, out of breath, when we reach the end of the swimming pool again. 'I don't want this to end, not yet.'

He puts his hand on the nape of my neck and kisses me on the forehead.

'Neither do I,' he says and within twenty minutes we are in a taxi on our way back towards the Viaduct and I feel like I am in heaven.

Chapter 29

The taxi drops us at Gerard's place and we walk side by side in silence down the riverbank to his studio home, where he leads me inside to find a tidy, white-walled workspace with a bed in the middle, a TV and a makeshift kitchen with a kettle, toaster and all the usual basics.

A radio plays softly in the background and I stare in wonder at the paintings that are hung so gracefully and with such pride around the walls. It is like a mini gallery, so perfectly thought out and not the messy hovel I had anticipated of someone mid-exhibition.

'I will leave you to it,' he says. 'I get embarrassed when I show my work, so if you don't mind, I'll disappear outside and hopefully when I come back you will have seen as much as you want to.'

I nod, still in awe at the arrangement of masterpieces, and he makes his way out a side door that leads onto a deck with a view of the river, similar to the decking patio at the *gîte*.

Les Personnes – the people who have touched his life are like ghosts around me and I cannot wait to take it all in.

The first painting is of his father, Benoit, and there is a

284

mixture of sadness and strength in the portrait, which has been created in oil on canvas. A brief description in Gerard's handwriting is pinned to the wall beside it but it is in French so I cannot translate.

I move on to the next one, which is of his younger self on a little blue tractor and the hope and joy in his innocent eyes makes me want to learn even more about his early life here in France.

The unmistakeable vision that is the late David Bowie is next and I move on around the room to see portraits of a boxer, the fisherman Pierre, an old teacher of his, his niece, his sister and then I come to the final piece, which I notice hasn't quite dried properly yet and I step back to get a proper look.

It is a woman – a red-haired woman on a boat, smiling with her head back like she is looking at the stars.

I gulp as the picture takes life before my eyes – the girl in the denim shorts and grey vest top looks all too familiar and then I look at the caption for confirmation.

It is *me*. It is unmistakeably me. The caption reads just 'Maggie'.

I am dizzy. I need to sit down.

'Why? Why did you choose me? Why did you paint me?' I go outside to Gerard when my heart has stopped racing.

He doesn't answer me at first.

'I mean, you could have at least warned me. I have a very lustful look on my face right there. Is that really how I looked out on the boat? Jeez. Sorry, I am just in a bit of shock right now. You really could have warned me.'

He laughs and I can tell he is nervous.

'That was the moment just before we kissed,' he says and he takes my hand to sit beside him. 'It was a moment I just had to capture. I hope you like it.'

I can smell his freshness, a mixture of cologne and soap and... of man.

'I... I... of course I like it. I am just shocked. Honoured, but shocked. I had no idea...'

He doesn't respond and when I look at him, I want him so badly right here, right now. Oh God help me. Oh good God and Lucy Harte and all the angels and saints who I pray to, please help me because he is such a beautiful creature. His eyes are so full of longing that they could almost speak for themselves and his jawline is strong and firm.

'You look... like a dream,' I tell him and I am not sure if I am actually breathing any more. I lift my hand and take a moment to touch his face and just look at him, properly, for what feels like the first time.

Then I run my fingers across his chin, then his lips and up onto his dark, damp wavy hair and my eyes follow my hand as I run my fingers through his hair and then back down past his eyes, his jaw and then his lips again, which I part and he lets me touch him so closely, then he wets his lips slowly with his tongue when my fingers let go.

I don't have to say another word because he pulls me closer towards him and brushes my hair off my shoulder. His breath is on my face and his lips when he kisses me make me catch my own breath again. Then he lets his hands do the talking as he leans me back onto the soft cushions, cups my breast firmly and urgently in his hand and moves against me to let me know exactly what he wants from me.

And I really, really want it too. I want this more than anything I may have ever wanted in my life. This man... this gorgeous, eccentric, moody son of a bitch, who has captured me in so many ways has got me exactly where we both want to be.

I lie back as he lifts my white lace-and-linen dress over my hips and shows me, in no uncertain terms, that this is what he has wanted all along.

He moves in me and I gasp.

'Don't close your eyes, Maggie,' he says to me in a breathy whisper. 'Don't close them. Look at me. I don't want you to miss a thing.'

'Do you think you might ever come back here?' asks Gerard as we lie in post-coital bliss, his strong arms enveloping my body against his. Our love-making began outside, but we moved into the studio and finished in perfect ecstasy on his bed. 'My exhibition opens in Toulouse on July the first. It would be fun if you could come to the launch and celebrate with me.'

I lean up on my elbow and cannot resist the urge to touch his face as I look into his beautiful eyes.

'I do think that if I ever return here, I will never go back to Ireland,' I say to him. 'You said it and so did Starling on the first day I arrived here. She warned me about this place. She said it gets under your skin – the food, the wine, the sun, the *men*...'

Gerard laughs and kisses my shoulder.

He makes some juice and toast and we sit on the bed to have it, then I lie down on his chest, cursing the crumbs that have found their way everywhere and I fall into a deep slumber, waking at six in the morning to see him at work on my painting, touching up dots of colour.

He is magnificent to watch, playing the knives like a musical instrument, totally focused, totally not here and I am afraid to make a noise in case it takes him out of his zone.

'You awake?' he asks. 'I was going to suggest some breakfast? And don't say you aren't hungry.'

He puts down the painting knife and comes towards me on the bed and he climbs across it to kiss me, lightly biting my lip as he does so. I have had worse ways to wake up, I must admit...

'I take it you aren't meaning food?' I say, but he is already on top of me and we are on our way again.

Chapter 30

Starling wakes me around eleven am back at the *gîte* with her persistent knocking on the door and calling through the letterbox.

My night with Gerard has exhausted me, unsurprisingly, and I crawled into bed for a morning snooze the moment I got back here.

'Mademoiselle Maggie! Are you there? It's Starling. Good morning!'

I have been looking forward to seeing Starling again, but right now, I am so cosy and she has taken me from a wonderful state of slumber, where I was back in Gerard's arms again and the world as I know it had stopped, leaving just the two of us alone together.

'Hello, darling!' I say to the contrary, shuffling through the *gîte* while trying to disguise that my t-shirt is on back to front and I haven't zipped up my shorts properly in my haste to answer the door.

'Oh I am ever so sorry!' She puts her hand over her mouth when she sees me. 'Were you asleep? I do apologise! I can come back later!'

'Come in, come in!' I tell her. 'It's lovely to see you!'

She is carrying a picnic basket and we go into the living room, where I feel the need to tidy the cushions on the sofa, stack up my novels and take empty coffee cups over to the kitchen area.

'Sorry, the place is very… lived in, let's say. I will clean it all properly before I go tomorrow.'

'Relax, Maggie,' says Starling, making herself at ease on an armchair. 'I haven't come to inspect! I know you are due to go home soon, so I just wanted to make sure you do not want to stay longer?'

There is a twinkle in her eye when she says it. There is something about Starling that makes her always look like she is up to something and I love it.

'I should really get back, but just for now,' I tell her. 'This place has stolen a piece of my heart and I will definitely come back.'

'And a good heart it is too, Mademoiselle.'

That look again… she has said that once before.

'So, how have you been?' I ask her. I need to redirect the conversation because sometimes when Starling looks at me like that, it's like she knows stuff that she cannot possibly know.

'I am sorry I haven't come to see you earlier to show you around a little, but we have been so busy at the café, but today we are closed, so it's the only day I could come here.'

'Honestly, I have been absolutely fine,' I assure her. 'I am having such a wonderful time just… well, just getting to know your wonderful town, and today I plan to totally relax and make the most of the sunshine, then clean up, pack up and make my way home to Ireland early in the morning.'

Starling hands me the picnic basket, which is neatly covered in red-and-white gingham.

'A gift for you before you go.'

'Ah, thank you so much, Starling. That's so kind!'

I can't resist a peep, so I lift back the gingham and find a note from Anton.

'*I hope you enjoyed your time here, Mademoiselle Maggie. Here is some local produce to enjoy on your last day. Bon appetit!*'

'My goodness.'

I am growing to love the Florval family more and more and not just because of Gerard. Their kindness from my first moments here has been like a warm, snuggly blanket of comfort and is making me have second thoughts about going home tomorrow, but my six weeks of time out from work is almost up and I have some major decisions to make now that Lucy's list is almost complete.

'It's just a few things from the restaurant – I hope you enjoy them!' says Starling.

My tummy rumbles at the sight of such elegant delicacies, which will make up the perfect lunch. A selection of pâté, a fresh baguette, some Emmental, Brie and Camembert and a hearty bottle of Beaujolais to wash it down... *delicieux!*

I so don't to leave here, but something tells me that it is time. I have done so much in Lucy's name lately and I feel totally fulfilled and happier than ever, but I also remember that there is one more thing on her list for me to do.

'Starling, I know this is incredibly short notice,' I say to her, 'but would you and your family like to come here tonight for dinner before I go. Say at 8.30 or so? No pressure if you have other plans, but I'd honestly love to give something back for all your kindness to me.'

Starling's face lights up at the invitation.

'Oh thank you, Maggie! Yes, count me in!' she says with a bright smile. 'I'll check with Anton and Bernard and maybe we could also invite Gerard? He has been given an extension on his exhibition, so he is much less grumpy these days. In fact, he seems very happy for a change! Would you mind?'

I feel the corners of my mouth twitch at the suggestion that Gerard has changed lately for the better.

'The more the merrier,' I tell her. I was hoping she would suggest him. 'I will set the table for five people, then. Let me know when you can if they all can come.'

Starling almost skips to the door and I walk with her to see her off.

'This is such a treat for us to be invited out for food as we always seem to be serving our customers! I'll bring dessert!' she says to me. '*À bientôt*, Maggie. I'm so glad you came here to our town and I hope your friend is happy that you saw the bridge.'

I open the door for her and we walk outside and the bridge, as always, catches my eye.

'I bet she is happy, yes,' I reply. 'She will never know how much she changed my life by bringing me here and in the weeks that have led up to this.'

Starling blinks in the sunshine.

'I'm sure you cannot wait to tell her all about it,' she says in earnest and her words surprise me at first.

'Yes, I hope I get to tell her all about it one day,' I whisper. 'But I have a feeling she already knows. I think she sees it all already.'

The reality of hosting the Florval family for dinner hits me like a ton of bricks when I reach the supermarket later that afternoon. What on earth was I thinking? They cook for a living and are experts at French cuisine, while the most people I ever cooked for was my Mum, Dad and Jeff and that was two years ago when they visited for Sunday lunch shortly after our wedding.

Throw a dinner party for strangers is what Lucy said on her list, so I think I've well and truly hit that one on the head by setting myself up with this challenge. Apart from Gerard, I really don't know these people at all. What do they like to eat? Or drink? More importantly, what do they not like to eat or drink?

I try to think of a suitable menu but the layout of the supermarket and its foreign brands baffle me, so I text Flo for advice.

'Dinner-party food suggestions. Five people. Quickly.'

Like any best friend should, she messages me back at the speed of lightning.

'Keep it simple. Roast a chicken, mash some potatoes, steam some good old veg and add gravy. Voilà.'

I get a second message from her right away.

'And lots of wine, of course, but I don't need to tell you that, do I?'

I am not going to complicate matters. I will do exactly what Flo says so I grab the ingredients and get back to the *gîte* as quickly as I can to start my preparations, all the while trying to ignore the herd of elephants that dance in my stomach.

I am so nervous I could cry. I am planning to cook for restaurateurs. I am about to finish the last thing from Lucy's list.

And I really cannot wait to see Gerard again.

'Bon soir!' Starling chirps in a high-pitched voice when my visitors arrive later that evening. The table is set to perfection, the candles are lit, the red wine is breathing and the white wine is chilled. Even the food has obeyed me so far and I am very, very proud of myself. Once I got settled into the cooking I actually enjoyed it and even managed enough time to change into some fresh clothes, spray some perfume, tidy my hair and add a bit of lippy. As the French would say, *parfait!*

'You remember Anton,' says Starling, as her future father-in-law crosses the threshold.

Anton greets me with a warm hug and the customary kiss on each cheek, looking like a different person than the stressed-out, perspiring restaurateur I met on my arrival here. He wears a grey suit with a white shirt and pink tie and I can see a resemblance between him and his younger brother.

'You look very dapper,' I tell him. 'Please make yourself at home.'

It is practically his home, or one of them, I realise, once I've said it.

'And my fiancé, Bernard,' says Starling proudly as Anton's son, Bernard, greets me politely and makes his way inside.

'So you are the magnificent Maggie!' he says, air-kissing me as Starling looks on with her hands clasped in delight.

'And Gerard?' I ask, trying to hide my enthusiasm.

'*Non*, sorry, no Gerard,' she says.

What? I don't have Gerard's phone number and I hadn't heard from him all day so I was really relying on Starling to let him know about tonight.

'Really? He isn't coming?' I feel a weight hit the bottom of my stomach.

'He isn't coming, no,' says Starling flippantly. 'It looks like he is back to his usual grumpy self so we'll have more fun without him as always, won't we?'

What? No, please God, no. I really wanted him to be here! I let out a deep sigh but Starling doesn't even notice. She has no idea. I was sure earlier when she called here that she knew something about Gerard and me. I'd thought that maybe the nosey checkout girl had filled her in, or that Gerard had told her himself, or that we had been spotted together, but no. It seems the Florvals know nothing of our recent romancing, so it is no big deal to them that he is not here.

But it is to me.

'Are you sure he can't make it?' I ask, trying to twitch my mouth to form a casual smile. 'I have set the table for five and there's plenty of food to go round? Maybe you could call him to be sure?'

Starling is already seated, as are the others and my plea seems to fall on deaf ears. I feel a chill of agitation run through my veins as my final evening here comes to a close. Why wouldn't he have come? Did Starling definitely tell him? I

should have invited him personally. My God, what a disaster!
I don't have any other time to see him after tonight.

'Starling?' I ask again.

'Sorry, yes Maggie? I can't believe you have gone to such
effort. The place looks so cosy and inviting.'

I do my best to show my appreciation for her compliments
but it's true. I have busted my gut all day for this dinner party
and now he isn't going to make it?

'I was just wondering if Gerard –'

'Seriously,' says Bernard. 'When he says no, he means no.
He is painting and when he is like that, he is best to be
avoided.'

That's not true and I know it. Yes, of course I know he can
be moody. He has shown me his moody side, but this is my
last night and... oh why am I wasting my energy thinking
about it? He was invited and he didn't come. I should just
focus on the present and on those who *are* here rather than
those who are not.

I should know better by now that people will let you down
just when you don't expect it.

'Wine anyone?' I say and I fill each of their glasses with a
lump in my throat. 'I'll just go and make a start on serving up.'

When I get to the kitchen, no matter how hard I try, I can't
help it that my eyes keep filling up with tears of disappointment.

I dab the sides of them with my fingers and plead with my
emotions not to take over but I can't stop thinking that this
is somehow my fault. I got so caught up in shopping and

preparing and cleaning the *gîte* but I really should have called with him and told him about tonight instead of leaving it up to a third party to relay the invitation.

I know his type. He would want to be invited personally. He would want it to have come from me. It's my own fault that he is not here and now I have to just suck it up.

'Can I help?'

Starling's voice startles me and I fake a quick smile and grab some kitchen roll to wipe my nose.

'No, not at all,' I assure her, praying she doesn't notice the damp around my eyes. 'I'm almost there. Please just relax and I'll be right with you.'

'Wait a minute. You're crying,' she says in a whisper. 'Is it because you are leaving tomorrow? What's wrong, Mademoiselle Maggie? Please don't cry.'

I shake my head and laugh at her innocence.

'No, no, I'm not sad at all,' I sniffle. 'I'm just overthinking things, but it's nothing serious. Here, maybe you could help me serve the veg? That would be of great help to me.'

I figure that her presence here in the kitchen might take my mind off Gerard and I am right, before I know it we are seated at the table and tucking into a very Irish-style home-cooked dinner, which they all seem to relish and enjoy.

Apart from me, that is. I force the food into me and do my best to keep up with the conversation but my eyes are constantly drawn to the empty seat and to the door, which I hope and pray will open at any time.

It doesn't. And soon the evening is over and it is time for them to go.

Chapter 31

I see my guests off and look around the *gîte*, cursing myself for getting so attached to Gerard so quickly.

It was part of Lucy's wishes to throw a dinner party and though I did it, I don't feel good after it at all.

I sit down on the sofa and curl my feet under me, but I can't settle. I try and remind myself of how complimented I was on the food and the room and the effort I had made, but it is not enough without him.

Damn you, Gerard, for getting so under my skin.

I want to run right now up to his studio and see him and for him to have a good explanation as to why he didn't want to see me on my last night here. Okay, so he didn't have to come to dinner at such short notice but he could have popped by. He could have showed some sign that he wanted to see me. He knows I leave early in the morning and that there will be no time then for real goodbyes, so why didn't he just show up and explain himself? Why didn't we make proper plans before I left his place this morning?

Why is time always against us?

Or maybe that's what he wants? No fuss. No pain.

Or maybe I was just an idle distraction, after all. Maybe I was just some way to pass the time in between his inspiration for his work.

But I know I wasn't just that to him. He painted me for his exhibition. He took me to that special restaurant. He even asked me to stay here for longer, or at least to come back really soon. He looked at me like he was looking into my soul and I have never experienced that before, not even with the man I married. Gerard, I truly believe, is different.

I just wish he had come to say goodbye.

I go outside onto the decking and look out onto the night-time view of the River Tarn for the last time. This place has filled me up inside in a way I could never have imagined. It has made the blood pump through my veins and my adrenaline flow and it has made me love wildly and freely so much that I thought my heart might burst for him.

And now, after all of that, I will be leaving tomorrow, with only memories and the thought of what could have been, and I have enough of those – thank you very much.

I sit down on my favourite chair outside on the deck, pull a rug around me and when I wake up a few hours later, I really do think I am dreaming.

For when I wake up, just as I had hoped, he is there.

'I'm drunk,' he says, but I need to wake up properly to make sure he is real and not just an illusion of my overactive imagination. 'I'm drunk and I am sorry.'

'Am I dreaming?' I ask him. I check the time. It's just gone midnight.

'You may be dreaming,' he replies, 'or you may be having

a nightmare. It depends on how angry you are with me right now. Just how angry *are* you with me right now, Maggie?'

A bottle of whiskey sits in front of him, half empty, or half full, whatever way you want to look at it. He has already filled a glass for me, but I have no interest, plus I have a journey to the airport to make early in the morning so I can't be drinking at this hour even if I wanted to.

'I don't want you to go, Maggie,' he tells me emphatically. 'I have only just found you and now I am going to lose you again and I am sorry but I got upset today at the thought of that and I went to the pub and, well, the rest is history. That is it, how do you say it, in a nutshell?'

'In a nutshell? You got drunk because of me?' I ask him. 'Because I am leaving? You got drunk instead of calling to see me to say goodbye?'

'Well, yes, but I am here now.'

I want to kill him, but I want to kiss him more.

'It's late, Gerard,' I say, stating the obvious. 'We could have spent the evening together but instead you choose to get pissed and turn up when I'm sleeping? This is so unfair of you!'

'But you're not sleeping now, are you, Maggie?'

'You woke me, that's why I am not sleeping!'

'I didn't wake you. You were snoring,' he says and he starts to laugh.

My eyes widen in defence.

'No I wasn't snoring! I was not indeed! I don't snore!'

He laughs more. I don't.

'Maggie, my sweet Maggie!' he says and he leans across

and puts his hand on my knee. I want to move it away but it feels too good. I want him close to me. I have longed for this all day and night.

'I thought you didn't care, Gerard. You hurt me tonight.'

'No, no!' he says and he moves towards me now and holds my hands. 'I'm so sorry if I hurt you, but do you think I don't care? If you can think of the very opposite of that, then that's how I feel! I am hurting so much inside at the thought of you leaving. You have distracted me from my work. No woman has ever done that before. You distracted me so much that the only way to finish my exhibition was to paint you and have you as part of it. Don't you know that?'

I shake my head. 'Is that supposed to be a compliment?'

He laughs at my response.

'A *huge* compliment,' he says. 'A fucking huge compliment!'

Now, it's my turn to laugh, whether I like it or not. I have never heard him swear before and it is so... well, it's so fucking cute, that's what it is.

'My heart,' he continues, 'well, I feel it broke a little today because I am so afraid that I will never see you again. I was too afraid of saying goodbye, but then, with some good old Dutch courage, I came here and I'm sorry if I woke or frightened you but I couldn't stay away.'

He holds up the bottle of whiskey.

'It's getting late,' I tell him. 'I have an early start tomorrow so I can't join you for drinks, I'm sorry.'

'Okay, no *I* am sorry,' he says, standing up in front of me. 'You're sorry, I'm sorry, we are all so sorry! I will go, then. I have dreaded this moment for ages now. I will say a quick goodbye Maggie and you won't ever have to see me again. Ever.'

He mumbles something in French, which of course I don't understand so I have to interrupt him.

'I'd like you to stay with me, Gerard,' I reply and I look right into his eyes. He stops talking instantly. 'Please stay with me till morning.'

His new-found silence lingers but he doesn't have to say another word. He just leads me to the bedroom so tenderly and soon we are saying goodbye in the way that lovers do.

And once again, it makes me feel like I'm on top of the world.

Lucy, Lucy, Lucy Harte, I write when I'm on the plane home to Ireland.

What have you done to this heart of ours? What have I done to it? I never thought it would even beat again after Jeff, but boy, oh boy you have proven me wrong with the past few weeks and all the love and joy you have brought me.

I return now to Ireland a very different Maggie O'Hara than the one your brother met almost six weeks ago and it's all for the better. It's all down to you.

Thanks to you, I have rediscovered the power of uncon-ditional love with my brother, I have discovered in Dublin the overpowering energy that lust can bring and how it can boost your self-esteem to simply be desired and wanted, I have discovered the sheer feel-good factor of giving to others through token gestures like baking a cake or bigger efforts like cooking dinner for strangers, I have discovered that although I don't have to forget I can always forgive with Jeff, but most of all I have discovered a place so magical to me and I fear I may have left part of my borrowed heart behind there with Gerard.

He has given me part of his heart in return so I will cherish it until we meet again and I do believe we will.

Your list is done, Lucy Harte, and I hope you know now how much your gift of life has meant to me. I hope it has made you as happy as it has me.

You saved my heart once before, but now you have saved my soul.

Please take care of me as I continue with my own hopes and dreams.

Forever your friend,

Maggie x

Chapter 32

I am meeting Sylvia Madden for a coffee before I hook up
with Kevin to train for our run and I am like a nervous
kitten as I sit in the café across from Powers Enterprises
waiting on her arrival.

I needn't be because when she comes in to the coffee house,
she is as graceful and gentle as she has been on our previous
meetings and I am immediately put at ease.

'So, I don't even need to ask if you had a good time,' she
says. 'As usual I am between appointments, but I can see it
was good for you. You are looking pale, though, Maggie. You
must be tired?'

'I have been resting a lot since I got back in between training
sessions with my friend for a mini marathon we are doing
soon. It's just a mixture of all that.'

'Okay, well, I hope you are looking after yourself?'

Sylvia and all the management team at Powers' know of
my heart condition and I guess that's why they have been so
lenient and understanding lately.

'A few more days back in Belfast and I'll be back on track,'
I assure her. I need to get my hair done again. I need to keep

refreshing how I look and doing new things so I don't slip back into any sort of feel-sorry-for-myself mode.

We order coffees and get down to business after I thank her profusely for giving me the nudge to get away from it all just over a week ago.

'I have a request,' I say to her, not wanting to waste any more of her time. 'If it is pushing the boundaries, I am sure you will let me know, but if you don't ask, you don't get and all that jazz...'

'Hit me,' she says, sipping her coffee.

'I would like to request a career break,' I tell her. 'A proper one. Unpaid, of course, but something a bit longer, to get myself really on the up, like really get it sorted. I feel like I am so close, but there are other things I would like to do now that I have the courage and strength to do them. I want to take some time out and live in France.'

Sylvia smiles and her silver bob shakes a little, but not a hair goes out of place.

'You know, I was telling my husband about you the other night,' she tells me, leaning across the table. 'He works in sport, so he gets to travel lots but I showed him the photo you sent me and he said to me that you looked like you had found your wings. He says you should travel more.'

I like the sound of that.

'Your husband sounds like he is well clued-in to the world,' I reply. 'I suppose you could say that I have found my wings, and now, without sounding all cheesy, I'd like to fly a bit more. I met someone, Sylvia.'

'I thought so,' she says.

She is impressed but not surprised and she lets out a hearty laugh.

'Have you ever thought about being a writer?' she asks me. 'I always enjoyed reading your reports, which, let's face it, weren't on the most creative of subjects, but you always managed to make a property come to life with your descriptions of interiors and locations. You will be a big loss to Powers if you decide to never come back to us.'

'I used to write when I was younger, but I am going to take one step at a time,' I tell her. 'I just want to explore more. My divorce will be through soon and I'm due a settlement from Jeff on the home we bought together. I will have enough money to last me for at least a year, so I want to make the most of the opportunity to see the world.'

Sylvia lifts her handbag from the back of the chair and sets it on her lap.

'I think you are a very wise young lady,' she tells me. 'I will see that your request is submitted to HR if you send me an email and we can take it from there, but I don't imagine it to be a problem. Will Powers has a lot of time for you. He will miss you, of course, but he will love that you have found your drive again and that it is taking you in a completely different direction.'

I finish my coffee quickly, aware that Sylvia has to get on with her day and I have a family reunion, of sorts, to go to in Loch Tara.

'I have so much to thank you for,' I tell her as we leave the café. 'You are quite an inspiration, Sylvia. I'm glad I got to know you in the way that I do.'

She swishes her hair again.

'I know they call me a serpent in there,' she says, nodding across to the Powers office block. 'But I kind of like it that way. Always keep an ace up your sleeve, Maggie. Don't give it all away in the workplace and you will go far, but I don't think I need to tell you that.'

'I appreciate your advice,' I tell her. 'Goodbye, Sylvia, and thanks for everything.'

'You're welcome, Maggie O'Hara,' she replies. 'Now go spread your wings and get yourself back to that handsome man in France!'

'I cannot wait!' I tell her. I have a plan in place already.

Simon and I have been on the phone for two hours now, but I do believe it would take another two to fully catch up with everything we have to tell each other.

I tell him about Dublin, about Tiernan Quinn, about John Joe and Vivienne in Nashville and of course about my life-changing trip to France and the Florval family, who I hold so closely in my heart. I have been continuously exhausted since my return from France, so I am lying on my bed with my feet up high on pillows, just like my mum used to make me do when I came home from school every day.

'It's hard to believe that this all started with a list from Lucy,' he says to me. 'In fact, it really started when we found each other a few months ago, though it seems like a lifetime. I am sorry if I ever put you under any sort of pressure, Maggie. I didn't mean it to be like that.'

'No, no you never really did,' I assure him. 'You didn't pressure me at all, I swear you didn't. I just got panicked along the way, but I have only gratitude for how you and Lucy have changed my life for the better. God knows what sort of mess I would be in now if you hadn't come along when you did. I would probably still be begging and screaming at that asshole Jeff to come back and would still be breaking my heart over and over again every time I thought of him and his precious baby on the way. Oh, and there's something I've been meaning to ask you for ages now, and it keeps slipping my mind!'

'Shoot,' he says.

'You said you found me because we had a mutual friend? Who on earth was the mutual friend?'

'Ha!' he laughs aloud. 'I thought I'd got away with that one. You work with a lady called Sylvia Madden, right?'

'Yes... well I did. What's Sylvia got to do with this?'

'Her husband is someone I know through reporting on Irish soccer games. We got talking one day on a plane from Belfast and by the time we touched down in Inverness, we'd made the amazing connection. Small world, as they say.'

'Ah,' is about as much as I can find to reply. Sylvia Madden, you dark horse you!

I can hear Andrea in the background.

'Andrea says hello,' he says instead. 'She is itching to hear all about your travels, so I hope you know that I will have to tell her every detail again and it will probably mean I don't get to sleep until the early hours because there is so much to go over. You women don't settle for any less than every detail, do you?'

Andrea shouts to him.

'Don't you doubt it for a second, Simon!' she says in her Spanish accent. 'I hope there are plenty of lust-filled European romances to tell me about too! I need some romance to keep me going at this stage before I die of boredom with being fat and pregnant!'

I can imagine her, totally drop-dead gorgeous with her neat bump and not one bit boring or fat at all.

'Is she keeping well? Not long to go now,' I say to Simon.

'She is doing my head in, isn't that right, darling wife? Ow!'

I hear her hit him playfully and I take it as my cue to wrap up.

'Simon, I am looking after Lucy's little memory box carefully but I'd like to return it to you sometime soon,' I tell him. 'It's all intact, all as it was, but it's me that has changed for the better.'

'No, no it's yours now, Maggie,' he tells me. 'Look, just let it be a reminder of how far you have come. Put it away but take it out when you need some courage or strength along the way. You're a strong, special lady, Maggie O'Hara, and I'm so glad I got to meet you.'

'I'm a whole lot stronger now, thanks to you,' I reply. 'Your sister saved my life and then you came along and saved it all over again with her little list of things to do. I will be eternally grateful to you, Simon. I've always wanted to say thank you to your family, so I hope in a way this shows how much it means to me.'

I can hear him choking up as we prepare to say goodbye.

'You know, I was warned by so many people against meeting you,' he confesses, and I hear the deep emotion in his voice as he speaks. 'I was told by social services, by my father for years, by my aunt, even by Andrea at first, to just let it all go, that it would be too emotional to meet the person who lived after Lucy.'

I nod my head, even though he can't see me. I can only imagine how they would have felt if they had seen me walking, breathing, living through Lucy's heart. Simon was the brave one and I'm glad he got some closure from it.

'Losing her was unbearable,' he continues. 'I was supposed to forget that somewhere out there, another life was living because of Dad's decision to donate Lucy's young, perfect organs but I couldn't forget it, not for a second, and when I heard her heart beat inside of you and saw your pain but your hidden lust for life, I knew he had made the right decision.'

I gulp and close my eyes, trying somehow to imagine his pain.

'Look after Andrea and let me know when baby Harte comes along,' I say to him. 'Look at this as your new beginning. He or she will be a real superstar, that's for sure.'

'Thank you, Maggie. I've exciting times ahead.'

I am about to leave it at that, but there is one more thing I need to say to him.

'Can I ask you one last favour, Simon, before I go?'

We sound as if we are having the last conversation we will ever have and I know, of course, there will be many more, but I just need to clarify a few things as we close this chapter of Lucy's precious young life.

'Of course you can. You know you can ask me anything, Maggie.'

I pause. I try to speak and then I pause again. I take a deep breath. I take another one. And another.

'The next time you visit your dad's grave,' I say to him... Oh God, I want to say this so badly but it's killing me inside when I think of what that poor man went through all those years ago and the loneliness that followed. I shut my eyes tightly but the tears trickle through.

'Yes?'

'The next time you visit his grave,' I whisper between sobs, 'will you please tell him that I said thank you... please tell him thank you, from me, and that I think of him every single day now. Thank him for saying yes on the worst day of his life. Thank him from me for my life. He has taught me so much about human nature and I am so, so grateful.'

'I will do that,' replies Simon. 'I will go do that right now. Are you okay, Maggie?'

'I'm just really tired, Simon. Grateful, but tired.'

My eyes are closing.

'You go get some rest and we will talk again,' he assures me. 'We are forever connected and please don't ever forget it. Goodbye, Maggie. Look after yourself, now, and good luck with your big run! I know you can do it! Do it just for you.'

I put down the phone and I let the tears flow as I let Lucy and Simon go for now.

It's now time for me to get on with the rest of my life.

Chapter 33

'You look fresh,' says Kevin on the morning of the mini marathon a few days later. 'Feeling any better?'

I have been complaining to everyone who will listen to me of sheer exhaustion since my return of a tiredness that I just can't shake off no matter how much I rest up, but I'm not going to let that beat me, not today especially.

'I'm good to go!' I tell him. 'I've been eating well, I've been resting and I've been exercising, so I'm as fit as I am going to be. The tiredness will have to just wait.'

'Are you totally sure?'

'Sure, I'm sure!' I reply. 'I was probably jet-lagged and tired out after all my travelling lately, not to mention the heavy emotional journey I've been on, but I've been really looking forward to this, big time.'

A hot soak in the bath, some celebrity magazines and a few early nights, plus a surprise call from Gerard this morning to wish me well, has got me psyched and is helping me deal with this exhaustion. His exhibition opens in Toulouse in just a few nights and I am planning to turn up and surprise him. I have booked my flights and packed my bag and he has no idea.

'Perhaps you will make it to see me soon?' he said this morning in his glorious accent that still drives me wild.

'Yes, for sure,' I promised him. 'I'm making plans to get back to you as soon as I can.'

I can't wait to see his face when I get there.

We finish our registration with the other runners, pin our numbers to our chests and the crowds are gathering to cheer us all on, including my mum and dad and my brother and his wife, who have flown in to put the final touches to their wedding celebrations at Loch Tara.

Vivienne has planned the most exquisitely tasteful party for our immediate family and a few old friends from down the years. There is a marquee in the garden, a barbecue ready to be fired up and a string quartet and jazz band all set for a lake-side gathering that I really can't wait for. My parents are beside themselves with excitement and to see them happy is the most magical thing of all.

They wave at me in the distance like two giddy school children and for just a second their faces blur as my head does a quick spin.

Whoah. That was scary. But then they are back again. I stall. Phew. It's okay.

'Are sure you are feeling okay, Maggie?' asks Kevin, adjusting his wrist bands and the sweat band on his head. 'You look like you're about to faint. You don't have to do this, you know? If you're not feeling great –'

He points me to a chair at the side of the road, but I refuse.

'I'm fine, Kevin. Stop fussing. My parents are watching.'

I smile at them and wave. My mother is taking photographs. My mother never takes photographs.

'Sip on some water,' says Kevin, so I do that to please him. The cool water trickles down the back of my throat and brings me round slightly, but I can't deny it. I feel like shit.

'I'm so up for this run,' I lie to him, but I'm feeling breathless and we haven't even started.

'You don't look like it. You're freakin' me out.'

'You're freakin' me out by fussing!' I reply. 'Look, I'm just tired, but I won't let that stop me, not a chance. It's my big start on the new me. I've done Lucy's list and now this is one of the things I want to do for me.'

He doesn't believe me, but he knows not to push it.

'Okay, then, let's jog lightly to get the muscles warmed up,' he says. 'Did you do your stretches this morning?'

'Exactly as you said, Captain! I'm stretched and warmed up and ready to hit the road.'

We start to jog on the spot and he looks so serious in his full running gear, with every gadget you can think of attached to him, that he makes me feel giddy.

'What are you laughing at?' he asks me. 'You won't be laughing when you hit the last leg and you are so near yet so far and you're begging for mercy.'

He jumps onto the ground and does some weird type of yoga pose.

'You just look so focused it is funny,' I say again and now I am definitely pushing it. Kevin takes his fitness challenges very, very serious, it seems.

'Never mind me and focus on your own preparation. Did you make a playlist, like I suggested?' he asks me.

'Of course I did.'

Of course I didn't.

'That's a lie,' he says, launching into some light sit-ups. 'I have mine all ready – I'll start off slow with a bit of Fleetwood Mac, build up to some classic eighties rock to get the adrenaline going and then cruise to a selection of pumping dance tracks to get me across the finishing line.'

'Bully for you,' I say to him, ever so slightly jealous of his pinpoint preparation, but then again, he has done this a million times before so he knows every trick in the book.

'Right! Let's do this,' he says, checking his phone and setting the time as the announcer asks for all runners to approach the starting line. 'You are going to fly through this, Mags. I just know you will. Think of Lucy. Do it for Lucy, but most of all do it for you.'

For a change, I am not thinking of Lucy. I am not thinking of Simon, nor am I thinking of me. I am thinking of Simon's poor dad, who made such a huge decision on the day he lost half his family and who has let me get this far in life. I will do this for him. I will think of him every step of the way.

But then, no, it's back again. The wave of nausea... the scary blurred vision. I think I am going to be sick. The dizziness is back again too. I take a deep breath.

'Maggie, are you okay?' Kevin asks me. 'You're really, really pale, love. Look, just sit it out. You can do the next one. These races are two a penny and we can sign up for one in just a few weeks' time.'

'I'm okay!'

'Don't do it if you don't feel well. You're pushing yourself to do this, I can tell. Maggie, do you hear me?'

I won't let it beat me.

'I'm just nervous,' I tell him and I drink more water, then jog lightly again. 'I'll be okay once we get started. Let's do this.'

Kevin and I start off slowly to begin with for the first mile and then he ever so slightly picks up the pace, which I match accordingly, just like we had agreed in our training sessions.

'You're doing good, Maggie. No rush, no panic. Take it at your own pace. Am I going too fast?'

I shake my head at him and smile. I am so not doing good. The dizziness keeps returning and I feel so sick. My heart is racing. It feels like it might jump out of my chest. I should really stop, but I don't. I keep going...

By the second mile, I am really getting worse but we had discussed this in training and apparently feeling nauseous is common and it's mainly a mixture of adrenaline and anxiety when faced with such a challenge.

I give Kevin two nods as we approach the third mile – which is an agreed signal to say that he can run ahead if he wants to. I don't want to hold him back, as I know he wants to beat his own personal best.

'Do you want me to stay with you? Are you definitely okay?'

I shake my head.

'Maggie, is that yes or no? Shit. Maggie? You're scaring me. Do you need to stop?'

I start to slow down now and I can't deny it any longer, I

am finding this really tough. My feet trip along as I slow way, way down. I put my hands to my head and slow down further. I wonder what song Kevin is listening to. He is probably on his eighties selection at this stage and I wish I had been smart enough to make a play list. It may have distracted me from this sickness and the jabbing pains I am having in my chest. And this tiredness that just won't go away... and the dizziness...

I have to stop now. I... I really have to... stop.

'Maggie, can you hear me? Maggie!'

His voice sounds so distant. I can just about see his face. I try to focus, then I bend over and put my hands on my thighs, but my vision starts to blur and now I can't see properly at all.

My God, what is happening? I can't see!

'Kevin!'

I reach out for him. I don't know if any sound is coming from my voice, but I try again.

I touch his arm.

'Kevin!'

I can't hear anything and the world goes white. And then I fall down.

I hear birdsong.

I blink slowly, but the light is too strong so I close my eyes again and focus on the sweet, chirping sounds that fill my ears, drowning out the bleeping noise that has irritated me in the distance for what feels like days now.

A woman's muffled voice takes over and I recognise that

also. She has been here before, lots of times. I like her voice. She says nice things to me even though I cannot see her.

'It's stuffy in here,' she says. 'Do you mind if I open a window?'

I wish I could answer, but I can't. I have no idea where I am or what I am doing here.

'Open it, yes,' says the whispered voice of a man, which sounds like home. 'Open it and let her hear the birdsong. It might help. Do anything. Do anything which might bring her back to us.'

My eyes flicker. The whiteness... then black... a ceiling light... a green hue...

I remember the run and the people and the voices and the faces of all my family, but who is here with me? Am I alive? Where the hell am I?

'Open your eyes, Maggie. Listen to your heart and open your eyes.'

It is her. It is Lucy. I can hear her and see her somewhere in my hazy, dream-like state. I try to reply, but I cannot speak and she smiles at me as she floats away, further and further away from me, waving goodbye – waving and waving until she totally disappears.

'Oh my God, she is opening her eyes. Nurse! Nurse, she is opening her eyes!'

It's the man's voice. A voice I once loved when I was a child... the voice of home and warmth and familiarity from when I was just a little girl. I open my eyes and I see him cry and he is holding my hand up to his face.

It is my brother.

It is my big brother by my bedside and he looks like he has been here for a very long time.

'You're back, Maggie,' he says, as tears drip from his cheeks onto my hands. 'Oh thank God! Mum! Dad! She is okay! Maggie, you are going to be okay!'

I look out onto the windowsill and the little bird flies away.

I have been at enough hospital appointments to automatically sense if the news I am about to hear is good or bad.

I can tell that by the mood in the air, by the hopeless dread, by the silences in between questions and answers.

I can tell that this time it's bad.

Mr James, a new consultant with the reddest hair I have ever seen, is flicking through my notes, glancing up at me every so often and pausing a lot. He goes to speak, but doesn't, then does again. That's not a good sign.

'You mentioned stress, Maggie,' he says eventually. 'On a scale of one to ten, how stressed would you say you have been in the run-up to this... to this incident?'

I look at my mum, who, just as she did when I was a child, speaks for me.

'Her husband left her and she had to move house, then she took time off work and travelled a while. She met with her heart donor's family too. Ten out of ten for stress. Definitely ten.'

'Mum!'

Mr James puts his pen down.

'You met your donor's family?' he says, taken aback. 'That's quite rare. Was this arrangement supervised or monitored by a third party?'

'It doesn't matter,' I tell him, finding my own voice at last. 'Look, I have been through a lot, yes, but what we all really want to know now is what happens next? To cut to the chase, Mr James, how long do I have left?'

The consultant takes off his glasses and takes a deep breath. Deep breaths – not good. Glasses on and off – not good.

'You are in your eighteenth year since transplant,' he reminds us. 'Every single day from now on should be treated like a bonus, with absolutely no stress, whatsoever. I urge you to do the things that rest your heart, Maggie. Go to the place where you find yourself most at peace. Cut out any negativity, and for goodness sake, don't attempt any more mini marathons. Not at this stage of your condition.'

'Every single day is a bonus?' I say to him.

'So, what you are really saying is...?' My father tries to get the man in front of us to tell us clearly, to just spit it out.

I don't have long left. My dad needs to hear it. He needs to hear the black and white of it all.

'What I'm saying is that you should make every second count,' says Mr James. 'I'm sorry. That's as much as I can tell you all. I wish I could be more specific, but I don't have a crystal ball. Your heart is very, very weak and unless a new donor comes along in the meantime... what I'm saying is, it could be days, it could be weeks, it could even be a couple of months...'

We wait for *'it could be years'* to come next.

It doesn't.

I cough, just to break the silence.

'Thank you for your time,' I say to the consultant. Ironic,

really. Time. It's all we need in life, really, if we want to get stuff done. The clock ticks on the wall and I want to cover my ears. I don't know how much time I have, do I? That's scary. That's really scary.

I can hear both my parents sniffle as they gather their coats and I bite my lip and shake the consultant's hand with a wry smile.

'I'm sorry,' he says to me.

'Don't be,' I whisper, and I mean it.

It's not his fault I'm at death's door. It's not anyone's fault. I always knew I'd get this news one day and at least I've got a bit of time to prepare, unlike so many of us here in this world. It's not like I died right there on the roadside, is it? It's not like I was killed almost straight out, like poor wee Lucy and her mother. I have a little time. I don't know how much, but it's some and that's a bonus in itself.

'John Joe and Vivienne will be wondering where we've got to,' I tell my parents when I see them stall at the door with more questions on their lips.

'Yes... yes, I suppose they will. Thank you, Mr James,' says my father, his poor ageing face crumpling as he speaks. 'Please pass on our sincere thanks to your team here. You have all done... everything you –'

And at that he can say no more, so I usher him out.

'Come on,' I say in the cheeriest voice I can muster. 'Let's go home to Loch Tara, Dad. We have a wedding party to attend and we'll dance and sing and eat and be merry. You heard Mr James. Every second counts from now on and I don't intend spending any more of them in this hospital.'

'That's my girl,' says my father, wiping and blowing his nose with his faithful cloth handkerchief. 'Elizabeth Taylor wouldn't hang around hospitals either, I bet. She knew how to live her life to the full and so does our Maggie.'

'And then like us all, she died in the end,' I mutter with a smile, but he doesn't hear me. Maybe that's for the best.

'Do you have my phone, Mum?' I ask, trying to bring some normality into the day. 'I need to check my messages.'

'Your brother has it,' she tells me. 'He has been minding all of your valuables. Your father and I are too long in the tooth for that.'

'Don't lie, Mum, I saw you taking photos at the race the other day.'

She laughs back at me and I can see in her sweet face that she has aged more in the past few days than I could ever have imagined.

My heart is giving up, but my poor mother's heart is breaking and my dad's is too. She links my dad's arm and he holds her up as I walk behind them and silently cry for them both.

Chapter 34

'When we were young we used to play Blind Man's Bluff over there amongst those trees,' I tell Flo at the wedding party a few days later. 'Or pretend we were Cowboys and Indians. I was always an Indian... I had my first birthday party here, and my second, and my third... and when my big eighteenth came, in the midst of my recovery, my family threw a party just like this one and the whole village came along. Probably out of sheer nosiness, mind you, but it was a hell of a party.'

'Keep talking, Maggie,' says Flo. 'I love hearing your stories about Loch Tara.'

'Ah there are so many,' I reply. 'I can't believe my brother is married. I am so proud of him, Flo.'

John Joe told me to invite all of my friends to his big day and it's no secret as to why. This is more than a wedding party. This is my unspoken big farewell and aren't I lucky to have such a chance to go out in celebration?

'Then there was the time the cow calved right over there and John Joe got his hand stuck and I've never seen so much blood in my whole life,' I say to Flo. 'Are those the type of stories you like to hear?'

Flo pats me playfully on the arm.

'You are an eejit,' she says. 'You know how squeamish I am. Stick to the birthday stories and the fun and games you had. Oh, it really is idyllic here. I hope I can give Billie a home like this one day soon instead of being cooped up in a housing estate forever.'

I look around at the open space, the green fields, the dark blue of the lake in the near distance and I can see exactly what she means.

'I have left you some money,' I tell her and she flinches in surprise.

'What?'

'The divorce money,' I explain. 'It's yours. All of it. Go build a nice house. It won't be as idyllic as this, but it will give you both a chance to start over again, you and Billie.'

'Maggie, I don't know what to say…'

Flo wipes a tear from her eyes and gives me a hug. She deserves it – and more. Damian left as quickly as he returned and I want to give her some sort of independence from him – a chance for her and Billie to have a better life.

'You know, when they told me I didn't have much longer,' I explain, 'my first instinct was to run to the airport – well, not run in a literal sense because, let's face it, I'm not very good at that, but you know what I mean. I wanted to run away, to run and run and run, but this is where I need to be. Here at Loch Tara is where I will spend my last days. Here with my family. I couldn't leave them sooner than I have to. It would break my mother's heart even more if she was left here wondering when…'

I look across the gardens to where my mum is fussing over someone who she believes hasn't had enough to eat. I wonder if you can miss things when you die... little things like my mum's fussing over food is the type of thing I will miss – if you do.

'And what about your apartment, Maggie?' asks Flo. 'Have you been back there since?'

I shake my head and sip my lemonade from a straw. Well, it's gin and lemonade, to be precise. There's no way I'm going out of here without making the most of the time I have left and that includes eating and drinking what I want – within reason, of course. I am not planning any more wild parties, for one, where I text the universe my problems and shout out windows about how much I love Belfast...

'Kevin arrived with boxes of what he thought I might need from there,' I explain to my best buddy. 'Just the important things and a few books I told him to grab for me. He's been so good to me and the next person who lives in that apartment is going to love having him as a neighbour. Maybe I could have liked it there one day...'

'Speak of the devil,' says Flo as Kevin appears with more drinks and a selection of chicken wings from the barbecue. 'You must have read our thirsty and hungry minds!'

'Your brother sure knows how to throw a party,' says Kevin. 'The food is to die for.'

'He sure does,' I say, trying to find John Joe in the small crowd on the dance floor.

I find him waltzing with one of my aunts and he is looking so, so handsome in his navy suit and crisp white shirt.

We had a good chat after breakfast this morning when he joked that once again I had stolen his limelight by causing all this fuss.

'That's what little sisters are for,' I grinned back at him.

'And mine is the best,' was his reply, kissing me on the forehead as I had warned him not to ruin my make-up with any sentimental hugs or tears.

I really do love him so. Many times I have caught myself just staring and staring at him on his big day, even though Vivienne, naturally, is the belle of the ball and the neighbours are salivating over her French accent. We don't get a lot of foreigners around Loch Tara. The last one was our postman, who was American, and who my father was convinced was related to Elvis Presley just because he said he once lived in Memphis, Tennessee.

'Cool band,' says Kevin as he devours another chicken wing. 'That singer is shit hot. I thought you said it was all jazz and swing music by the lake?'

I shrug and laugh as Tiernan Quinn toasts his pint towards me from the band stand.

'John Joe and Roisin got him here as a special guest appearance, especially for me,' I laugh. 'Roisin thought it would be hilarious.'

'Are you and him?'

Kevin turns to me quickly, looking like he might wet himself at the possibility.

'No!' I laugh. 'Definitely not. He has his new girlfriend with him, so we're all above board, but yes, he's shit hot. *Really* shit hot, believe me.'

My friends laugh together in agreement and we spend the next few moments watching Roisin and my dad boogie to 'Sweet Child of Mine' on the dance floor. One of the elderly neighbours is covering her ears with paper cups and another is grooving along to the rhythm of 'GnR' like she was born to rock. It's going to be a great party.

'And speaking of lovers, what about the delightful Gerard?' Flo asks me, when the song is over. 'I've never seen you so loved up before, Mags. Please say you are going to see him before... you know...'

'Before I die, you mean, Flo. You *can* say it, you know.'

'I don't want to say it. I don't have to if I don't want to,' she replies.

I shake my head and stare at the ground. I would have given anything to spend some last moments with Gerard but I didn't have the heart, pardon the pun, to tell him what has happened to me. It would be so unfair to do it, since he hates goodbyes so much.

'It's better that I just slip off out of this life and out of his,' I tell Flo, 'and maybe someday he will find out, though I do not know how. He'll forget about me one day soon, I hope.'

I close my eyes at that and see his face. I can't forget about him and I know he won't forget about me easily either. He is likely in his studio now, watching his phone, taking his moods out with splashes of paint on his sheets of canvas and wondering why the hell I am not returning his calls. The urge I have to hold him once more is so overpowering but it upsets me too much to even think about it.

'I can't talk about him, I'm sorry,' I whisper to Flo and she puts her arm around me so that my head rests on her shoulder. 'It's too painful.'

She holds my hand and we sway together slowly to the next song which Tiernan Quinn, much to my surprise, dedicates to me and it makes me smile, despite the hurt I feel inside.

'A while ago in Dublin I met the most amazing woman who said she would come back to me, but she never did,' he announces. 'All she left me with was a song, so this one's for you, Maggie O'Hara. Next time when you tell a man you'll be back, don't leave him hanging!'

All of my relatives and friends and family are looking at me and I go wide-eyed – to maintain my innocence. '*Sorry*' is all I can mouth back to him, but he is joking of course. If you saw his new girlfriend with her sexy tattoos, voluptuous chest and tiny waist, you would know that he is joking.

He strums the beginning of Eva Cassidy's 'Songbird' and I close my eyes, resting on Flo's shoulder and tears roll down my face despite my resistance. I don't want to move. I want to stay here and listen to the words and relish all the good times I have had lately.

I have lived a good life. It may not have been a long life, but it was good fun. I passed my driving test, thanks to Lucy Harte. I saw my first opera when I was eighteen, thanks to her. I got to experience a full-blown white-wedding day. I felt the white sand on the Caribbean coast on my honeymoon. I have laughed, I have sung, I have danced – a lot – and most of all, I have loved with all of my precious heart. All thanks to Lucy, who gave me extra, if only borrowed, time. And now my time is up.

But I don't want the song to end. I don't want to stop dancing. Oh please God, I just want to see him again.

And when I open my eyes, he is there.

I hear Flo gasp. I look at her, then at him. She is crying and so is he.

'Gerard! Oh my God, Gerard!'

He nods slowly to me, smiling and his big beautiful green eyes are filled to the top with tears. Then he tenderly takes me by the hand and leads me onto the dance floor.

'How...' I ask him, waiting for the shock to subside. I want to keep touching his face, just to make sure he is real and that this isn't some cruel dream.

'Your brother and I have been talking a lot,' he whispers to me as he rubs my hair, holding me so close to him like I am a precious stone. 'I called you to see how the race had gone the day you got ill and he answered your phone. I have tried to call you many, many times since, but I understand if it was too hard for you.'

I put my head on his shoulder and breathe in his familiar smell. He holds my right hand and we sway to the music. I feel like I am floating. This could be heaven, for all I know.

'You said you hate goodbyes,' I say to him. 'I didn't want to put you through the pain. I didn't think my heart could stand any more pain either.'

Gerard tilts my chin back, like he did that day on the riverbank and looks into my eyes.

'We don't ever have to say goodbye, Maggie,' he whispers to me. 'I'm going to be here for as long as you need me.

Right here. I will stay with you until it's time... to go.'

'But what about –?'

What about his exhibition, I want to ask him? It's due to open in just a few days.

'Ssh, Maggie,' he whispers into my hair. 'Rest your heart now and let me love you while we still have time.'

I lie beside Gerard and I watch him sleep.

He looks so content, so perfect lying in the half light, here in my bed into the small hours of the morning.

My life is complete, that's all I can think of as I look at him now. He came for me. He loved me so much that he came for me and he promised to stay. No matter how long I have lived, no matter where I have been, I can well and truly say that today was the best day of my life.

My heart is full. My heart is smiling.

I slip out of the bed and put on my dressing gown and a pair of old sandals I have been using as slippers and I tiptoe out of the room, lifting a pen and notebook from my side table as I go.

I open the door, carefully and quietly, to make sure I do not wake him. I do the same as I go through every step of my childhood home and down the wooden stairway. My parents have always been light sleepers, they've had to be on the farm, and John Joe and Vivienne are out for the count too after their big day, so I dare not wake them.

The big clock in the hallway catches my eye as I make my way past and I see that it's just gone 4.20am. Perfect. It is my favourite time of a summer morning; not quite light but not totally dark and just enough visibility to make you feel safe, just before the break of dawn.

I walk along the little pathway outside and take a moment to marvel at the morning dew, which wets my toes. Then I tilt my head back and look up at the dark-blue sky as the last of the night-time stars twinkle above me.

I want to be by the lake. I want to watch the sunrise, the beginning of a whole new day and drink it in and, as I do, I want to write a letter to someone I do not know. I want to make a pledge to pass on a gift that will let someone else watch new sunrises and feel what I feel now for a lot longer than they ever thought they could.

I want to leave behind a gift. I want to give someone more time.

I find a little spot where I used to sit as a child and I think of Lucy and her little bridge. This was my bridge, I suppose. This might actually be my favourite place in the whole world, right here by Loch Tara.

This will always be my home.

Loch Tara, Ireland, June 24th

Dear Friend, I write

You may never get this letter, but if you are as curious as I am, you probably will find it one day and I hope you do because I know you will have many questions, just like I did almost eighteen years ago.

My name is Maggie and I am passing you on a part of

me in order to give you more time with the people you love. I don't have a bucket list for you, I don't have a list of life-long dreams for you to chase. I don't have any advice to you on where to go, on what you do or on who you choose to do that with. All of that is up to you and only you and I trust you will choose well.

What I do want to do is pass on a few little things that I have learned, perhaps a little later than I wish I had…

Life is about people and sometimes we forget that we are all that we have. Look after each other. Look out for each other. Care a little more. Forgive a little more.

Life is about giving. Give hugs, give kisses, give respect. Give what you can afford. Hell, no, give more than you can afford, always. It will make you a better person in every way.

Life is about time. Spend more time than you do money on others. Give time more than any other gift. Also, take time when you need to. Take time for you when you need it. Sometimes time is all we have with the people we love the most. I ask you to slow down in life. To take your time, but don't waste it.

Life is, most of all, about love – follow your heart, live out your dreams, smile, be happy, see the good in everyone you meet and rise above those who try to make you feel low. Love yourself. Fill your heart and fill your soul – love, no matter what, is always the answer.

It will hurt you, it will break you, it will bend you, it will make you. Love with all your heart and soul and never forget those who, in return, love you.

My time may be running out now, but yours is only just beginning. I hope this extra time brings you all the love in the world.

Please don't waste a single second.

Your donor, Maggie O'Hara, age 34

I tear out the pages from my notebook and go inside to my childhood home, where I am automatically enveloped in the love that seeps from the walls and I realise that all I care about is here right now. I shudder to think of how careless I was with life until Lucy Harte saved me for the second time around. I was throwing it away, I was selfish and self-destructive. I was on a road to nowhere until she reminded me that we aren't here for that long, really, none of us, and while we are here, it's nice to make a difference for all the right reasons.

I think of the old saying –

Live every day as your last, because one day, it will be.

Then I go back into my room and I slip under the bedclothes.

'You're freezing,' he says to me. 'Come, let me warm you up.'

I snuggle into him and my heart sings. I have lived and I have loved.

Oh, how I have loved...

Epilogue

'I'm so cold, Josh. I'm really, really cold.'

Claire Bryans held her husband's hand as the dialysis machine pumped through her body for the third time that week. She was more than exhausted; she was literally drained as she lay there, waiting for her bodily waste to be filtered out by a machine to help her live a little while longer.

'Well it is summer in England, babe,' said Josh. 'What do you expect? Tropical heat?'

'Oh hush,' she said. He knew what she meant and he always told the worst jokes, especially when he got nervous.

'Play my favourite song again for me,' she whispered as she lay on the hospital bed, the same bed she had been lying on for four hours a day, three days a week for almost two years now. 'Every time I hear it I wonder if it will be the last time I do.'

'Now, it's your turn to hush,' he replied, flicking through the iPod. 'Don't say things like that.'

'It's true,' said Claire. 'I don't know how long I can take this any more... I'm so, so cold...'

She tried to concentrate on the lyrics of the Elvis Presley classic, to ignore what was really going on inside her.

'Don't say that, Claire, please don't,' said Josh, letting go of her hand and rubbing his own tired eyes. 'I mean, you aren't going to die at twenty-nine, are you?'

Claire looked out of the window as sleet and rain pelted down.

'People of all ages die every day,' said Claire with a sigh. 'It's the only way I can live, if someone dies. And I can't do this forever.'

'No, you can't, but we still have to keep hoping,' Josh replied. 'Close your eyes and imagine the twins' birthday party next week. Think of them opening their presents, of them tearing the house apart, of me messing up the cake like I did last year and you getting mad, of the sounds of your father's usual jokes, which are way worse than mine. Do you think we could do all of that without you?'

Despite her husband's attempts to cheer her up, Claire knew the reality as well as he did and she couldn't deny it any longer. Kidney failure was a killer and she had been waiting for long enough now for a donor to save her life. Her time, it seemed, was almost up. Her birthday parties and family celebrations, without a donor, were becoming fewer.

'You would do it all without me if you had to,' she said, fixing herself, now that she knew her dialysis was done for another day. 'Anyhow, I thought you had shopping to do for the boys today, you promised? I've told you a million times that I really don't need you watching over me here every time I have this done. Waiting and hoping and waiting...'

Josh shrugged and Claire knew that no matter how many times she said it, he wasn't going anywhere. He would wait with her forever if he had to and when the consultant's secretary asked them to wait on their way out of the ward, Claire knew by her face that it was to be no ordinary discussion.

'What do you think he wants?' whispered Josh. 'Is there something wrong?'

Claire didn't answer. They would find out soon enough. She always felt a bit sick and faint after dialysis, but a rush of nerves made her need the loo really badly this time.

'Mr and Mrs Bryans, please take a seat in the waiting area and Mr Henry will be with you shortly,' said the receptionist.

'Is everything okay?' asked Claire, afraid of the reply.

'Have a seat. He won't be long,' said the lady with a neutral expression.

Moments later they were led into an office, where they sat side by side at the end of a long mahogany desk and they waited as the consultant finished a phone call to another doctor. Claire overheard Mr Henry speak of a hospital with an address in Ireland and he wrote on a pad of paper as he spoke. She shouldn't have heard that much, she knew that, and her heart leaped in anticipation.

'What's going on?' Josh whispered to her, but Claire just clasped his hand. 'Do you think –?'

'Don't say it,' she whispered back. 'Just wait and see.'

Could this really be happening? She didn't want to get her husband's hopes up in case she was wrong. She didn't want to get her own hopes up in case she was wrong, but Claire Bryans had been to enough hospital appointments down the years to tell if it was good news or bad news and this was good news.

She just knew it.

She knew it by the atmosphere. She knew by how Mr Henry hung up the phone. She knew by how he rubbed his hands before he shook theirs to greet them. She knew by how he didn't pause between his sentences. She knew by how he didn't fidget. She knew by how he got straight down to business. She just knew.

'We've found you a donor,' the doctor told them and Claire looked at her husband to make sure this was real.

'Oh my God!' she exclaimed, putting her hands over her face in disbelief. 'Really?'

No matter how much she 'just knew' she still couldn't believe it was finally happening. Sweet heavens, it was finally happening.

'Oh my God!' she said again and she almost lost her breath momentarily. 'Are you sure? For me? Are you absolutely sure?'

'Yes, for you, Claire,' said the doctor. 'I'm absolutely sure. We'll have you in and out in a week, just in time for your boys' birthday. You did tell me it was their birthday soon?'

Claire nodded and tried to reply as tears rolled down her face.

'It's next Saturday,' she told him. 'They will be six next Saturday.'

She swallowed and closed her eyes and the fatigue and nausea she always felt after dialysis faded away until it was no longer there. This would soon be history to her. She could live a normal life again.

'I can't believe this is really happening. Are you really sure?' she asked Mr Henry once again.

'I'm really sure, Claire,' said Mr Henry with a gentle smile. He had become a big part of their lives over the past two years and now he was giving them the news they had always hoped for. 'Now what will happen is, you'll be admitted to the ward and...'

Claire looked out of the window behind the doctor at the clear, blue August sky but she couldn't absorb all the formalities Mr Henry spoke of. She would leave that up to Josh, who was drinking in the doctor's every word. She wanted to go outside and dance and scream and thank the heavens for her second chance of life. She wanted to hug her baby boys and let them know that everything was going to be alright again. That Mummy was going to get better.

Two birds landing on the windowsill outside caught her eye.

She stared at them until they blurred, feeling the whole world slow down as she breathed and smiled and she blinked her eyes and let the news she had been waiting for sink in at long last. Dates, procedures, risks, side effects, chances, success rates, life... she had dreamed of this moment. She had literally clung on to her own life for this moment. And now it was really happening. Somebody, somewhere had decided to save a life, and that life was hers.

Me... Claire Bryans from the Wirral in the north of England; a humble part-time cleaner; a mummy of two rascal boys; a wife; a daughter; a sister; a friend; the owner of Chico the rescued dog and Penny the runaway cat. A lover of science, of Elvis Presley, afraid of the dark, a fan of Mills & Boon novels and of eating too much chocolate ice cream until I almost get sick. Me?

'Thank you, whoever you are,' she whispered as she closed her eyes and said a silent prayer to the hero who she would never meet but who had given her the most precious gift of all – life. 'I don't know how I will ever get the opportunity to say thank you, but I really hope I do.'

Her husband gave her hand a gentle squeeze and they held each other tightly.

'I told you we had time,' he said to her but she couldn't speak, so she just nodded and held him closer.

'We have now,' she said as she wiped her eyes. 'Let's not waste even a second. I need to tell the boys. I need to tell my babies that Mummy is going to be okay and that we are going to have the best birthday party ever.'

Then she looked out of the window again and the little birds flew away.

THE END

Acknowledgements

It has taken me much longer than I planned to write this book (a *lot* longer!), but I can safely say it has been worth all the blood, sweat and tears to really explore the sensitive, emotional subject of donating life.

I've learned a lot on the subject over the past couple of years and I'd firstly like to thank Ciaran and Geraldine Campbell as well as Patricia Kelly for allowing me to hear their story and for answering questions at all hours at night when I was in the zone.

I'd also like to acknowledge little Juniper and her family in the US for the insight into their life and for helping me to fully appreciate the wonder and miraculous gift that is organ donation.

Thanks to my editor Emily Ruston who really pushed me to make sure every drop of emotion I could spare was put into this book. You are simply the best and it was an honour to work with you.

Thanks also to Charlotte Ledger and Kimberley Young for giving me the opportunity to get this story out there with HarperImpulse and for their patience as I wrote around a very busy, bumpy time for me and my family.

Big thanks to all the readers, Facebook friends and all those who sent me messages of encouragement as they waited for 'Lucy Harte' to hit the shelves, especially Grace Girvan and Kerry Davidson for reading an early draft and giving me some very constructive feedback and to my aunt and Godmother Kathleen McCausland for being there all the time to listen to story ideas and also for babysitting duties lately! Thanks to my sister Vanessa for helping out with Sonny too. It really means a lot.

My cousin Charlene Greensword helped me come up with the title of the book – it was so long ago she probably doesn't remember, but cheers cuz! It's a good one!

Thanks to Sherry Perkins and Kerry Burak for being so supportive in promoting my work to their friends on the other side of the Atlantic. Every little helps and you girls are a great support team to have!

Thanks to all the bloggers and printed/broadcast media who make sure the work us authors do gets out there, especially Annamay McNally, Jenny Lee, Gail Walker, Martin Breen, Ronan McSherry, Ian Greer, Kerry McKittrick, Laura McMullan, Cliodhna Fullen, Annette Kelly, Joanne Savage and Gillian McDade.

To the booksellers across Ireland and the UK, thanks so much for your support with a special thanks to my friends at Sheehy's in Cookstown, Easons in Belfast, Easons in Craigavon, Co Armagh and Dean & Tom at Kenny's in Galway.

Thanks to Keith Acheson at Belfast Book Festival for giving me a platform to read from my work and also to Arts Council of Northern Ireland (Gilly Campbell, Damian Smyth and

Angela Warren in particular) for financial support in recent years.

Thanks to Catriona Corrigan at Divine Photography and Eadoina McHugh at In Haus Make Up for the fantastic promo photos! You really did make me look fab at 40!

To all my family and friends in Donaghmore and beyond, thanks for your continued support in my career as an author especially my cousins Kathie & Brenda, my sisters Vanessa, Rachel, Lynne, Rebecca, Niamh, my brother David and of course daddy cool himself, Hugh.

Finally, huge thanks and big, big love to my children Jordyn, Jade, Adam, Dualta and Sonny James for allowing me the time and space to write and for just being the best kids in the world ever. I love you all so much x

And to my partner Jim McKee, thanks for listening, for reading, for all the road-trips, celebrations, encouragement, hugs, mopping up of tears when the going got tough, for believing in me and for loving *The Legacy of Lucy Harte* as much as I do. I love you pa x

#donatelife

CPSIA information can be obtained
at www.ICGtesting.com
Printed in the USA
LVOW08s0034030717
539986LV00013BA/16/P